THE SEARCH FOR
SARAH OWEN
and Other Western Tales

EMERY MEHOK

iUniverse, Inc.
New York   Bloomington

The Search for Sarah Owen and Other Western Tales

iUniverse books may be ordered through booksellers or by contacting:

iUniverse
1663 Liberty Drive
Bloomington, IN 47403
www.iuniverse.com
1-800-Authors (1-800-288-4677)

ISBN: 978-1-4502-4990-4 (sc)
ISBN: 978-1-4502-4991-1 (ebook)

Printed in the United States of America

iUniverse rev. date: 08/18/2010

DEDICATION

This second collection of stories is, like the first, dedicated to my Mother and Father.

What I've become and what I've done is due in large part to them.

Neither lived to see any of my work in print, but I know they would've loved it.

PREFACE

As I wrote in the forward to "Johnny Bluehorse and other Western Tales", this book too is a dream fulfilled for me.

This collection is also my view of the Old West as I would like it to have been.

This viewpoint was honed through years of reading Western Stories, and watching Western movies and television shows. It is rooted in a real love of history and an education in Social Studies.

If the stories seem somewhat cinematic, they are meant to be. I imagine them as movies in my mind. I really believe that some of them, especially the Grant Kirby tales, would transfer well to the screen.

I have had people comment to me that some of my stories are very short, and they have wondered why. There are a couple of simple answers:

1.) I felt I had written enough,
2.) I had more luck selling short, short stories.

I imagine they were easier for editors to fit in a publication. They didn't have to worry about editing much because of limited space. I actually enjoy telling a satisfactory story in a modest number of words. It's not something a lot of people can do very well.

Some of these short stories have similar themes. Keep in mind they were written as stand alone pieces at different times and published in different magazines. I wasn't writing them as parts of a collection, but I think they work well as parts of this collection.

As always, some heartfelt thanks are due to some important people. My wife, Helen, has been supportive all along in all ways. My brother, Frank, has given me good ideas. The story titled "Elijah and the Highlander" was his brainchild. My pal, Dennis Nielsen, has been a great sounding board and even part time editor.

I have a group of lifelong friends who have always been "in my corner". These include: Dan and Mary Ann Dwornik, Al and Cindy Marazas, Dennis and Jan Nielsen, Mike and Jo O'Neal, Tim and Barb Osmulski, Tom Pancheri, Jim and Mary Kay Sisson and Larry and Stephanie Sterling. Sincere thanks to them. Some of those friendships go back over fifty years, and I treasure them.

A final thank you to Doug Sharp who gave me and many others a chance to get published for a few years when he produced a labor of love titled Western Digest up in Calgary, Canada.

So, once again, it is my pleasure to furnish you with some more "Campfire Tales", stories at home being told and listened to around a crackling fire by people cradling hot cups of coffee in their hands. I hope these tales will provide you with some moments of escape and relaxation.

HAPPY TRAILS
Emery Mehok

Table of Contents

The Search for

Sarah Owen

PROLOGUE

I know many people were disappointed in the last election. Hell, so was I. I lost. First time in four terms.

Friends of long standing have come to me and pleaded with me to answer my opponent, Peter Anderson's accusations about my past. I put them off with rhetoric and evasive answers.

The truth is I loved my wife and family too much. I had actually become complacent about what happened those many years ago. I had become too confident in my power and position as a senator to believe that anything could harm me. I was wrong.

I have learned that one must never underestimate an opponent. An opponent is imbued with overwhelming ambition, but is sometimes not cautious. Anderson wanted my job and now he's got it. He'll learn that his exuberance won't count for much in the halls of Congress. It's the cranky, old bastards like me who get the job done. We know which arms to twist. We know when to give and when to take; when to grant favors and when to call them in.

But, I'm not crying. I've done a lot of good for this state, and I am approaching my 76th year. How much more time have I got? I don't know. Enough, I hope to tell the story I must. Then, the complete record will be down for all to see, I am not ashamed.

My wife has passed on, God rest her soul. My children are mature enough and their lives well-established so that my story shouldn't upset them to any great degree. In fact they've urged me to tell it.

I ask only these things of the reader: remember I am not an author, maintain an open mind, and, if I digress, or tend to philosophize, accept it as one of the idiosyncrasies of an old man.

Grant Kirby
1918 Santa Fe

Chapter I

I've lived in two centuries. Two different worlds, though, might be better terminology. But, for this story, I have to take you back to the first world: the frontier. I am not writing an autobiography, but I think a little background on my upbringing might be helpful.

My roots go back to Indiana and a farm a little outside the city of Terre Haute. The family consisted of four: my father, Frank; my mother, Elizabeth; my brother Joseph; and me. I was the oldest.

My childhood and youth were uneventful. Education and work were stressed. My father was great believer in both.

I was easygoing and got along with most people. I loved school and read whatever I could, whenever and wherever I could. I did manage to finish all eight grades.

But, the life on the farm as I grew older became a dull routine. So, like many other young men of the time, when the Civil War erupted, I was swept up in the pageantry and patriotism of the time. I joined the Union Army, hoping to get into action before it was all over. I got more than I bargained for.

When the time came for me to leave, my mother cried. My father walked with me down the road toward town. He was never a man of many words, but he talked a lot that time. He said some things I still remember today. His voice was sort of thick and raspy when he spoke.

"Son," he said, "you are walking down a road that will change your whole life. In a very short time you will long for the life you now think is so unexciting. War will change you, I am sorry to see you go, but I am proud of your decision. Now you must stick by it. Never go back on your word. When you get into a fight, finish it. God go with you, and may He bring you back to us."

We embraced then, tears filling both our eyes. I turned and walked away without looking back. At that point I didn't want to leave any longer. I was afraid if I did look back, I might not be able to leave at all. I never saw my Mother or Father again.

My Father was right. War did change me. It changed everyone to some extent. I learned to hate, I learned to kill, I learned to survive.

My idea of the glory of war was dispelled quickly. There is no glory in shivering in the winter cold and sweating in the summer heat. There is no glory in dead and mutilated bodies or the screams of soldiers in pain. There is no glory in shooting a rifle at an unseen enemy, unseen because the gun smoke is so thick a man's eyes burn and sting, and he can't distinguish between friend or foe.

To this day I loathe even the sound of the word war. In my work in Congress I have tried to avoid sending American troops into battle anywhere. I have not always been successful. Right now United States soldiers are fighting in the European War. I hope it will be the last war I live to see.

When I returned home after the war, Mother and Father were no long there. Instead, I found two gravestones perched atop the little hill behind the house. Some sort of fever took them, I was told.

Joseph had married. He and his wife, Elizabeth, had a baby girl Mary, and they had settled into the family house.

I tried to stay, but it was no use. Even though Joseph and Elizabeth did their best to make me feel at home, I was never comfortable. Farming was not for me. I wanted to forget the war, I needed a fresh start. In this country at that time, the West was the answer.

I bid my brother and his family good-bye and headed for new land and new opportunities.

CHAPTER 2

Over the next few years I held a variety of jobs as I worked my way westward. I was a store clerk in Terre Haute, a bouncer in a bawdy house, a riverboat gambler and a peace office. I even tried my hand at cowboying, but oh, how I hated cattle.

I did learn to handle a horse pretty well. Guns were never a problem for me. I was always a decent shot, a sharpshooter in the war. For the time, I was pretty well-educated and had a pleasant personality. I was able to get along.

After some adventures in Texas with the Tenner family whom I love dearly, I finally settled, more or less, in Wichita, Kansas. My job was deputy marshal under Samuel Lane.

Even though he was getting older, Sam was still quite a man. He had been a lawman for many years, and his experience was priceless. I learned a lot from him and I'm thankful he chose to share his knowledge with me.

Sam helped me improve my skills with a handgun. He showed me how to perform the border shift and the road agent spin. He cautioned me about trying to be too fast on the draw.

"Don't hurry," he used to say, "it's not getting that hog leg out fast that counts. It's hitting what you aim at that's important."

A fellow lawman from Texas, Clay Ellis, had told me much the same thing and they were both correct. Those old Colts were notorious for inaccuracy. The man who was deliberate rather than anxious usually won in a fight.

The early 1870's were wild times. Texas cattle herds were being driven up the trail from the southwest. Businesses catered to the drovers, supplying them with whiskey, women and gambling.

Our job was to protect the town and to try to keep everyone in line. It was during this period that the events took place for which Peter Anderson labeled me a murderer and my late wife a harlot.

Abraham Marx, president of the Homestead Band and Trust Company, was killed during a robbery when he reached for a pistol in his desk drawer. Witnesses identified the killer and leader of the bandits as a man called Cletus. He had no other name as far as we knew. He rode with a rather ragtag assortment of cutthroats and thieves. All of them were known men to steer clear of. Lyle and Charles Terk were a pair of retarded twin brothers. They were close to being imbeciles but were good shots. Cherokee Bill Mullins was a good tracker. Johnny Otis was a baby faced outlaw who fancied himself a lady's man.

As we stared at each other across the desk in the Marshal's office, Sam Lane's face reflected worry and concern. He spoke slowly and carefully.

"Grant, someone has got to go after them. It will have to be you. I can't spare any other men. Besides, I think you can do it." I nodded indicating that I understood.

He continued, "They were seen heading northwest, but my guess is Lannon's though. There's nothing for them to the north. That's just a decoy, I think. They want to try to throw us off the track. They probably figure no one from town will trail them very far anyway. You follow my hunch and ride for Lannon's. You should be able to get there ahead of them.

"What do I do then?" I asked. "One on five ain't exactly good odds."

A hint of a smile glimmered on Lanes' face as he answered, "You'll think of something."

"Thanks," I said, "but that's no help."

Sam was quiet a moment then his eyes lit up.

"Didn't Cletus use to come visit Squirrel Sally when she was here?

"I think so," I answered.

"Isn't she working down at Lannon's these days?"

Now I knew what Sam meant.

"Sally will do most anything for money won't she?" I asked.

Sam nodded affirmatively.

"Marx's son is offering a one thousand dollar reward isn't he?" I asked again.

Sam nodded once more.

We both laughed then because we knew there was a good chance

Squirrel Sally would help us, especially since there was reward money to be had.

To some this may seem too easy to be true, but it is. In those days outlaws didn't have much fear of the law outside of towns. In fact, there wasn't much law outside of town law.

Lannon's was a good guess too because it was one of the few places where men could rest and gather supplies in that country. Anyway, it was worth a try. Sam's hunches usually were pretty accurate. After so many years in the marshalling business, it seemed almost as if he could read the mind of an outlaw.

As I've professed that what I'm writing here is the truth, I must include one more point. It was not only a sense of duty that behooved me to try to catch those outlaws. It was also that one thousand dollar reward.

That very day I saddled my dun horse, gathered provisions, weapons and cartridges and rode towards Lannon's.

Chapter 3

Lannon's was situated on the southwestern Kansas-Colorado border. It had originally been built as a trading post, but over a twenty year period it had been considerably altered. The post looked like a small fortress or stockade. The Plains Indians, who were engaged in a struggle against the ever increasing white men, never threatened Lannon's. Perhaps it was too formidable for the light Indian cavalry. Perhaps they respected the owner who had never cheated them. Perhaps they preferred fighting on their own terrain. The real reason was not known.

Lannon's catered to the plainsman, buffalo hunter, and an occasional wandering cowboy. A variety of foodstuffs, clothes, blankets, tack, hardware, and ammunition was stocked in the store building. In the adjacent two-story structure were housed a saloon and several sleeping rooms. It was here that Squirrel Sally and four other "soiled doves" plied their trade.

Squirrel Sally had been around a few years. At one time she had been quite beautiful. Now the years had begun to take their toll. She was still pretty, but now she had to resort to powder and rouge to provide what nature no longer did. She got her name from the pet squirrel she had. The little animal used to sit upon her shoulder and be fed by hand. One day, however, the fury little creature made the mistake of biting the hand of one of Sally's customers.

He became enraged, took his pistol, and shot it. But Sally still carried the nickname.

I had done some hard riding. And, as Sam figured, I had arrived before Cletus or any of the others. If, in fact, this was their destination.

We sat at a corner table in Lannon's saloon. The only other occupant of the room was Lannon himself. The short, fat, balding proprietor was taking an inventory of his whiskey.

I had explained the proposition to Squirrel Sally. She sat thinking. Her chestnut hair tumbled down over her shoulders to rest upon her pale yellow dress.

"How much did you say is being offered?" she asked.

"There is a thousand dollar reward," I answered. "We'll split it; five-hundred for you, five-hundred for me."

She sat silent. I could tell she was worried.

"Look, when are you ever going to get a chance like this again?" I continued. "I know its dirty money, but what is Cletus to you anyway? If it wasn't you, it would be someone else. He has no friends nor does he deserve any."

She thought for a moment longer, and then spoke quietly.

"You're right Kirby. I'll do it. I really would like to get out of here. But, you've got to fix it so no one will suspect. Otherwise, Johnny Otis and the others will kill me for sure."

"Don't worry Sally, " I said, "we'll take him like I told you. No one will ever think ill of you. After Cletus is turned in, I'll come and get you myself and take you to Wichita. The money will be there and so will the train. You can start fresh wherever you want."

Sally's eyes were wet, and she wiped them with a lace kerchief. I could see them clear then, and I knew her mind was set.

"Cletus will be here in one day, two at the most. The window will be left open. Just don't make any mistakes, Marshal, "she said.

She placed her hand on mine and squeezed she rubbed her knee against mine, smiled, and raised her eyebrows, "Care for some relaxation?" she queried.

I just answered, "No thanks." I don't really believe in mixing business and pleasure then or now.

Chapter 4

Cletus and his men arrived on schedule. They slumped in their saddles like fellows who had ridden hard for a very long time. They dismounted and straightened their bowed legs with noticeable effort.

I was not worried about being recognized. My badge was hidden and I was dressed in the normal fashion. I was an average sized man. My hair and beard were black. My hat, pants, shirt and vest weren't unusual. Besides, in those days people weren't' nosy. No on asked questions as long as you minded your own business. It was dangerous to do otherwise.

That night the moon was half full, and the silvery stars dotted the black velvet night sky. I led my dun and a small bay I had procured, saddled and provisioned, to the back stairs of the hotel building. I tethered them there and looped my spurs over the saddle horn, a little trick Sam had taught me. The sound of jingling spurs doesn't help when you want to go unnoticed. I quietly mounted the stairs that led to the second floor balcony.

The cold March air felt good in my lungs, and the wooden stairs didn't creak or complain under my weight.

I reached the window, tested it, found it unlatched, and raised it slowly. I climbed through and stood a moment, allowing myself to get accustomed to the surroundings.

From the adjoining room a shaft of light peeked under the door, and sounds of heavy breathing and rustling bed sheets could be heard.

I moved to the door, opened it slowly, and looked in. Sally and Cletus were in bed oblivious to anything going on around them.

I paused a while, drew my Colt, and then slipped into the room. In three steps I reached the bed. In one movement I put the gun to Cletus' head, thumbed back the hammer, and whispered, "Don't move or make a sound."

Sally opened her eyes, gasped, and looked about to scream.

"One word out of you miss and I'll kill you both, " I threatened. "Keep your mouth shut and you won't be hurt."

Cletus looked pretty miserable. He was short, skinny, and naked. A scraggily brown beard covered his pock marked face.

"What is this anyway? What do you want?" Cletus cautiously asked when I backed away.

"I'm a deputy U.S. Marshal," I answered. "You're under arrest for the murder of Abraham Marx and the robbery of the Homestead Bank and Trust. Now get your clothes on and don't ask any more questions."

Cletus dropped his jaw open and seemed absolutely dismayed, but he obeyed.

Sally was doing a fine job of acting. Fright was written across her face like a banner headline.

I ordered Cletus to tie and gag the girl with strips torn from the bed sheets. I then handcuffed the outlaw, stuffed his mouth full of cloth, and tied a neckerchief over his lips for good measure.

I grabbed Cletus's saddlebags that were resting on the table. I unstrapped one side and looked. It was filled with money. I didn't know if that was all, but I wasn't going to wait around to find out.

We went back out the window, across the balcony, down the steps, and mounted the waiting horses. We moved quietly through the main gate and headed Northeast at a trot. The night closed around us, and we were swallowed up by the darkness.

CHAPTER 5

The day dawned gray and cloudy. The country was hilly; extensions of the sand stone hills in the Indian Territory. They ranged in height from about 250 to 400 feet. Small stands of cottonwood, dogwood and post oak were scattered around in the most unlikely spots. They seemed to be huddled together for protection against the cold. The wind whistled through the still-naked branches. There was very little color spread across the landscape except the drab tone of receding winter.

Cletus and I rode silently. The collars of our heavy coats were pulled up about our ears. Our hands were gloved, and steam puffed regularly from the horse's nostrils. The creak of saddle leather and the footfalls or hooves combined in sort of a rhythmic pattern; kind of a relaxing, hypnotizing union of sounds. Only the jingle of a spur or a snort from one of the animals interrupted the pattern.

Finally Cletus spoke. "Kirby?"

"Yeah," I answered. "What do you want?"

"Look, I ain't never met anyone like you. Why don't you just take the bank money in the saddle bags. There's more there than you'd earn marshalling in five years."

I had to laugh to myself. Cletus did have a point. So, I had to offer him an answer.

"Cletus, I've been telling you I've got one big weakness, I'm honest. I can't help it. I may end up in a Boot Hill grave somewhere without a penny to my name, but it'll be by my own choice. Besides, there's a little reward I'm going to collect on you anyway."

"Just my luck. Of all the peace officers operating in this country, I got to draw you."

"Looks like your luck is running real bad all right. There's a jail cell and then a rope in your neck size waiting for you in Wichita. You shouldn't have let your face been seen. You're too well known," I commented.

"Don't be too sure Marshal. The boys ain't awful smart, but they'll figure this out right quick. Cherokee Bill will sniff out our trail plenty fast. After all, there's money at stake. You're gonna have to ride looking over your shoulder. You'll get the goddamndest stiff neck you ever had. And no sleep either." Cletus smiled, showing a row of yellow, rotting teeth.

I now turned hard. "You let me worry about that," I said. "Talking time is over."

"Wait," Cletus interjected, "Can't we stop a minute? I've got to relieve myself. This damn cold and rough riding horses play hell with my insides."

I reined in my dun. "Go ahead," I said, "but don't waste any time."

"Are you kidding?" Cletus chuckled to himself, dismounted.

Shuffled a few feet, and began to urinate.

I watched my dun lower its head to crop grass, find nothing and then sniff at the semi-frozen earth instead. Then, abruptly, the animal's head came up quickly, and its ears pricked forward. The little bay followed suit.

Anyone who has worked around horses knows that the ears are very important. They can tell you when he's mad, when he's asleep, and when his attention is focused forward.

I told Cletus we had a problem and that he better hurry up.

"I'll be right there, "he answered as he fumbled around with handcuffed wrists, cold fingers and tricky buttons.

When Cletus mounted, he looked out in the direction the horses were staring. He saw the man I had been watching, the man that was to pose a problem for us. You couldn't miss him. His pinto pony and the blue blanket he held about his shoulders stood out-strikingly against the neutral sky.

"A little far south for Cheyenne, don't you think Marshal?" Cletus' voice wavered ever-so-slightly as he asked the question.

"It seems so," I answered. "Could be Kiowa though. Maybe even Comanche. The tribes are all raiding these days."

Slowly, more horsemen joined the lone brave.

They rose up from behind the high ridge to the North like figures emerging from the bowels of the earth. The group numbered nine. They sat like gaudy sentinels; watching, waiting.

The ridge ran somewhat parallel to the path Cletus and I were following. About a half mile ahead, the high ground receded to meet the flatland. A rather thick grove of cottonweeds stood along the base of the ridge.

"Cletus, listen to me," I said. Even in the chilly air, beads of perspiration formed on my forehead. I grabbed the stock of my Henry rifle where it rested in the saddle boot. "We can't run from them. Our horses are tired and are carrying too much weight. They'd catch us in an open flight sure. We wouldn't stand a chance. We've got to make for that bunch of trees. We'll have some cover there, and they might think twice before trying to take us then. When I say so, move! Don't spare the spur. If we're caught before we hit cover, it's all over. When I start, you fall in behind me."

"O.K. Marshal, I'm so goddamned scared, I'll do whatever you say."

I dug my spurs into the dun's flanks. Cletus yelled, and the two horses pounded over the dormant grass.

While at the gallop, I drew the Henry from the saddle boot. I knew how important the long gun would be, and I didn't want to risk losing it if my horse was downed.

From what I could see, the Indians looked to be Comanche from their point, trappings and horsemanship, but I wasn't sure. A couple were armed with old-time muskets. They could not afford to waste powder, I guessed, so they didn't fire. They did, however, use their voices effectively, as all the braves joined in screaming cries.

Most rode with reins loose, guiding their ponies with knee and leg pressure. This left hands free to work with bows and arrows. And, as they thundered nearer to us, the arrows began to fly.

I took a shaft in the meaty part of my right thigh. It bit through my leather chaps and pants to bare flesh. The warm blood oozed thickly out and down my leg, but I hardly felt any pain, It must have been shock, fear or the fact that there just was no time to think of it.

Coming down off the hill, the braves could not ride as swiftly because of the terrain. Consequently, Cletus and I reached the grove ahead of them.

The outlaw dropped down and held the reins of both horses while I flattened myself on the ground and let loose with the Henry. Two shots kicked up dirt in front of the charging Indians. They stopped out of range knowing better than to challenge the long gun.

"Goddamn, goddamn, Kirby," Cletus yelled, shaking uncontrollably. "They'll get us for sure! They'll wait us out!"

"Shut up you sniveling bastard, or I'll kill you myself!" I shouted back. I was now becoming aware of the pain and blood loss from my leg.

Cletus quieted down. He just sat and shivered. The braves sat their ponies and waited. Time was on their side.

I lay on the frosty ground wondering if they would try to outflank us and hoping I wouldn't become too weak or pass out from pain.

CHAPTER 6

The braves dismounted and sat cross-legged upon the ground. They began some sort of an animated discussion. They gestured emphatically toward us but made no moves that we could see or understand.

Cletus sat with his back resting against a good sized tree. He virtually had the reins of the two horses tied to his hands. I guess he feared losing them. I know he feared the Indians. Our situation was a grievous one.

"Kirby, please unlock my cuffs," he pleaded. "Give me a gun so I can help out, so I can defend myself."

"Go to hell," I answered. I won't trust you. If I pass out for if I'm killed, you're welcome to the handcuff keys and my weapons, but not until then. I've never turned a prisoner loose nor do I intend to now."

I switched my position slightly to ease the pressure on the wounded leg. I tied my neckerchief about the wound to help stop the flow of blood. Oh, how I hate the sight of blood! Especially my own. To this day it upsets my insides.

It was well into morning, but the sun had not yet shown itself. The temperature had risen though. A slight breeze blew intermittently from the south.

I tried to take my mind of the pain by thinking of other times and other places. My thoughts wandered back to my boyhood on our Indiana farm; cornstalks reaching to the sky and the smell of freshly baked pies cooling on the window sill. I thought of my mother and father and brothers and the peace and quiet of that life. I remembered the horror of the Civil War and father's prediction that I would never be the same after taking part in that conflict.

My reverie was interrupted abruptly by what seemed to be a muffled explosion from somewhere in the distance. I could not gauge the direction, but I looked up to see the brave in the blue blanket stiffen clutch his throat, and fall backward.

Following rather quickly was another sharp report. The legs of the Pinto pony buckled, and the animal collapsed.

Confusion reigned supreme as the other Indian horses began to plunge and shy. The braves wasted no time mounting. The fallen Indian was placed upon a horse with one of his companions. They rode off to the north at a gallop.

I know both Cletus and I were relieved and thankful but puzzled. We didn't say word, just gazed at the fleeing Indians.

When the hostiles were out of sight, Cletus called to me, "Look to the West!"

Wincing in pain, I rolled over to face the appropriate direction. I saw a solitary rider about here hundred yards off.

"I think that's our saviour, Cletus," I said, smiling broadly.

The outlaw nodded in assent, but no emotion showed on his face. His fear of immediate danger from Indians was somewhat alleviated, but his future was still bleak. After all, death from an arrow or the hangman's rope is much the same. This was just a temporary reprieve for Cletus.

The approaching rider could be seen quite clearly by now, and large he was in height and girth. He looked to be well over six feet tall with a weight of around two hundred pounds. He was dressed in moccasins and buckskin leggings. His coat was heavy dark brown wool, and his hat was flat brimmed and open crowned with a solitary feather fastened to a horse hair hatband. He carried his rifle across his saddle in an ornately beaded and fringed scabbard. The saddle itself was of the old Sante Fe type. His sorrel horse was well-muscled and moved without any noticeable guidance.

His age was hard to tell, but I judged from the man's full grey beard and silvery hair that 60 years, give or take a few would probably be correct.

The man dismounted, leaned his rifle up against a tree, and walked toward us.

"My name is Ethan Owen," he said. "You seem to have needed some help."

"We sure did Mr. Owen," I nodded. "I am Deputy U.S. Marshal Grant Kirby. This man is my prisoner. I was taking him to Wichita to meet with a rope when those Indians set upon us."

Owen looked at Cletus momentarily, then turned his attention to my wounded leg.

"That arrow has got to come out."

"Yes," I answered, "I fear that I've lost a lot of blood. I fell weak."

"We'll have to take care of that quickly," the big man said with assurance.

From the corner of my eye I spied a swift movement by Cletus. He dropped the reins of the horses, grabbed Owen's rifle from its resting place against the cottonwood, peeled off the fringed scabbard, and pointed the big Sharps at us.

"Drop your gun Marshal," the outlaw ordered. "Do what I say else I'll shoot. I mean to be free."

Even though I saw it happen, in my weakened state I couldn't react quickly enough. As ordered, I let the Henry fall to the ground.

Then the big man did a strange and, at the time I thought, suicidal thing: he began walking straight at the armed bad man, talking as he moved.

"Boy, I just saved your hair. I didn't have to, but I believe in helping people who need it. Even death by hanging is better than death by Indian torture. You should be thankful. Instead, you threaten me with my own gun. No one does harm to me or mine without paying for it. Now, I am going to teach you a lesson. I am going to hit you right in the mouth hard enough to break out your front teeth."

Owen kept advancing. Cletus cocked the hammer of the .50 caliber and pulled the trigger. The hammer fell on an empty chamber. The click it made was ominous to the outlaw's ears. The look on his face is indescribable.

Ethan Owen hit him then the full force of his two hundred pounds followed through. His fist met Cletus' mouth, and I could hear the sound of bone on flesh and tooth. The smaller man thudded to the ground. Blood seeped over his lips. One large tooth dangled precariously from his upper gums.

"Hell," said Owen retrieving his Sharps and scabbard, "I must be getting old. I used to be able to knock both front ones out right off. By the way, I used my last two cartridges shooting at those braves.

"Boy, you best remember this if you ever entertain notions of trying to cross me again. I'll knock the rest out and you'll swallow. Now get some wood and make a fire."

Cletus wiped his bloody mouth on his sleeve and hastened to get some branches.

Owen turned his attention to me.

"Marshal, after I get that arrowhead out, we'll rig up a travois and haul you over to my place. It's not far, over by the south fork of the Cimarron."

I watched as the big man took his knife from its sheath on his right calf, sterilized it in the fire Cletus had built, gave me a branch to bite on, and began to dig out the arrowhead. Jesus it hurt!!

Afterward, he began to douse the wound with whiskey from his saddlebag. Thankfully, that's when I passed out.

Ethan Owen's home was not much to look at. Constructed of logs and sod with two adjoining corrals, it was situated only a short distance from the Cimarron. There was plenty of water, enough grass, and ample shade. It was comfortable in the broadest frontier interpretation of the word.

When we arrived, Ethan took my handcuff keys and escorted Cletus to a shed in one of the corrals. He handcuffed the outlaw to one of the posts.

"How the hell am I supposed to move around like this?" I heard Cletus ask.

"You ain't," Owen replied. "I'll bring some food out to you later. I'll let you loose to eat and tend to yourself. But, you won't be here long. You've got to keep a date in Wichita."

The big man returned to the travois, hoisted me up on his should with my arm about his neck and half-dragged and half-carried me into his house.

When he laid me on the bed, I said, "Mr. Owen, I can't let you do this. I can't take a man's own bed."

"The name's Ethan," he replied, "and I don't rightly see what you can do about it. You just lay there and in no time you'll be all right."

"What about my prisoner?" I asked. "I've got to get him to "Wichita."

"Well, I still ain't forgiven old yellow tooth for throwing down on me with my own gun. I think maybe I'll just take him on in for you."

"But Ethan," I argued, "his friends are sure to be following. I don't want you risking your neck."

"Hell Kirby, a man risks his neck just living out here. Besides, I covered our trail pretty well. And, I don't want that fellow around my family. You just relax and get well. My family ain't had no visitors in a long time. They're going to enjoy your company. You get some sleep now."

With that Ethan Owen left the room and closed the door. I'm sure it was only moments before sweet sleep overtook me.

When I awoke, Ethan was standing in the room. He had his arms around two very pretty women.

"Let me introduce you to the two most handsome women in the whole world," he said. "This is my wife, Anne, and my daughter, Sarah."

Their copper colored faces deepened in hue at the unexpected compliment. Then they both smiled broadly.

I spoke. "I am very pleased to meet you both and I certainly agree with you, Ethan. I thank you for your kindness and your hospitality."

Then Ethan took each woman by the arm and guided her to the door. "I think our guest is hungry," he said. "I know I am. Will you fix something to eat?"

The two women went out quickly and busied themselves with cooking chores.

Owen pulled up a chair and sat down. "How's your leg?" he questioned.

"Much better," I answered, "thanks to you I'd probably be dead meat now if you hadn't come along. What made you want to get involved anyway?"

Ethan thought for a moment before he replied. "Ah, that's the trouble with civilized people, Kirby. Don't want no part of nothing but their own. I don't have much, but I'll share with them that needs or wants. Trouble is most in this country take instead of ask. I can't abide that. I've lived most of my life among Indians, Blackfoot and Cheyenne. My wife is Cheyenne, sister to Dull Knife. Those so called savages don't have some of the problems we do. There's no stealing, cause any wrongdoer is punished quick. When times are hard, all suffer. When times are good, all thrive. I can't shake that way of thinking. I couldn't have passed you by without lending a hand, no more than I could fly. This time my help was enough. Another time it mightn't have been. A man's got to judge that for himself.

"I've talked enough for now. I think you better rest a spell while the food is fixin'. I'll send someone in when it's ready. We'll talk more later."

Ethan rose and slipped out the door.

I lay thinking. I knew my string had almost run out. I also knew that I was safe and secure. It was a good feeling. What I didn't know and couldn't imagine was that one day Ethan and I would be on opposite sides.

CHAPTER 7

The door squeaked open and Sarah entered carrying a tray. Her long black hair was tied back with a white ribbon. The fresh blue gingham dress covered her well-rounded body but could not hide it. The girl's glowing copper skin contrasted beautifully with the brightly colored cloth. She smiled, and the sparkle of her teeth against the background of her dark facial features was dazzling. She was quite a vision.

My experience with girls was limited mostly to the Squirrel Sally type. Their beauty was artificial and painted on. Their smiles were false and so were their feelings. This girl was clean and new. Her smile was natural and so were her looks.

"Mr. Kirby," she said, "here is some stew if you feel up to it. It is quite tasty, and I'm sure you'll like it."

"Why, thank you Sarah. I am quite hungry."

She set the tray on my lap and turned to leave. I stopped her.

"Wait, don't go. Keep me company for a while."

Sarah moved a chair closer to the bed, seated herself and watched me eat.

I felt a little self-conscious but tried to keep the conversation going.

"I've not tasted anything this good in a long while. Did you make it?"

She nodded her head.

I continued, "I got the buffalo meat nailed down, but what else?"

Sarah smiled, obviously pleased at my interest.

"Oh there's some venison, onions, and potatoes. Father does a lot of hunting. Would you like some more?"

"No thanks," I answered as I cleaned the last of the gravy with the remaining crust of bread. "This is enough for now. But if you have any coffee, I could go for a cup."

"Certainly," she said, "I'll be right back. Do you take anything in it?"

I shook my head and watched her walk out of the room with the tray. She returned with a steaming cup of black coffee.

I let the fragrance of the brew tantalize my nostrils. I sipped and the hot liquid burned my tongue but still tasted delicious. I continued the conversation.

"Have you lived here long?"

"Most of my life, Sarah answered. "When I was small, we traveled. We used to spend some time in the camp of my uncle, Dull Knife. Did you know my mother was Cheyenne?"

I nodded, still drinking my coffee.

"My father calls her Anne after his own grandmother, but her Indian name is Singing Bird. She has a beautiful voice."

"And a beautiful daughter," I added.

Sarah blushed momentarily, cast her eyes down, soothed her skirt, retained her composure, and then looked at me again. I thought it best to change the subject.

"Have you had much schooling?" I asked.

"I've not been to a regular school," she answered, "but father has taught me to read and write and cipher. He says that is enough for me to know. Mother has taught me to cook and sew and all the things a woman should know. So I guess I've had a lot of schooling. How about you?

I gave her a little information about my 8th grade education and my life as a boy in Indiana. It was a thoroughly pleasant conversation. I found myself definitely attracted to Sarah.

"More coffee, Mr. Kirby?" she asked.

"No," I answered, "no more coffee thank you. Would you please call me by my first name, Grant?

Sarah grinned at that and said, "Surely. Now Father said he wanted to talk to you when you were finished."

She walked out with a swish of her skirts, and I began to feel more like a well man than an injured one. She made my heart beat a little faster, and her sweet scent lingered in the room.

Ethan entered the room and said, "Good food and rest will do the trick, Kirby. You look better already."

I winked as I spoke, "I'll think you better add your daughter to that list of cures."

"Yes," Ethan said, "she takes after her mother."

"I want to leave tomorrow with your prisoner. I'll need to have some sort of authorization."

"I'll write a letter explaining the situation," I replied. "You can carry my badge also if you wish."

Owen brought me paper and pen. I wrote the whole story.

"Ethan," I said, there is a reward for Cletus. I'd be glad to split my share with you. It comes to two hundred fifty dollars apiece.

The other part goes to one of the girls at Lannon's, Squirrel Sally."

The big man's face changed slightly. It became stern.

"I'd appreciate it if you'd drop Sally's share of the money off at Lannon's on your way back," I said.

"That I will not do," said Ethan.

I didn't know how to react for a moment. His sudden change in attitude surprised me. I didn't feel I should ask why.

"All right then," I continued, "just leave the money at the bank, and they'll follow my instructions."

I added a postscript to the note informing the bank that two hundred fifty dollars should be deposited in the name of Ethan Owen.

"How long do you think it will take?" I asked.

"Depends on what I run into. At most I should be back in ten days," Ethan answered.

"You're sure you want to do this Ethan?"

"Well, you'll be stove up here for a time, and I'd rather have that vermin out from around here and my women."

I nodded in agreement.

I'll leave at first light, so I better get to bed. Good night Kirby."

"Ethan," I said, "you seem to place a lot of trust in me, leaving me here with your women. Ain't you worried?"

"Nope. You're not the kind to take advantage," he answered. "you trust me don't you?"

"I must," I replied. "You've got my prisoner, my badge, and the bank's money." We chuckled at that.

"Kirby, my friends, the Cheyenne, keep an eye on this place. They visit off and on. Anyone who meddles here better sell his horse and traps cause he ain't gonna need'em where he's going. There's women like those sorts at Lannon's can be bought, and they deserve what they get. What's your thinking on it?

"I'm thinking I'll stay in bed for about ten days," I answered.

We both laughed at that and said our goodnights.

I didn't fall asleep right away. Ethan Owen puzzled me. He was loving and gentle with his family, but I knew he could also be the opposite. I certainly wouldn't want to cross him. His reaction about Squirrel Sally puzzled me too.

I decided I was tired and needed sleep so I cleared my mind except for visions of Sarah. I slipped down in the bed, pulled up the covers and closed my eyes. Ethan Owen's daughter was in my dreams.

Chapter 8

There was a small window in Ethan Owen's bedroom. Through it I watched Ethan and Cletus ford the chilly Cimarron as the light began to pour over the eastern horizon. Frost was on the ground, and the horses looked reluctant and rank; but the crossing was achieved with no incident. I saw the two figures scramble up the north bank and head into the sun at an easy lope.

I did not try to rise until a couple of hours after the duo's departure. There was some pain and stiffness in my leg, but in general, I felt much better. The big, brass bed was warm and comfortable. The softness of the feather pillow and the crispness of the sheets made me feel sorry for Ethan who would have no such comforts on the trek to Wichita.

I slipped to the edge of the bed and stood, testing the wounded leg. It hurt but not too badly. I was able to move around slowly if I kept most of my weight on my good limb.

I got my trousers on with some difficulty. I was very careful, because I didn't want to start the bleeding again. I decided not to even try my boots. They would require too much effort. I slipped on my shirt and shuffled to the door.

The door opened out onto a short hallway which led past another bedroom and into the main room of the house which was quite large. A huge stone foreplace almost covered the south wall. An assortment of rough hewn furniture including a table and chairs was scattered about. A stove and a bed completed the furnishings.

Anne was seated at the table sewing when I came in.

"Good morning Mr. Kirby," she said.

"Good morning to you too Mrs. Owen. I haven't slept so well in a long time," I replied.

"Should you be up on that leg so soon?" she asked.

"I think that as long as it doesn't start to bleed again, I'm better off moving around than staying in bed. But I've got to walk cautious and slow," I answered.

I eased myself into one of the chairs.

"Where's Sarah?" I asked.

Anne looked at me, and the faintest trace of a grin crossed her face.

"She is out feeding the chickens and tending our little garden. Would you like some breakfast?"

I could feel the emptiness in the pit of my stomach, and the promise of food was a welcome thought to me so I said, "Yes ma'am I would."

Anne busied herself at the stove. She cut strips of bacon and placed them in a skillet. She cracked three eggs in a bowl and poured a cup of coffee which she set before me.

"You're a rather young-looking man Mr. Kirby. If you don't mind me asking, how old are you?" She went back to the stove to turn the bacon.

I thought for a moment, then answered. "I'm right around thirty. But, to tell the truth, I haven't celebrated my birthday in so many years that I tend to forget."

"Do you have a family?" Anne questioned again.

"My folks are dead, but I do have a brother, Joseph, and his family back in Indiana. I have no other family."

A few moments later Anne gave me a plate covered with strips of hot, crisp bacon and bright yellow-yoked eggs. Conversation halted while I proceeded to consume mouthful after mouthful.

I had gone along with Anne's questions for a while then I decided it was my turn. Through some rather deft inquiries of my own, I found out that Ethan was quite a bit older than Anne. They had married when he was 41 and she was 18. I also learned that one child, a boy, had died as an infant.

As the days passed, I grew stronger. I was able to walk farther and longer. The pain lessened and my feelings for Sarah Owen strengthened.

Sarah was someone completely different. I guess she filled a need in my life that I had not allowed myself to recognize. It wasn't a physical need. Any of the girls at Lannon's or numerous women in Wichita could've done that. It was something else: an attitude of feeling, caring, listening I had never experience before.

We were together most of the time; talking, joking and laughing. I almost became thankful for the Indian arrow that necessitated my stay at Ethan Owen's.

We had made a habit of walking to the river every morning; more to exercise my leg than out of need for water. This morning I held Sarah's hand as we strolled; an innocent gesture, but the warmth and softness of her made feel a little nervous. We sat down on a tree covered ridge overlooking the river.

The sky was an azure blue, and the breeze carried the warmth of the spring. The rush of the river water and the songs of the birds completed a most beautiful scene.

I kissed her, softly. She slipped here arms around me and returned my kiss and held me close. Not a word was spoken. I knew then that my life would never quite be the same.

CHAPTER 9

The weather grew warmer. The pain in my leg subsided, and all that remained was a little soreness. I should have been getting restless, but I wasn't. I think Sarah had something to do with that. But, since we were somewhat low on meat, I decided to try my hand at a little hunting. I saddled my horse and slipped the Henry into its boot.

"You're not going," I heard Sarah say.

I turned to find her standing behind me.

"No, I'm not leaving," I answered. I pulled her toward me and hugged her.

"You Indians sure can sneak up on a man," I said.

She chuckled and kissed me. "Where are you going then?" she asked.

"I thought I would hunt for a little fresh meat," I replied.

I mounted my dun and rode off at a trot, looking over my shoulder watching Sarah walk back to the house.

I knew something was wrong the moment I caught sight of the house. The door was open. There were no pies on the window sill and no smoke rising from the chimney. The corrals were empty.

My heart began to race as I levered a shell into the Henry spurred the dun into a gallop.

I slid the horse to a stop in front of the house, dismounted, and ran for the door. I never even thought to proceed cautiously.

The interior was a shambles; furniture broken, drawers pulled out, items strewn across the floor. Whoever had been there had been searching frantically for something.

I walked down the short hallway to the bedroom. Anne was on the bed naked. Her head had been literally smashed in. The dried blood had formed into a crust. Even her fingernails were red from blood. It looked like she had put up quite a fight. I thought I was going to be sick.

I turned to run but the doorway was blocked. Two Indian braves stood just inside and two others were in the hallway.

Before I could think to use my rifle, the first two grabbed me. It was no use struggling, but I tried anyway. The second two entered, and I was wrested to the ground. My hands and feet were bound.

I was terrified as I listened to their angry conversation. They looked at Anne's body then gestured toward me. I knew they thought I was responsible, but I could not defend myself.

I wish I could explain to you just how frightened I was.

You cannot imagine the feelings of sheer horror and helplessness.

After a few more moments of discussion by the Indians, I was picked up and carried outside.

The largest of the four braves, an Indian with a solitary feather affixed to his hair, pulled his scalping knife from its sheath and approached me. I began to scream. He bent down and slit my shirt from neck to waist, baring my chest. Two other Indians pulled my pants and drawers down to my knees, exposing my privates. The three other Indians also drew knives. I knew then what was in store for me. They planned to do a little carving and cutting before they killed me.

The Indians sat down cross-legged, two on each side of me. The largest of them leaned forward and drew his blade across my chest. He didn't pierce deeply, just enough to bring forth a trickle of blood along the slash mark. The Indian sitting across from him followed suit, and then the other two. It looked like they were going to take turns and make it last quite awhile.

My chest, stomach and upper thighs were covered with cuts, but they were all minor as of yet.

I have never been extremely religious, but I never stopped praying. This was going to be a slow, agonizing death and one I didn't deserve.

I didn't really pray for salvation, but, rather, I prayed for strength to endure. I even prayed that God show me a way to make them angrier so that they would kill me quicker.

I heard another Indian calling from some distance away. At least it was Indian language, but the voice was familiar.

The four braves stood up. And, from my position, flat on the ground, I saw Ethan Owen's sorrel horse come into view.

I guess I cried then. The Indians had to be Cheyenne because they knew Ethan and he knew them. They released me after just a few words had been exchanged.

They continued to talk as I arose and pulled on my clothes.

Ethan turned to me and said, "Anne is dead."

"Yes," I answered.

"Where is Sarah?" he asked.

"She is gone," I replied. "She either ran away or they've taken her."

"She would never run," said Ethan. "I must see my wife."

Ethan exchanged a few more words with the Indians, and then they mounted their horses and left.

Ethan walked toward the house. And expressionless look was on his face.

I heard a cry of anguish that sent chills through me come from the house.

It was sometime later that Ethan emerged. He carried a chimneyless kerosene lamp in his hand, spilling its contents. He struck a match, and within moments, the building was enveloped in flames.

The big man sat down on the ground, took out his knife and began stabbing the earth while he watched the fire.

Chapter 10

"I feel terrible, Ethan," I said. "If you hadn't taken me in, none of this would've happened. I should never have left them alone to go hunting."

"It's not your fault," Owen answered. "That's like saying I was responsible for the death of my little boy because I fathered him. No, the fault lies with the men who did this and took my daughter. They will have to pay."

He voice was firm, icy and left no doubt in my mind that he meant exactly what he said.

"I want to come with you," I said.

"Do you think you can make it?" he asked.

I nodded.

"Then you'll be welcome, " he added.

"We must stop at Lannon's for supplies and ammunition. Most of my things were taken, and your Indian friends ruined these clothes. By the way thank you for saving my life a second time," I said. "I hope I can return the favor some day."

"I wish the Cheyenne had happened by a little sooner. They might have been able to help," Ethan commented. "You know they were going to peel the skin off your body piece by piece."

I cringed at the thought.

Ethan continued, "Then they were going to cut off your privates and watch you die."

I really wanted to change the subject, but Ethan changed it for me.

"Do you have any idea who these men were?" he asked.

"I believe they were all men who rode with Cletus. They were probably looking for that bank money. I don't think they really cared about him," I answered. "There were probably four: the two Terk brothers, Johnny Otis, and Cherokee Bill Mullins."

"Will they stick together?" he asked.

"No," I said, "I don't believe so. I think they'll split up. That'll make it harder for us to follow."

"It won't do 'em any good," said Ethan. "It may take us time, but we'll find them in the end."

"I think the key is not giving up, Ethan," I said, "Most outlaws know that the law can only go so far, so fast. If they keep running, they also know that sooner or later, the law has to give up. Not enough manpower. Too many other duties. The men simply give up because of the difficulties. We won't have those problems."

I knew what I said was important to Ethan. An outlaw trail is hard to follow alone. A trusted companion is most welcome. It gives you a sense of security. He also knew that I would stay with it to the end. After all, I owed the man my life. But, I also had other motives. Ethan was not aware of what Sarah meant to me.

Owen cut a piece off of a plug of tobacco and inserted it into his mouth. He offered some to me but I shook my head. I never could stomach chewing tobacco.

"You know these men, Kirby," the big man said. "Will they harm Sarah?"

"I wish I could answer that," I replied. "I just don't know. I think their main concern is money. I know they'll be angry that they missed on their shares from the bank robbery. Other than that I can't figure. The faster we get moving, though, the better our chances."

"You are right," said Ethan.

He mounted his sorrel and I my dun. Shod hoof prints weren't hard to pick up on the untrampled earth. We set out on a journey with an unknown destination. We would not stop until we found Sarah Owen.

CHAPTER 11

I was wrong about the outlaws splitting up. They didn't, at least not right away. All tracks led toward Lannon's. I did appreciate that because I needed some new clothes, a new shell belt, and holster. Luckily, I always carried an extra handgun in my saddlebags, so I still had that weapon plus my Henry.

It was night when we arrived at Lannon'. No matter how good a tracker a man is, not much can be done in the dark. We had no street lamps to guide our way. Moonlight doesn't help much. We also figured this would be the last night in quite awhile in which we would be able to sleep in bed. We left our horses with the stable boy.

We entered the store side of Lannon's. I busied myself picking out the goods I needed while Ethan selected a supply of foodstuffs.

After paying for my purchases, I moved toward the saloon informing Ethan that I would secure a room for the night.

The saloon was dimly lit by kerosene lamps on the walls and tables. There were four men playing cards at a corner table. Lannon was behind the bar. Across the room from the card players sat an old whore named Rosy. At the same table were Lyle and Charles Terk!!!

I caught my breath and looked again. I had seen their likenesses on wanted posters. I was not mistaken.

I turned back from the saloon door an reentered the store. I motioned to Ethan. His moccasined feet made no sound as he strode over to me.

"We've had some luck. I don't know we deserve," I whispered. "Lyle and Charles Terk are sitting in Lannon's saloon drinking, big as you please."

Ethan's face hardened and his eyes narrowed. His grip on the Sharp' rifle tightened. He brushed past me on his way to the saloon. I knew he intended to hill those two.

I grabbed his arm, halting him momentarily. "What do you mean to do?" I asked.

"I'm going to kill them both," he answered. "Don't try to stop me."

"Use your head, Ethan," I said. "We need information. Maybe we can get some idea of Sarah's whereabouts. "Isn't that what we're really after?"

He halted and I continued quickly, knowing I had to keep him from spoiling a golden opportunity. Anything that might put us on the right track had to be explored. Ethan's desire for revenge could hamper us seriously.

"If you kill them now, we miss the best chance we have to locate Sarah. Hold off and let me handle it. Get a room from Lannon and go up and cool off. Those two ain't going anywhere. I'll find out what I can."

I know Ethan wanted swift vengeance. I did too. But, he saw my way was right. He made arrangements with Lannon for the room and went upstairs. I held my breath because I thought any moment he might break and blow the Terk brothers out of their chairs.

I stood in the store thinking. I knew the brothers were slow, so I figured I could outwit them if I went about it the right way.

I guess even the, without knowing exactly what I was doing, I was employing psychology. I know that in my years in Congress handling people was never a chore for me. A little common sense always helped also.

I know there was some talk in the latter part of my last term about making alcoholic refreshments illegal. Prohibition they called it. I just tried to convince people to use their heads. You can't legislate morals. What people can't get legally, they'll get illegally. If the do-gooders ever get that law passed, the criminals in this country will dance in the streets.

I'm sorry. I digress.

Anyway, I knew, the Terk brothers would be easy to manipulate. I only had to come up with the right kind of story.

First of all, I went to the bar and purchased a bottle of whiskey, figuring that a few drinks might be an aid in loosening the brothers' tongues. Then I put the friendliest smile I could muster on my face and walked to the table occupied by the Terks and Rosy.

"Excuse this intrusion on your privacy," I said, tipping my hat to the red-headed woman who grinned, revealing two chipped front teeth. "Ain't you two the famous Terk brother?"

I knew that would get me off to a good start. Flattery is almost always effective if not overused.

I don't think the Terks were used to being complimented because they just sat there and stared. I was amazed at how much alike they looked. I had had only one experience with twins before. I'd been told that there is no such thing as identical twins. But, the only difference I could see between Lyle and Charles was their manner of dress. They both had hawk noses, square chins and deep-set eyes. The only other twins I had known, the Belden brothers, had looked identical too.

"I would like to discuss something with you gentlemen over a drink," I continued, placing my whiskey on the table.

"I turned to Rosy, flashing my best smile and said, "Would you pardon us ma'am. I'm afraid your presence would provide a sweet distraction, and I must keep my mind on business."

That did it. Rosy's face blushed to match her hair. She got up without saying a word and walked toward the stairs casting what I had to surmise as a come hither glance my way.

I turned to the Terks, poured their glasses and mine full. I held my tumbler aloft and announced, "A toast gentlemen. To money. For you and for me. More than you've seen before."

I could see their eyes sparkle like children's on Christmas morning.

Finally, one of them spoke. I couldn't tell who was Lyle and who was Charles, but he said, "Who are you?"

I answered, "George Washington."

The other posed a question in slowly spoken words, each receiving the same emphasis. "What do you want with us?"

I launched into the most outlandish story I could think of. It was long yarn about hidden Confederate gold buried in the Indian Territory. I kept filling their glasses as I told the tale. By the time I was finished, the Terk brothers were drooling over the prospect of easy riches. They were also quite drunk.

Then I changed my approach. The smile disappeared from my face. "There is one problem," I said.

"What?" they asked in unison.

"I need four good men," I answered. "I was hoping your friends Johnny Otis, and Cherokee Bill Mullins would be with you."

"They are not with us," one of them replied hiccuping to sort of punctuate the last word.

"Where are they?" I asked trying to keep the edge out of my voice.

"They are going to Doan's Crossing," one of them answered.

I was anxious and tried to make my next questions as casual as possible. "Where is the girl?" What will they do with her?"

It worked as I hoped it would. The Terk brother who answered the last question answered this one too. I apologize for the language, but this is what he said. "She kicked Johnny in the balls." He chuckled at that then continued. "They will sell her to L.Q. Tyler. She will not kick him or he will beat her. I think they will make a good whore out of her."

The last words were hardly out of his mouth when a growl came from the staircase. Ethan was standing there, his Sharps in his hands. He only said one word, "bastard" and the rifle roared in the confines of the room.

The .50 caliber caught the one Terk brother full in the face causing his features to sort of explode, leaving a gaping hole where his nose used to be.

I was busy at the time also. The other Terk brother went for his gun belt. I pulled my colt from the newly purchased holster, hoping it wouldn't hang up on the new leather. A .44 is not very accurate, but at close range it can make one hell of a mess.

I shot the other Terk brother in the base of the throat. He jerked back in his chair against the wall as blood spurted forth splashing upon the table.

Remembering the card players, I spun around leveling my colt in their direction. "Don't do nothing foolish," I said. "Just keep your hands on the table."

With my free hand I pulled my vest open, revealing my deputy marshal's badge pinned on the inside.

"I'm a law officer," I said. "These men were thieves and murders and got what was coming to them."

Ethan stayed on the stairs. I walked to the bar and dropped a couple of coins on its polished surface. The jingle they made was rather ominous in the silent barroom. The girls upstairs stared over the railing but didn't utter a word.

"Lannon," I said, "this'll pay for the cleanup and burial. Sorry for the disturbance.

I holstered my gun and turned to walk up the stairs. My heart was still pounding and my mouth strangely dry as Ethan and I moved up toward our room as if nothing had happened.

CHAPTER 12

Ethan didn't explain till we reached our room. "I'm sorry, Kirby," he said. "I just couldn't hold my temper."

"I understand," I answered. "I've got a bad temper too. It's a curse. I'm just glad I was able to get some information."

"Why would they be going to Doan's Crossing?" Ethan asked.

"I imagine they just want to disappear," I replied. "They probably figure to hook on with one of the herds going north or with a bunch of drovers going home. An extra pair of hands is always welcome, and on one cares who you are or what you did as long as you do your job."

"What about this L.Q. Tyler? What do you know of him?" Ethan questioned.

"I don't know anything about him," I answered, "but I can imagine the sooner we get to her the better."

"It may already be too late." Ethan commented.

"What do you mean too late?" I retorted. "As long as she's alive, it's not too late."

Ethan Owen didn't answer me than because there was a knock on the door. We both reached for our guns.

"Who is it?" I asked.

"Sally" came the muffled reply.

"Hold on," I said.

I unbolted the door and swung it open.

Sally looked terrible. There were purple bruises over her face and neck. Her nose was puffed up and bent to the side as if it had been broken.

I said, "Come in. What happened?"

When Sally entered, Ethan rose abruptly and exited.

"Sit down," I said, "and tell me about it."

"Well," she said, "Johnny Otis figured I set up Cletus up, and he beat me until I admitted it. I guess I just can't stand pain. I'm sorry."

"You're sorry," I replied. "I should be the one who is sorry for getting you into a mess like this."

"No," she said, "I knew I was taking a chance. I'm sorry because I told 'em which way you was headed."

Tears began to well in her eyes, and she sniffed a little.

"Oh, that's all right," I said, "Johnny'll get what's coming to him. Cletus probably already has.

"Like I promised, your reward money is waiting for you in the bank in Wichita."

I thought a moment. "Sally," I said, "have you ever heard of a man named L.Q. Tyler?"

"Sure I have," she answered. "He's a real son of a bitch."

I guess I had a puzzled look on my face because she hastened to explain.

"L. Q. Tyler is a whoremaster. He buys and sells women. Sometimes he kidnaps them too. He's got a black snake whip he can pluck your eyebrow with. No girl refuses to work for him."

Suddenly, I felt ill, and I wanted to cry out; but I kept silent.

"Where does he stay?" I asked.

"He travels all around this country," she answered. "From Kansas down through Texas to Mexico. He likes to get them young Mex girls. He can buy cheap and sell high."

I thanked her for her help and rose when she left.

Ethan reentered and said, "Jesus Christ what a mess she is."

I didn't say anything.

"Damn whore," Ethan mumbled, "probably got what she deserved."

Suddenly I got angry.

"That woman was beaten because she helped me," I said.

"You looked at her like she is less than human."

"She is," Ethan shot back.

"And what are we?" I asked, the anger noticeably creeping into my voice. "we just shot and killed two men downstairs. What about that?"

"That was necessary." Ethan spat out the words.

"There are a lot of things that become necessary," I answered. Then I decided to drop it. I also decided not to tell him what I learned from Sally about L.Q. Tyler. Instead, I said, "Let's get some sleep. We'll head for Doan's tomorrow. Right?"

Ethan nodded his head.

We both crawled into our beds, I'm sure with our own individual thoughts. Two things worried me most: finding Sarah and wondering what Ethan would do if we did.

CHAPTER 13

Doan's Crossing was cluster of a dozen buildings on the banks of the Red River. The Doans made a small fortune furnishing supplies to the drovers. It was a fine location where the cattle could cross the river with a minimum of danger. As long as people desired beef on their dinner plates, the cattle would keep coming and the Doans would continue prospering.

As I wrote, earlier, I tried my hand at cowboying, but I hated cattle. I do believe they are less intelligent than horses, and horses are a far cry from being smart.

I had journeyed down to Texas not long after the war and worked on the Tenner ranch there for a short time. But there was no market for beef in Texas. The market was in the North.

In fact it was working driving a trail herd north that brought me to Kansas.

Damn that was hard work. Long hours in the saddle, and it was dangerous at that.

Longhorn cattle are nothing more than wild animals. You better be mounted on a good horse when you're around them. If you're on foot, you don't stand much of a chance.

Two things were feared most of all: stampedes and river crossings. Anything could set cattle to stampeding; a peculiar sound, a flash of lightning. You never knew.

The only way to stop the stampede was to turn the leaders back on the rest, making them move in a circle until they ran themselves out. It sounds a lot easier than it was.

It's a frightening thing to gallop alongside a thundering herd of cattle in the pitch black night, screaming and firing your handgun, hoping your horse wouldn't stumble or step in a prairie dog hole, throwing you under those beasts.

River crossings could be just as bad. Swift currents, slippery footing and balky, rank horses all combined to claim the life of many a cowboy.

Ethan and I sat our horses watching a sea of shaggy brown bodies splash through the muddy water of the Red and slosh up the far bank.

There was a lone rider on the south bank who looked to be supervising the crossing. He was not an imposing figure. He was dressed in the normal cowboy garb of the period; broad brimmed hat, shirt, vest, pants, chaps and gun belt. He was thin and wiry. A stubble of beard covered his face and almost hid the scar along his right cheekbone.

As we rode up to him, I pinned my badge on the outside of the vest. I figured we might as well get down to business right away.

"You've got quite a herd there," I said as I pulled my horse alongside.

"That's years of hard work on the hoof," the cowboy answered, "sweating in the summer and freezing in the winter. And we've still got miles to go yet before they can be turned into hard money. My name is Lafe Talon. The herd is mine."

We introduced ourselves and shook hands. Talon spit a glob of tobacco juice out on the ground and spoke again.

"Lawmen out here ain't riding just for fun or to admire a cattle herd. I seen the shine of your star a little ways off. Who are you after?"

"You don't miss much," I commented.

"Can't afford to," said Talon.

Ethan dropped his reins on his horse's neck, pulled a plug of tobacco from his pocket and offered it to Talon.

"Fresh chaw?" he asked.

"No thanks," said Talon, "there's plenty of spit left in this one."

He punctuated his comment by letting loose a spurt of juice that hit a spotted steer on the nose.

"Pretty good," said Ethan.

"Takes practice," stated Talon, "besides, I ain't got no spittoons to aim at."

Ethan Owen took a bite out of his plug and maneuvered it to the side of his mouth.

I felt I should get right to the point.

"We're looking for two men who did a killing in Kansas," I said. "One's a half breed with braided hair. Calls himself Cherokee Bill Mullins. The other's got sandy hair, looks young like a kid. His name is Johnny Otis. You seen any like 'em?"

Talon stood in his stirrups and bellowed at one of his men.

"Shortstuff! There's one bogged down in the mud on the far side Pull him out!"

One of the cowboys hastened to carry out the order.

Talon turned his attention back to us.

"I got no half breed, but I hired a young fellow a few days ago," he said.

Ethan's eyes brightened at such good fortune, but I was a little skeptical as Talon continued.

"I had lost a man in a stampede. A replacement was very welcome. I never ask no questions as long as a man does what he is told. This fella never give his name, so I just called him Kid. He does his work, causes no trouble, but he might be who you're looking for."

"When can we see him?" I asked.

"After the crossing," Talon answered, "we'll lay up a day, letting the animals feed and rest. The men can use the time too. You should be able to see him when the herd's bedded down."

"We'll come back tonight if it's all right with you." I said.

"Sure Marshal," he replied, "only, I'd appreciate it if there wasn't no gunplay. I don't want to chase cattle all night."

I assured Lafe Talon there'd be no trouble, casting a glance at Ethan while I talked. I was hoping the big man would cooperate and control his temper. I cautioned the cattleman not to say anything to the kid. Then we rode to Doan's to await nightfall.

CHAPTER 14

Ethan and I unsaddled and fed our horses at Doan's. Then we fed ourselves steak, potatoes, canned tomatoes, and deep dish apple pie. It was the best meal we had had for days.

As the red glow of sunset blushed upon the western horizon, we saddled our horses again and headed toward Lafe Talon's camp.

Ethan seemed strangely calm to me. I thought he would be nervous and anxious, but he had himself under control. I must confess I certainly felt jumpier than he looked.

Lafe Talon's crew of cowboys had finished their evening meal and were sitting around the campfire swapping stories as was the custom.

The cook was under a canvas that extended from the chuckwagon and was supported by two poles. He was tending to his pots and pans and listening with one ear.

The men were in a semi-circle sitting or reclining on their bedrolls, sipping cups of strong fragrant coffee.

A young man stood in front of his peers regaling them with a rather risqué story. The orange glow from the fire cast a dancing, burning light on him. The portion of his body facing the fire seemed to change in hue with each flicker of the flames. The six other men hung on the speaker's words as if they were Confucius' pearls of wisdom.

We heard the cowboys laugh in unison as we tied our horses to the chuckwagon.

Lafe Talon didn't look happy as he approached us.

"Marshal," Talon said, "I've got bad news. The kid lit out sometime between the crossing and supper."

Ethan let out a string of curses. They expressed my sentiments also. We had been close.

"How long of a start does he have?" I asked.

"Maybe two hours at most," Talon answered.

"Did anyone see him go?" Ethan questioned.

Talon replied, "Dippermouth did."

Talon motioned and a black cowboy with skin like a lump of coal emerged from the shadow. We could easily see why he as called Dippermouth.

The black man told us that he talked to Johnny Otis just before his departure. Otis had not told of his destination, but had ridden north. We didn't know who had told Otis of our visit, but I suspected Dippermouth did. He seemed almost too willing to cooperate.

One bit of information Dippermouth provided was helpful. The black man helped the horse wrangler with the remuda so he knew many of the mounts well. The roan Johnny Otis had taken had a cracked shoe on the left foreleg. It wasn't much, but it could make tracking a little easier.

Ethan came up with the plan that we finally followed.

"There is still light," he said. "A single man riding a string of horses could run him down this night."

"How the hell can that be done?" I asked. Lafe Talon and the black cowboy listened intently.

"It ain't gonna be easy," said Ethan, "but it can be done Kirby. You'll burn up some horseflesh but you can catch him.

We all waited for the big man to continue. We were still puzzled.

"We'll string three horses together, your saddle horse and two others. You'll ride one and lead two. They'll all tire, but not as fast as if all were carrying weight. You'll ride steady with no stopping. It's a little chancy, but I don't think he'll be expecting it. It's worth a try."

I pondered the situation a bit. I must admit I was a little hesitant thinking of the pounding my posterior would have to take.

Finally I said, "I just hope he's scared enough to ride straight and not try to do anything fancy: just put miles under his belt."

I wrote a voucher for payment for two of Lafe Talon's horses. I told him to present it to Sam Lane, and he would be paid for his animals.

Ethan rigged rope halters and used rawhide for reins. He employed a type of a slip knot that, when pulled, would allow the halter to slip off the animals, head, setting it free. Once I was done with a horse, I would turn it loose.

The light was beginning to fade as I slipped up onto the bare back of the first horse, a grey mustang with a hammer head. I took the rawhide reins in my left hand, wrapped the lead rope attached to the other two horses around my right hand and rode to where Ethan was sitting astride his sorrel. He had found the outlaw's track.

"Straight north, Kirby," he said. "Get a move on!"

I touched spurs to the flanks of my mount, pulled up the slack on the lead rope, and moved out at a lope. Ethan followed at an easy trot, and it wasn't long before the big man was just a rapidly receding speck over my shoulder.

Chapter 15

I was taught that one of the best ways to learn horsemanship was by riding bareback. It teaches the rider the importance of maintaining balance. But, I somehow never enjoyed horse riding without a saddle. I guess I like that extra sense of security.

After an hour and a half on the trail of Johnny Otis, my rump had already taken a pounding. That grey mustang had high withers and a bony back.

The night was clear and the stars sparkled like diamonds in the inky sky. The moon was full like a pale yellow disc.

I could travel no faster than a lope because of the darkness ,but an easy lope can cover a lot of ground in a couple of hours.

I paused to relieve myself and turned the grey mustang loose. I chewed on a piece of beef jerky and washed it down with water from my canteen.

My second mount was a bay gelding. He proved to be a little smoother than the grey horse.

Another few hours passed. I was tired and needed sleep but kept pushing on.

It was two o'clock by my pocket watch when I stopped to examine some horse droppings. They were fresh. That woke me up.

Otis couldn't be far ahead, and he just had to rest his horse. I knew I had a few more miles in my bay, and then I could switch to my dun. I was positive I could catch him.

By 4 a.m. I was mounted on my dun, a little more comfortable sitting in my own, good saddle.

I topped a ridge and halted, straining my eyes to catch any movement

I could. Down below me I saw him moving slowly. I figured his horse must have been pretty much done in. I was surprised he was still going. I figured he must've been planning on riding all night and not resting till morning.

I urged the dun into an easy trot while I pulled the Henry from its scabbard. I didn't want to go charging after him just yet. I wanted to close the gap a little more between us. I knew if I had to shoot from a moving horse that my rifle would be much more accurate than any handgun.

I kept gaining on him minute by minute. I was within shouting distance before he even saw me.

Otis snapped a shot over his shoulder. He spurred his horse into a lope and kept raking the animal's sides with his rowels, but the mount could not muster any more speed.

I had knotted my reins and now I dropped them on the dun's neck. I guided my horse with leg pressure only as I levered a cartridge into the Henry and began firing. I aimed high and low, not really wanting to hit him.

Firing from moving horses is a tricky business. The explosion of gunpowder around their heads can make them shy and veer off helping to create an extra dimension of difficulty in sighting and shooting.

I tried to direct my fire at the horse rather than Johnny Otis. Looking back on it now, I probably shouldn't have fired at all.

I shot the roan horse and saw it go down. The animal fell. Its impetus carried it forward, propelling its hindquarters up and over. It looked like a man performing a somersault.

Sometimes a man will purposely dive off a bucking or falling horse rather than be thrown or hung up in the stirrup leathers. Johnny Otis either didn't think of it or simple didn't have time to do anything.

He could've died from the broken neck he sustained or from the saddle horn crushing his chest under the weight of the animal.

The sight was rather gruesome, but I must confess I didn't feel sorry for him. He led a violent life and received a violent death.

What occupied my mind that night was Sarah Owen, and the fact that a doorway that might've led to her speedy rescue was slammed shut in my face.

CHAPTER 16

There was nothing I could do for Johnny Otis. I couldn't even bury him. Even if I had had a shovel, it would've been useless. I could never have moved the body from under the carcass of the horse.

I was exhausted and sore. I unsaddled the dun, and hobbled him. Even though that horse was good about staying put, I never took any chances. In those days in wild country a man's life often times depended on his horse. I never wanted to wake up and find that my mount had wandered off. That was like an instant death sentence.

Ethan arrived a little after sunup. I was always a light sleeper, but, in my days as a lawman, I was an especially light sleeper.

Ethan dismounted and surveyed the strange sight of the dead horse and the man under it.

"What a mess," he finally said.

"Yeah," I answered, rubbing the sleep out of my eyes.

"How did it happen?" Owen questioned.

I told the whole story while Ethan rummaged through his saddlebags and extracted a bottle of whiskey. He tossed it to me.

"You look like you could use it," he said.

"Breakfast," I said tilting the bottle toward him. I took a swig, and the liquid burned from my throat to my stomach. It sort of took my breath away but felt good anyhow.

"Join me?" I questioned.

"Hell, might as well," he answered. "Did you get any information from him before he died?"

I shook my head no. "He was dead when I reached him. I hit the horse like I wanted. It was just a freak accident."

Ethan Owen wiped his mouth on his sleeve. Then he spoke again. "You were right. Our luck was going too good. Now we are up against it. Where do we go from here?"

I still had not mentioned L.Q. Tyler. I wanted to keep that to myself for a while so I said, "I'm going back to Wichita for a few days. You should come with me."

I told him I wanted to check around town. Maybe there might be some information to be found. I was really planning on making the rounds of gambling halls, saloons, and whorehouses trying to check on the whereabouts of L.Q. Tyler. Squirrel Sally had helped me before. I thought she might help me again.

Ethan unsaddled his horse also. The animals both had to rest. And I guess the humans needed something too, because before long, we were both roaring drunk.

Drink tends to loosen tongues, and destroy inhibitions. We both ended up talking a lot.

After divulging much of my past, I turned to Ethan and inquired about his background.

In a voice slurred by whiskey, he launched into a rather long oratory.

"My mother died when I was young. My father had been gone sometime. I don't remember him at all. I was raised by my sister."

He spat out the word sister as if it were a foul object in his mouth and continued.

"She was a whore Kirby, goddamned whore. I was raised in a whorehouse. It made me sick. Night after night men coming and going at all hours. Fat, skinny, young, old, all looking for a good time. And my sister gave it to them. She enjoyed it!! Damn her soul!!!"

The last few words were actually a shout which revealed the depth of his hatred for his sister.

It was not use disagreeing, arguing, or even trying to reason with him. Sometimes people are just close minded on certain topics. They will not allow another opinion to enter their thoughts. I guess it's a little safer and more secure that way.

I had known many ladies of the evening in my days as a lawman. Not one of them enjoyed her work. The better ones were able to fake a passion or pleasure. It could result in better pay. Flattered male egos tend toward generosity.

Ethan calmed down a little then. I was going to inquire further about his sister but thought it more prudent to drop the subject. Instead if asked about Anne.

"I had been a trapper for some years," said Ethan, "I was friendly with all the Indians. I treated 'em fair. They respected me. And I needed them. I needed their protection so I married Singing Bird. I didn't love her at first, but it came upon me gradual like. You know the way the sun peeks over the horizon little by little, lighting the earth as it goes until it's a bright new day? Well, my feelings for Anne grew like that until she was the true brightness in each of my days."

The tears welled up in his eyes and spilled onto his cheek. But he wasn't just another drunk crying. He was an individual crushed with grief. He must've loved and needed Anne desperately, much more than I realized.

"You still have Sarah," I said.

"It's not the same," he replied. "Nothing will ever be the same again."

Owen would talk no more. We moved our gear under the sparse shade of a trio of post oaks and slept.

CHAPTER 17

I was very happy to get back to Wichita. I looked forward to a bath, a shave and sleeping in my own bed.

Sam Lane was glad to see me too. He pumped my hand until I thought my arm might fall off. His concern for me was evident and genuine.

"Grant," he said, "I was getting' mighty worried about you. When that Owen fella brought Cletus in, I was plenty relieved. He told me what had happened, and I was thankful for his help. Your scalp might've been decorating some Cheyenne's war lance."

"Yes, that was a close call," I answered.

"But that was some time ago, son. Where have you been since?"

I gave him a capsule account of what had happened since I had been wounded. I left out nothing because there was no one in the world I trusted more than Sam Lane.

When I had finished, Sam shook his head and spoke soberly.

"Damn, what is this world coming to? I can imagine what Ethan Owen is feeling. I can imagine what you're feeling. You plan to carry this through until you find her don't you?"

"Yes, I do," I replied.

"You know that L.Q. Tyler is a slaver don't you?" he asked.

I nodded my head affirmatively.

"I don't know how to put this delicately," Sam said as he shifted and fidgeted in his desk chair. "Tyler has already made that girl a wh..." He stopped in mid sentence, realizing that what he was going to say would hurt me, and rephrased it. "Tyler will have compromised the girl already. Can you take that?"

That was a question I had been asking myself for a long time. If she could be rescued, would I be man enough to accept her as she was, knowing what she had had to do? I wasn't sure, but I thought so. What she was going through now was necessary for her survival. Human beings can and will do many distasteful things to stay alive. Sarah was smart and she was a fighter. She would never give up trying to escape or hoping for rescue. She would never surrender to the life L.Q. Tyler thrust upon her. She would simply endure it, and to me that was the big difference.

"Yes Sam, I think I can," I answered.

I wanted to change the subject for a bit because I was beginning to feel a little uncomfortable. So, I inquired about Cletus.

"Cletus is under the earth," Sam stated. "He didn't die well. He cried and blubbered. He had to be dragged up on the scaffold. We had a good crowd that morning. Cletus was well-known and hated by many.

"He didn't die fast. His neck didn't break. The hangman said he choked to death."

"I'm sorry I missed it," I commented.

"There are others who deserved the same fate," I continued.

"We killed two. A third is dead and the other is still loose."

"Cherokee Bill Mullins is not the type to do this sort of thing. Take my word for it," Sam said. "Mullins is a thief and a good tracker. He's no killer and he pays little attention to women. I think you should turn your attention to L.Q. Tyler."

"You're probably right Sam." I winked at him and continued.

"You usually are."

He smiled and I knew the compliment pleased him.

You know, I'll never understand why people don't recognize the power of a well-placed compliment. It can surely help you, and it certainly makes the complimented fell appreciated.

"Did Squirrel Sally get her share of the reward?" I asked.

"Yes, she did," Sam answered, "but she didn't leave."

That surprised me. I thought she would've been long gone.

"Where is she?" I inquired.

"She is working for Fat Alice over at her house on Beacon Street."

I raised my eyebrows at that information. Fat Alice ran the most luxurious bordello in Wichita. It was also the most expensive. In Sally's rather sordid world she had achieved somewhat of a pinnacle. She could aspire to nothing finer than Fat Alice's.

Sally was really the only glimmer of hope I had. She knew L.Q. Tyler.

She just might be able to help me locate him. If she could not help, my chances of ever finding Sarah would be almost extinguished.

I excused my self and went to bathe. After all, a man had to look his best when visiting Fat Alice's.

CHAPTER 18

Fat Alice's was quite an elegant establishment. From the silver knocker on the door to the baby grand piano in the parlor, it was the classiest brothel a cowpoke was likely to see this side of New Orleans.

The ladies reflected the surroundings. They were genteel and demure, never brassy, loud, or coarse. Even though the product offered was basically the same that was offered in any of the saloons in Wichita, Alice's still had a certain aura about it. Her house of ill repute furnished customers with the totality of pleasure. The combination of the atmosphere and the seemingly refined women made a visit to Fat Alice's something really special.

It seemed as if I had just released the silver knocker when the door swung open. A tall thin negro dressed in a black cutaway coat and trousers ushered me in.

"Good evenin' sir," he said, "would you please follow me?"
the man took my hat and led me into the parlor.

The room was quite large. It had to be to accommodate a baby grand and assorted tables, chairs, and couches. Velvet drapes hung against the windows.

The color scheme seemed to include mostly reds and browns adding richness and heaviness to the appearance of the room.

I told the Negro doorman that I wanted to see Fat Alice. He suggested that I be seated while he went to fetch the lady.

It may seem strange to you now to read about a law officer visiting a house of prostitution and not making arrests or in some manner causing mayhem; but that is the way it was. As long as the ladies kept to their own areas of the city, we never bothered them.

Fat Alice entered the parlor with a swish of skirts and a hearty, "Hello there Kirby!"

She was truly a large woman. I'm sure she stood six feet tall and must've weighed two hundred pounds. Her huge body was enclosed by a beautiful blue brocade gown. Her bosom spilled over the low cut top.

Her face, framed by soft auburn hair, was full but pretty. A cigarillo was clenched between her teeth.

"What can we do for you Marshal?" She winked and her mouth spread into a smile.

"Alice, I need your assistance," I said. "I certainly hope you can help me out."

"I'll do what I can," she replied. The smile disappeared from her countenance as she spied the serious, troubled look on my face.

I launched into a somewhat edited version of the story I had told Sam Lane. I stressed the importance of finding L.Q. Tyler.

When I was finished, Fat Alice spoke. "I've heard of L.Q. Tyler, but I've never had any dealings with him. He mistreats his girls and cheats customers. I heard he beat one of his women to death."

That statement didn't make me feel any better. I was already worried that we might be too late, that Sarah might be lost to us. The thought that she was in the hands of someone like Tyler made me cringe.

"Have you any idea where he might be?" I asked.

"I don't know Kirby," Alice answered. "He is on the move quite a bit."

I asked her if I could speak with Squirrel Sally. She was my best chance the way I saw it.

"Sally is at the top of the stairs, first door to your right. I know she isn't busy yet. It's too early. I sure hope she can help you."

I think Alice meant what she said. Even though she was as hardened as they come, I believe she was real with me. I was serious about trying to rescue someone from a life like hers. I'm sure she respected me for that. I just knew should help me if she could.

"Alice, I'd appreciate it if you would check around with your other lady friends (I emphasized lady). Anything you can find out may aid me. Everyday counts," I said.

I stood and turned to head toward the stairs. Alice placed her hand on my shoulder and held me back momentarily.

"Tell me the truth," she said, "do you love her?"

I nodded my head and answered, "Yes."

"You better," she continued, "cause if you do find her and don't love her, it'd hurt her worse than if you never tried. She's better off where she is than with someone who won't be able to forget her past."

"I'll be able to do what I have to do," I replied. "She's a fighter and so am I. We'll make it. I know."

Alice dropped her hand from my shoulder, smiled and said, "I'll send someone around tonight to ask about L.Q. Tyler. You'll find him and Sarah too."

I thanked her and moved toward the stairs. I somehow felt more confident about things. I hoped Squirrel Sally would be able to add to that feeling.

CHAPTER 19

Sally answered my knock with a cheerful, "Come in."

As I entered, I saw her seated at her vanity table. She was applying the finishing touches on her makeup when she spied my reflection in the mirror. She turned, flashed a genuine but surprised smile, stood up and walked toward me.

"You're looking a lot better than the last time I saw you," I said.

"Yes, I was in a bad way then," she replied.

Sally did look remarkable well. The pale green dress she wore provided a contrast for her chestnut hair. She seemed relaxed.

"Have you had any luck?" she questioned.

I proceeded to fill her in on the details so far. She was certainly aware of the killing of the Terk brothers, but the demise of Johnny Otis especially pleased her.

I must digress again at this point and apologize to the reader. Age is sometimes a curse. I fear I've mislead you somewhat as to the passage of time and the distance involved in the search.

What I've told you so far took place over quite a period of time. I took Cletus prisoner early in March. I did not get back to Wichita until late in May.

Doan's Crossing is across the river from Texas, so I had traveled quite a ways. I did this for two reasons, I was positive I could get some information about the whereabouts of L.Q. Tyler and I felt a responsibility toward Sam Lane. He deserved to know about my plans to find Sarah. He deserved to know that I would search until I located her, no matter how long it took.

59

"Sally, I asked, "can you give me any more information on Tyler? Alice has already said she will check around with other madams in the city."

She walked back to her chair and sat down. She indicated for me to do the same. I perched myself on the edge of the bed.

"L.Q. Tyler and I go back a few years," she said. "I ran away from my mother because I thought I loved him. Well, I found out soon that it wasn't love at all. He just wanted to use me.

"I don't want to bore you with the details, but the first time he forced me to be with another man I thought I would rather die. His whip taught me different. From then till now it's him I've wanted to see dead."

"How did you get away from him?" I interrupted.

"I convinced one of my customers to take me with him. It wasn't hard. L.Q. was a little too confident he had me scared. He did, but I took the chance. I knew he wouldn't kill me if he caught me. A dead girl is no good for business. I haven't seen the bastard since.

I wanted to ask Sally why she had remained in her profession when she might have gotten out, but I didn't. I've always believed that a person's private life is just that --- private.

"L. Q. moves up and down the cattle trails from south Texas to Kansas," Sally continued. "His base is in a place called Elm Spring in the Indian Territory.

"When he's traveling, he usually has two or three wagons and about a half dozen men. It's like a whorehouse on wheels.

"He buys and sells girls along the way. He can make a dent in some of that cowboy money before they even reach the railhead. Most of those men don't have much cash. Sometimes their bosses have to loan them money. A cowboy seeing an available woman and then not being able to have her can get mighty ornery. If they've got the wherewithal, they're usually more than willing to let their men pleasure themselves. It sure enough beats having them rebel."

I questioned Sally further about the Elm Spring location and got the layout in my mind. It was centered on the Concho Trail which lay between the Western Trail and the Chisholm Trail. She told me that Tyler always kept a few girls there along with some of his men.

Since this was the season for moving cattle up from Texas, I figured Tyler would be somewhere along those three trails. The other, the Goodnight-Loving, went too far west. I thought he'd be too busy making money on his women to be concerned with selling them.

We talked for a few minutes longer, and I thanked Sally very sincerely for her help. I didn't expect that any information forthcoming from Fat Alice could add much to what I already knew.

I would have to inform Ethan of the situation. Then, we would be off to the Indian Territory.

CHAPTER 20

On our return to Wichita, Ethan had put up at Sullivan's Hotel. I told him I had things to check on and that I would get back to him when I had some information.

After my conversations with Alice and Sally I knew I would have to tell Ethan what I had learned about his daughter's captor. I wasn't sure how he was going to take it.

Sullivan's was a moderately priced, clean hotel. Rooms were generous in size, well kept and the food was good. The restaurant and a small bar with gaming tables were located on the other side of the lobby.

When I entered, the lobby was silent. A lone desk clerk was seated reading the newspaper. I could hear muffled noises emanating from the dining room and the bar.

I rang the bell at the desk and the clerk almost fell off his seat. The little man wearing frameless glasses stood bolt upright, his face gradually changing from flesh tone to full pink as he flushed in embarrassment.

"May I help you sir"" he stammered.

"Yes," I said, "I'm looking for a man called Ethan Owen.

A man like Ethan isn't hard to describe. He certainly was unique enough to stand out in a crown. The desk clerk knew immediately to whom I was referring, and he directed me without hesitation to the barroom.

I crossed the lobby and pushed through the swinging doors leading to the saloon.

I spotted Ethan Owen seated across the room, his back to the wall. Most gunfighters and lawmen liked to sit with their backs against the wall. It provided some protection against an attack from the rear. He sat with a half empty bottle of whiskey in front of him and a deck of playing cards scattered on the table.

A black haired girl in a tight fitting yellow dress leaned over Ethan, stroking his hair and whispering in his ear.

What surprised me most was the non-committal expression Ethan's face. He didn't telegraph what he was thinking at all.

In one continuous motion the big man stood up and lashed out with his right back hand. The blow caught the girl on the right cheek and knocked her over an empty table. Her scream blended with the scrape of wooden table legs on the wooden floor.

There were only three other men in the room counting the bartender. They must have been surprised as me because no one moved. It's as if we were all mesmerized by the big man's action.

Ethan slowly, turned toward the girl on the floor and in a drunken slur yelled, "You bitch! You filthy whore!"

He started for her, and I knew something had to be done. The bartender looked like he was frozen to the floor, and the two customers also weren't moving. They definitely were not about to interfere.

Ethan pulled the girl up by the hair and with the open hand slapped her across the face. It sounded like the crack of a whip as flesh met flesh.

I was running across the room as this happened, threading my way between tables and chairs.

"Ethan! Stop it!" I screamed.

The big man looked over his shoulder and muttered, Go to hell."

I don't know if he recognized me or not. What I did know was that he wasn't going to stop. He was going to continue beating that girl. Given his size and strength, he could easily do serious damage, even kill her.

I thought of using my gun, but too often guns are used in anger. After all, the man had saved my life. I was afraid I might have to shoot.

I've heard that Wyatt Earp successfully buffaloed many men. That is he hit them with is revolver. I never did believe in that. When I drew my gun, I was prepared to shoot it.

I had seen a few barroom brawls, and fair play was never a prerequisite, especially when the opponent was considerably bigger and stronger.

My first blow was a well placed kick to the back of Owen's left knee. His leg buckled and, as a reflex action, he let go of the girl so he could use both hands to keep from falling.

I followed with a left to his stomach summoning all the force I could put behind it. I've found it's much easier on the hands hitting soft parts of the human body rather than bony sections of the jaw.

Ethan doubled over with a groan.

I grabbed the whiskey bottle from the table and broke it over his skull. He collapsed, and hit the floor with a resounding thud and lay still.

The girl had taken a couple of good licks. I helped her to a seat and told the bartender to bring her a drink.

"Are you all right?" I asked.

"I think so," she replied. "I'm a little dizzy."

"Can you see?" I inquired.

She said her vision was all right. I asked her if she knew what brought Ethan's violent reaction.

"It's funny," she replied, "he'd been staring at me for sometime. I figured he might want some pleasure. I mean, even if he is old enough to be my daddy, it don't make no difference to me."

"What did you say to him?" I asked.

"I only said what I usually say, 'Do you want Sarah to show you a good time?' Then I licked his ear a little."

I understood then.

I left the girl where she was. I enlisted the aid of the two men in the barroom. Together the three of us managed to carry Ethan up to his room.

We laid him on top of his bed. I took a cloth, soaked it in the wash basin, and cleaned away the blood from the back of his head.

I sat down in the only chair in the room and waited, mulling the events of the evening over in my mind, wondering how Ethan would react to the truth about his daughter.

CHAPTER 21

I must have dozed off sitting in the chair because I awoke with a start. Ethan was groaning and trying to get up from the bed.

I turned the flame up on the kerosene lamp on the table, and the golden flow of the flame lightened all but the recesses of the room, casting silhouettes against the walls.

The big man sat upright, cradling his head in his hands. His face was puffy and his eyes red rimmed as he gazed across the room at me.

"What happened?" he mumbled as he rubbed the back of his head, tenderly massaging the injured area.

I slowly explained what had taken place earlier in the evening. When I had finished, Ethan shook his head gingerly and muttered, "Jesus, what's wrong with me?"

I let that remark pass by because I didn't know how to answer it. Instead I went downstairs and got a pot of coffee and two cups.

When I returned, Ethan was washing his face. He sat back down on the bed while I poured the strong black coffee.

"We've got to talk." I said.

Ethan blew the steam from his cup, took a sip and nodded.

"I've got some news you've got to hear," I continued, "It's about Sarah."

"Bad news?" Owen interjected.

"Not good," I replied.

His face twisted into a grimace and he winced in pain as if recoiling from a blow.

"Might as well tell me," he said. "It can't make me feel much worse than I already do."

I knew he'd change his mind after he heard what I had to say, but I plunged ahead anyway.

"As far as I can tell, Sarah is being held captive by L.Q. Tyler."

Ethan's face was blank. Even though he had heard the name of Tyler, it obviously meant nothing to him now so I continued.

"He's a slaver. He buys and sells women.

At that he let out a low moan, and I knew it wasn't from the pain in his head. His worst fears had been realized.

"Tyler runs some wagons between here and Texas," I said. "He follows the cattle trails, catering to the cowboys. He's got a place at Elm Spring in the Indian Nation. This is spring. A lot of drovers will be heading our way. I think the chances are good that we can catch them either on the trail or on his home ground."

Ethan looked a little more in control now. His face showed a stern façade. His speech was steady.

"How many men?"

"I heard a half dozen or so with the wagons and a couple more at Elm Spring," I answered. "They are tough men I've been told. I don't think they're liable to give her up without a fight."

"Then we'll fight," Ethan said. His voice cracked a little as he went on. "Damn that Johnny Otis' soul!!! Why did he have to do this to my little girl?"

That was something else I couldn't answer. You can never tell why people do what they do. All you can do is guess.

I've found that to be true throughout my life including my tenure in the Senate. Bills I've worked on and sponsored have been defeated by the people I thought I could count on for support.

"He was a mean one, Ethan," I replied, "and a little crazy too, but he paid with his life."

"It's not enough," Ethan muttered. "The Cheyenne know what's right to do. Peel the skin off him. That's what to do."

His comment made me think back to what had almost happened to me. I swallowed hard because it still frightened me.

I changed the subject because I knew I must. We couldn't change the past, but we could sure do our damndest to alter the future.

"Will you be ready to ride tomorrow?" I asked.

"I'll be ready if you have to tie me in the saddle," he answered.

"I figure the horses have rested up enough," I continued.

"We should probably take another horse along too. We can pack provisions on him and use him as a riding horse on the way back.

"Kirby, do you really think we'll find her alive?" the big man asked.

There was an emphasis on her that upset me. It was as if Sarah no longer existed and had been replaced by a phantom her.

"We'll find Sarah and she'll be alive," I replied.

If you call it living," Ethan commented.

Ethan's detachment frightened me. The odds were good that she was alive. L.Q. Tyler wouldn't kill or even beat her badly. She was too valuable. And yet, Ethan talked like Sarah was already dead or lost forever.

"She's waiting for us, Ethan, I know it," I assured him. "We can't let her down."

I received no answer from Owen. He had reclined on the bed. Intermittent snores pierced the air. I don't really think he wanted to hear what I had to say anyhow.

I let myself quietly out of the room. I returned to my own lodgings behind the jail and tried to sleep, but my slumber was troubled. Ethan had changed. I was hoping it was just a mixture of whiskey, and the news of Sarah, but I couldn't be sure.

CHAPTER 22

I awoke early the next morning from a troubled slumber to the noise of rattling pans followed by the sizzle of frying bacon. The aroma of cooking meat mixed with the scent of freshly brewed coffee drifted through the half opened door of my room. It tickled my nostrils and chased the sleep from my eyes.

I slipped on my socks, pulled on my pants and shuffled into the marshal's office.

There stood Sam Lane cracking eggs into a frying pan. He flashed a smile at me and announced cheerfully, "Good mornin', How many will you have? Three? Four?"

I smiled back. "Good morning to you too. Make it three."

I walked out back to the outhouse, returned, and washed my hands and face. I was buttoning my shirt when Sam called to me to eat.

The desk top was covered with plates, pans, cups, and a coffee pot. I attacked the food with gusto not realizing how hungry I was.

When we had finished eating and were draining the last drops from the coffee pot, Sam finally spoke. "Did you find out what you needed?"

"Yes, I did," I answered. "She's with Tyler. He's somewhere between here and south Texas, either on the road or at his home place, Elm Spring."

Sam slurped the last of his coffee and placed the cop back on the desk.

"Do you want to kill him?" he asked.

Same Lane didn't have to wait long for his answer.

"I want to rescue Sarah," I replied. "If Tyler gets killed in the process, I won't cry."

Sam grinned and nodded his head up and down slowly.

"Good, he said, "that's what I wanted toe hear. You're still a lawman, but that don't mean you've got a license to go around killing, even no accounts like Tyler."

Sam leaned back in his chairs and crossed his feet on the desk top.

I unpinned the star from my vest and reached out, handling it to the old man.

"Sam," I said, "I don't know how long I'll be gone this time. I'll be no help to you here. I don't be going my job so I'm turning in my badge."

Sam held up his hand a signal to stop. "You keep it," he said, "you'll be back."

"I don't know," I mumbled. "Won't there be trouble for you for keeping me on the payroll like this?"

The aging marshal shook his head. "Why hell no! you're still on the trail of the rest of that bank robbery outfit aren't you?"

"No, I'm not," I answered. Then I caught the wink of his eye and understood his meaning.

"Thanks Sam," I continued, "this means a lot to me. A deputy marshal's badge might come in very handy where we're going."

"How do you figure to handle this?" he asked.

"We'll head down to Elm Spring first," I replied. "If we're lucky and she's there, we'll do what we have to do to get her out. If not, we'll find out what we can.

"We know Tyler is traveling much of the time. He follows the cattle trails and journeys down even as far as Mexico to get women. Those young Mexican girls are supposed to be favorites of his. We'll ride those trails if we have to."

"That could take you all summer," Sam commented, "maybe even longer."

I nodded in assent. It might certainly take a long time. That's really why I wanted to turn in my badge. I didn't know when I'd be able to return to my job in Wichita.

The door swung open and the figure of Ethan Owen filled the frame. He looked none the worse for wear. In fact, he looked much the same as he had when I first saw him. He offered a polite greeting and accepted the dregs of the coffee pot in the cup.

"You'll have to chew it," Sam chuckled.

"That's fine with me," Ethan replied. He then turned his attention to me. "You ready?" he asked.

"I've got most everything packed. I do have to secure another horse though," I answered.

Sam volunteered to go and purchase an animal for me while I finished preparations. That was really better because a lot of people owed Sam Lane favors that he rarely called in. I was sure he could pick up a sound horse for a good price. I was correct. He returned with a fine looking bay gelding and would take no payment. It was a "gift" he said.

When we were provisioned and the horses saddled, I bid another goodbye to Sam Lane. He wished us both luck.

We headed south toward uncertain territory, I prayed that our quest would end rapidly and successfully.

CHAPTER 23

A long horse ride can be dry, dusty, and back breaking or cold, wet, and back breaking. When we set out for Elm Spring at least the weather was with us. The sun was warm. The breezes were fresh. All around us nature was awakening. We were traveling at that in-between time. Winter had dissipated and the heat of summer had not yet arrived. The journey would have been pleasant but for its purpose.

About five days out of Wichita we came upon a sight that upset Ethan quite a bit. If the wind had been blowing toward us, the odor would've served as a warning.

We topped a rise and below us in a small basin were a group of four buffalo hunters skinning the carcasses of a herd of about twenty bison.

I am not condoning their work but, in a way, it was rather fascinating. They moved quickly and knew exactly where to make the cuts so that the hides could be peeled off with less difficulty.

Ethan was angered at the sight. "Damn them," he said, "they take those hides and leave the rest to rot! The Indians use every bit of the buffalo, hides, and bones. These bastards kill them for money just because back East some fancy folks have decided they want buffalo coats and are willing to pay for them."

I couldn't argue with him there. Working these last several decades in government has reinforced in me what I already knew then: what the public is willing to pay for someone will definitely be willing to supply.

It puzzled me how so many animals could be shot down in the same spot. From the close proximity of the bodies it looked as if none had even tried to escape. I asked Ethan about that.

"The buffalo is not smart," he replied, "It depends a lot on smell. You'll notice the wind is blowing toward us."

I nodded my head in agreement and he continued.

"The hunters will set up so the wind isn't with them. Otherwise the scent might start the herd to running. They fire as fast as they can and buffalo just keep grazing while others drop dead around them.

"I've heard they can shoot a long day if everything is with them. Their gun barrels get so heavy they rest them in stands while they shoot. And the barrels get so hot they have to constantly be cooled with water."

I was amazed, but the explanation certainly seemed plausible to me. Ethan went on.

"They'll kill the Indian eventually, Kirby," he said. "When the white man wipes out his food, he'll be beat. Can't fight well on an empty stomach. It just don't seem fair, taking away a man's food."

I didn't know it at the time, but Ethan Owen was right. The extermination of the buffalo did sound the death knell for the existence of the Plains Indian life as it was then. Lack of food, lack of fighting men, lack of weapons all contributed to the defeat of the red man. The one thing he never lacked though was courage or spirit.

I apologize again. I tend to philosophize too much on this topic. I think because of association with Ethan Owen I've become a champion of Indian's rights in the halls of Congress. (much to the chagrin of many of my colleagues, I might add).

The men working on the carcasses stopped and looked up, their hands and forearms covered with blood and their knives gleaming red in the sun.

"They've spotted us," I said, "we better ride down slow so they don't get nervous."

Ethan agreed and we urged our horses down the hill.

When we reached their wagon, we dismounted. One of them approached us. He was a short, stocky man with hair and a beard the color of a raven's wing.

"Howdy," he said, "my name is John Turner. You'll excuse me if I don't shake hands."

The blood dripping from his fingers insured no handshaking on my part, but I did introduce Ethan and myself.

"I hope you can help us," I said.

"I will if I can," Turner answered.

"We are looking for a man named Tyler," I stated.

I thought it best not to state our real reason so I made up one. I also kept my badge hidden. It's funny but sometimes people are reluctant to give information to the law, but they'll give the same information to a complete stranger.

"I hear he buys and sells women. I have some women and a couple of Indian brats for sale and I'd like to locate him."

"Do you mean L.Q. Tyler?" Turner questioned.

I answered affirmatively.

"We seen him about a week ago," the buffalo hunter replied.

I became excited but tried to keep my voice calm. I cast a quick glance at Ethan and his face displayed no emotion. He just took a bite out of his tobacco plug.

"Where?" I asked.

"A little south of here," Turner replied. Then he winked and continued. "He's got a nice black-haired young gal with him. Cost us a bunch of buffalo hides but we had us a fine time that night."

It took some doing, but I fought to keep control of myself. I fully expected Ethan to explode, but he just kept chewing hard on his tobacco.

"You should be able to catch him in a few days if you ride steady. He moves sort of slow especially if he has business."

I thanked him for his help. Ethan and I mounted our horses and rode south, thankful to be moving away from the stench and the blood of the slaughter.

John Turner's information must have been both helpful and unsettling to the two of us because we rode quite some time in silence.

CHAPTER 24

Over the next few days there was a tenseness between Ethan and me that I couldn't quite figure out then. But, the fact that we were nearing our goal, I'm sure, had something to do with it.

Up until now and end wasn't in sight. With L.Q. Tyler only days ahead of us that was no longer true.

Around the campfire at night we discussed what course of action we would follow when we finally caught up with Tyler.

It was agreed for safety's sake that I would go in alone, posing as a man who wanted a woman or as a dealer in women. I would pay for a night with Sarah if I had to. Sometime during that night I would try to sneak her out of camp. If that proved impossible, at dawn Ethan would come charging into camp and we would try to take her by force.

We finally caught up with them just inside the Indian Nation. Thank God Tyler did follow the cattle trails. It not, we could've been riding for months.

L.Q. Tyler and his men were camped in a small basin somewhat similar to the one in which we had seen the slaughtered buffalo. It was sort of oblong, running east to west. The wagons were set toward the western end.

From what we could see, the men didn't use hobbles on the animals. Instead, they constructed a rope corral using both wagons as two of the sides. It was much harder for marauding Indians to make off with a horse or mule that way.

I rode in boldly, carrying Ethan's Sharps across my saddle. We decided that Ethan should use my Henry if I couldn't get Sarah out. He could shoot many more times and a lot faster than with his own gun.

I counted six men around the campfire. They watched me closely, hands on guns, as I dismounted and approached the fire.

"I am looking for a Mr. L.Q. Tyler," I announced.

A pot-bellied man in a derby hat spoke. "I'm L.Q. Tyler. What can I do for you?"

"So you're the famous L.Q. Tyler, I'm very glad to meet you sir," I said.

I smiled broadly and shook his hand firmly. I was so warm and friendly I almost made myself sick.

"My name is Kirby and you and I are in the same business," I continued. "I think I can be of help to you."

The five other men relaxed visibly. I could see their gun hands move away from their Colts. They were a motley look crew. They weren't the type of men you'd trust behind your back.

Tyler beckoned me to sit with him by the fire.

"Won't you join us for some supper?" he inquired.

Anxious to put him at ease I agreed to eat with him.

During the meal which consisted of bacon, beans, tortillas, canned peaches and coffee, we discussed our mutual "business." Even if I do say so myself, I lied convincingly.

"So you see Mr. Tyler," I said, "I get across the border quite frequently. I can supply you with young Mexican girls without much trouble."

Tyler's eyes squinted as he drank the last of the coffee from his cup.

"Well, Mr. Kirby," he commented, "your proposal sounds good but what will the price be?"

"One hundred dollars a piece," I answered.

He laughed until he coughed, spat into the fire and said, "That's pretty steep."

"You won't regret it," I promised. "In fact if you're not satisfied with my first delivery, the deal is off. Fair enough?"

"That does sound fair," Tyler said. "How far will you come?"

"I'll bring them as far as the Red River," I replied. "They'll be yours from then on. I'm not at home in this country. This is more your territory than mine."

"How about a drink on the deal?" asked Tyler.

"That sounds just fine," I answered.

"Juan!" the fat bellied man bellowed, "bring us the jug."

While we were talking I had observed Juan taking a plate of food and coffee over to one of the wagons. That meant there was only one girl with them. My heart began to race a little faster.

Juan came over with the jug and poured whiskey into our cups. Surprisingly it tasted good. I had expected the worst, but it seemed to be good sipping whiskey. I commented on it. "Mighty good."

"Yes," Tyler said, taking off his derby hat and revealing a bald head with a fringe of red hair.

"These men you have – are they good?" I asked, looking them over for the tenth time.

"They'll do," Tyler replied. "They can all handle their guns well. Why do you want to know?"

His voice had a little edge in it. I hastened to smooth over my last comment.

"I can always use good men too. I thought I might try to bribe them to come with me."

I flashed a grin and Tyler seemed to relax. I figured it was time to try to get to see Sarah.

"Your reputation says you handle only the best," I said.

I could see his chest swell as he spoke.

"Yes, that's right. Would you like a sample?"

It was what I had hoped for. I prayed that I wouldn't ruin it by acting over anxious.

"Do you mean you have one of your girls with you now?" I questioned.

L. Q. Tyler nodded his head and pointed toward the wagon on the north side of the basin.

"She's young and lovely, Kirby," he said. "She'll show you a most pleasant evening. She won't give you no trouble. She knows better."

He patted his blacksnake whip that lay next to him on the ground.

I wanted to shoot him then, but common sense overcame anger and I sat still.

"This will really seal our bargain," he said as he stood up. "You enjoy yourself. Don't worry. None of my men will disturb you."

I stood and shook hands with L.Q. Tyler.

I wanted to squeeze as hard as I could. I wanted to try to break his fingers, but I didn't.

"Thank you," I said instead, "I really appreciate this. I've been riding a long time. A little unexpected relaxation will be most welcome."

"You won't be disappointed," the bald headed man promised. "Good night."

I said good night and headed toward the wagon. My heart thumped wildly in my breast, and my legs were a little weak. I was only a few steps from Sarah and at the end of our search.

L. Q. Tyler had a guard posted at the wagon. He was a tall, thin man with a sallow complexion. He held up his hand and I approached.

"Hold up there, friend," he said in a slow even voice, punctuated by the twang of a southern drawl. "You best leave your weapons out here with me."

That was something I hadn't counted on. I certainly didn't want to chance breaking out at night without a gun. I tried to humor the guard.

"Leave my guns!" I stammered, "why I never leave my guns anywhere. They're always with me. I don't feel right without them."

"You won't need 'em," the guard responded. "Besides," he continued, "we had a girl a few months back who stole a man's gun. She shot him, wounded one of the men, and then killed herself. Now we wouldn't want to take a chance on that happening again, would we?"

I registered a sufficiently shocked look on my face and emphatically replied, "No sir."

I handed over the Sharps, unbuckled my shell belt and passed that over to the guard too.

I watched carefully to see what he did with the weapons. The guard simply leaned the rifle up against the wagon and placed my holster and shell belt atop one of the wagon wheels. I made a mental note of the placement because I knew I'd have to get to them quickly early in the morning.

The guard motioned to me to enter the wagon. I took a deep breath, pulled the flap aside, and climbed inside.

She was sitting in the back on what looked like a mattress covered with blankets. Her head was downward so that her hair obscured her features.

"Sarah," I whispered. I stood still, waiting for her reaction.

She didn't move or say a word.

I whispered the name again a little more urgently and with a slight increase in volume.

She tilted her head upward. The black hair fell away from her face. The long search was not over. It was not Sarah's face that I saw.

It took me a few minutes to get over the shock and disappointment. During this time, the girl began to disrobe. Obviously, she was well-trained as Tyler had indicated.

I held my finger to my lips signaling her to silence as I approached.

"I'm here to help you," I said, keeping my voice barely audible.

She looked at me in disbelief and drew her robe around her body. She said nothing so I continued.

"At dawn all hell will break loose. My friend will ride down here creating quite a ruckus. He'll shoot whoever he can before they have a chance to wake and fight back. During the commotion, we will get out of this wagon. I don't think they'll suspect me so I'll be able to get my guns and help out. With a little luck we may get out of this alive."

After listening to my speech, the girl finally spoke. In a voice trembling with emotion, she asked, "Why?"

I told her about the search for Sarah and asked her if she knew the whereabouts of Ethan Owen's daughter.

"I don't know," she answered. "We were held together for awhile, but about a week ago she was taken away. I have no idea where."

"How was she?" I inquired hesitantly not really sure whether I wanted to know or not.

"As well as can be expected," she answered.

I could see she didn't want to talk about it. I didn't press her.

"You know I won't be able to go with you," she said.

I looked at her in amazement. I could not believe what was saying. Then she raised her leg and I understood her statement. She was shackled to the floor of the wagon. There was a cuff locked about her ankle attached to a chain which, in turn, was fastened to a ring in the floor.

"Who's got the key?" I asked.

She told me the guard had custody of the keys and that Tyler also had a set.

"I guess we'll have to get them in the morning," I stated as matter of factly as I could. "Look," I continued, "I'm supposed to be taking my pleasure with you. We must be convincing."

For a moment, fright returned to her eyes. I hastened to allay her fears.

"We only must make them think they know what we are doing," I reassured her.

She smiled then. I think I spotted a tear in her eye.

I commenced to rock the wagon a little and moan a bit. The girl joined in.

I caught snatches of conversation an a few chuckles, but, after a short while, everything was quiet. The rest of the night we talked and waited for dawn.

CHAPTER 25

Her name was Maria Flores. L.Q. Tyler had purchased her from some Commancheros down in Texas. They in turn had stolen her from her father's ranch near Bandera.

"How long has it been?" I asked.

"Over a year," she answered. "No one knows where I am or what has happened to me," she continued.

"Don't worry," I said placing my hand over hers, "when this is over, I'll see to it that you'll get back to your home."

"Thank you," Maria whispered, "Long ago I gave up any hopes of ever seeing my home or family again."

"You'll see the," I assured her. "Now you better try to get a little sleep."

She flipped down under the blankets and soon her breathing became steady, indicating sleep.

I sat and thought, knowing that for me sleep was impossible. I was too tense. If anything ruined the element of surprise in the morning, our chances would be drastically diminished. These were tough men we'd be up against, two on six. We needed a little edge. Surprise was that edge.

The waiting that night reminded me of similar nights during the war. After fighting all day, exhausted we would collapse where we were and wait for morning and resumption of the battle.

I could remember the moans and cries of the wounded on the battlefield and the screams of the patients being operated on by ill-equipped doctors. And always, there was the realization that in the morning it would start again.

Sleep would never come to me on those nights. No matter how fatigued I was, my mind would not allow my body the rest it needed. So, it was not unusual to me that I remained awake this night while Maria slept.

I kept watch, and, when the blackness of night began to turn grey, I awakened Maria and cautioned her to stay low during the shooting.

I moved to the entrance to the tent, pulled the flap open, and peeked outside. Five of the men were arranged in a semi-circle around the smoldering campfire. I figured L.Q. Tyler would be sleeping in the other wagon.

I slipped outside quietly and took my guns from their respective resting places. I slid underneath the wagon behind one of the wheels.

I watched the eastern horizon, and, as the sun began its ascent, it illuminated a long figure on horse back moving steadily toward the camp.

Just then one of the figures around the fire stirred. The man stood up. As his blankets fell away, I could see it was the tall, thin guard.

He poked at the ashes, coaxed a flame to life, and tossed on some more wood to fuel that flame.

I held my breath, hoping that his attention would not be drawn to the approaching rider.

Ethan kept coming steadily closer.

I cocked the hammer on my Colt, after inserting a sixth cartridge.

The tall thin man finally saw Ethan. His warning to his compadres was cut short by my bullet. It hit him high in the chest and he fell headlong into the newly rekindled fire.

At almost the same instant a wild savage scream erupted from Ethan Owen's throat. His red horse was urged into a gallop, and my Henry rifle spit fire and lead as the big man worked the lever.

With the morning sun behind him, he was like a devil riding out of a blazing hell. The men simply couldn't look long enough to take careful aim. They fired wildly, and our bullets dropped them one by one.

I imagine it was all over in a couple of minutes. They fell unceremoniously, not even having enough time to wipe the sleep out of their eyes.

This may not seem fair to you, but that was how it was done. Those men deserved no chance, and we gave them as little as we could.

I spied L.Q. Tyler as he slipped from his wagon. He grabbed a bridle and tried to catch one of the horses moving about in the rope corral.

He swung up on the animal's back not bothering to even try to saddle it. He had no time. I knew I couldn't let him get away. I took aim with

Ethan's Sharps and shot the horse in the head. The horse collapsed and Tyler slid free.

Ethan dismounted, and I crawled out from underneath Maria's wagon. We reached Tyler simultaneously.

The pot bellied man didn't even make a move toward his gun. He knew he was dead if he did.

"Just stand still," I ordered. "Don't even breathe heavy."

He did as he was told. We took his weapons and made him sit on his hands.

I relieved him of his keys and went to unlock Maria. She was a little shaken but was all right.

I introduced her to Ethan. He barely acknowledged her with the briefest of hellos.

He did, however, extract a whiskey bottle from his saddlebags and offered us a drink. We each took a sip. Ethan drank at least a capful in one swig.

We turned our attention back to Tyler, who looked pretty miserable.

"We have no time to waste," I said. "We're looking for Sarah Owen."

Tyler's countenance was blank.

"I don't know on one like that," he mumbled.

"That's a lie," interjected Maria. "She was with us a week or so ago."

"Lies won't help you now," commented Ethan. "Where is she?" he shouted. The big man took another swallow of whiskey after he spoke.

"You're going to kill me aren't you?" surmised Tyler.

Before I could say anything, Ethan stated, "That's right bastard, but first you're going to tell us where Sarah is.

"Like hell," said Tyler. "Why should I? I'm going to die anyway. I ain't about to help you." I believe it was false bravado that made him say that because his voice cracked as he spoke.

"You will," said Ethan, taking another drink from his bottle. He drew his skinning knife from its sheath. Ethan looked at me and said, "It's time for a little peeling."

It took a moment for what he said to register in my mind. When it did, I grabbed his arm.

"But you can't do that!" I said. "That's inhuman."

"The hell I can't," Ethan replied. "Don't try to stop me."

I was sure the drink was taking hold of him.

I didn't even see the punch coming. I felt pain, then nothing. Black unconsciousness claimed my mind.

Chapter 26

I awakened to the touch of a wet cloth on my forehead. Maria had my head cradled in her arms.

"Are you all right?" she asked.

"I think so," I replied, shaking my head back and forth.

I saw Ethan's huge form on the ground an few feet away. His loud snores pierced the silence. The empty whiskey bottle next to him indicated that he wasn't just tired.

As my mind began to clear, I remembered what happened. I sat up quickly. "Where's Tyler?" I asked.

Maria directed my attention to one of the wagons.

It was truly a gruesome sight. L.Q. Tyler's body was tied to one of the wagon wheels. The area of his chest that had once been covered with flesh was replaced with the redness of life's blood. In his forehead was a round hole. It looked like Ethan had finally put the slaver out of his misery.

"Oh my God!" I exclaimed.

"He talked almost at once," Maria explained. "But I don't think that's what Ethan wanted. He just wanted the man to suffer and he did. He just kept cutting and cutting. Tyler kept screaming and asking to die.

I hated Tyler, make no mistake, but I wouldn't wish that kind of death on anyone.

"Your friend seemed a little crazy to me," she continued. He kept repeating "You made my daughter a whore' with almost every cut."

"Did you watch it all?" I asked.

"No," Maria replied, "but I heard it all."

"Did Tyler tell him where Sarah was?" I questioned.

"He said she was at Elm Spring," Maria answered.

"That's where we were headed," I commented.

Maria told me that she had been at Elm Spring for a while. She knew the layout. I was very thankful because I thought that might come in handy later on.

I did my best to bury what was left of Tyler and his men. All the while Ethan snored.

We rummaged through the articles belonging to the bad men. We took money and weapons. We found some men's clothes that sort of fit Maria and replaced the rags she wore with them.

I didn't want to ride into Elm Spring in Tyler's wagon. I thought that would look too suspicious.

Along towards evening Ethan finally roused himself.

Maria had fixed a meal which Ethan devoured. One would never have known that he drank almost an entire bottle of whiskey that day.

That puts me in mind of one of my former colleagues, Senator Randall Carson. That man drank damn near a fifth of whiskey a day! Everyday! And yet, he never missed a vote on the senate floor. He was more consistent than any other man I knew in Congress.

He used to carry a sterling silver flask with him wherever he went. In fact, that's how he got his nickname, "Silver."

"Silver" never let his drinking color his judgment though. It's funny his love of alcohol never seemed to injure his health. He died in a freak accident. He was run over by a runaway beer wagon.

I'm sorry. I've gone far afield again. I must get back to the story.

I didn't feel I could really talk to Ethan anymore. The torturing of Tyler was simply the last in a series of changes the big man had been undergoing. I wondered if he was really responsible for what he was doing.

After supper was ended, I tried to converse a little with Maria.

"So, Sarah is at Elm Spring I hear," I said.

Ethan grunted in answer.

"We will get her out of there then," I continued.

"Yes, we will," he answered. "What will we do about this girl?" he asked indicating Maria.

"She'll come with us to Elm Spring. She knows the place and can help us locate Sarah. After that I'll see she gets back home to Bandera, Texas."

Ethan turned to Maria.

"What did you want to go home for?" he asked. "Do you think your family wants you the way you are now?"

The look of disgust on his face was unbelievable.

Maria's eyes filled with tears and she quickly left the campfire and entered one of the wagons. I could still hear her crying inside. I turned to Ethan.

"You unfeeling bastard! Why did you have to say that anyway?"

"I'm just speaking the truth," he said.

"How do you know that?" I shouted back. "Do you know all the truth there is to know?"

He saw that I was angry and backed down slightly.

"I think I know what I'm talking about," he said.

I was becoming quite livid now.

"That's the trouble with you – you think you know! You only allow the parts of the truth you want into your mind. All others are blocked out.

"From now on you keep your mouth shut around Maria. She's got trouble enough without having to listen to you and your truths."

I only paused for a second to catch my breath and I lit into him again.

"We're going to find Sarah and rescue her. She's going to be feeling bad like Maria. You just make sure you watch your tongue around her too."

Ethan got up, went to his saddlebags and extracted another bottle of whiskey. He didn't say anything more. Perhaps that was the most infuriating thing he could have done. It certainly kept my anger burning.

I went to the wagon to comfort Maria. She was calmed down already. It turned out that she comforted me instead.

CHAPTER 27

Elm Spring was L.Q. Tyler's headquarters. According to Maria Flore's description it was a collection of ramshackle buildings in the middle of nowhere. She was right. There was a barn, some sort of a shed, and a long low main building.

Even though we were anxious to move when we arrived, we camped instead and observed the place.

We saw no women at all. Chances were that they were not allowed to go outside. We did see three very tough looking fellows make trips between the house and the barn. A young boy of about thirteen or fourteen was noticeable, out getting water. Maria explained the procedures at Elm Spring.

"Tyler's uncle runs Elm Spring," she said. That's his son getting the water. The boy supplies water and firewood and any other special needs for the girls. He takes out his payment in trade.

"The girls are housed in rooms toward the back. In the front there's a barroom and a sort of general store. Off to the side are a couple of sleeping rooms."

"How many girls does he usually keep here?" I asked.

"There are usually three," she answered.

"How about guards?" I questioned.

"Tyler usually left three or four men to watch the place," she replied. "Looks like there are three there now."

Ethan sat. a chaw of tobacco bulged in his left cheek. He hadn't said anything only listened. Finally he spoke.

"What about Tyler's uncle? Will he fight?"

Maria shook her head. "He won't lift a finger to help. You'll have no trouble from him," she replied.

"Well, Kirby, what do you think?" Ethan asked.

"I think we might as well ride straight in. Nothing fancy. Maybe they won't even put up a fight."

"Don't count on that," Maria interjected, "That's what they're paid for and they earn their pay."

"We'll have to try to get them all together in one room. Then, perhaps, we can get the drop on them and convince them that fighting is useless."

"And when they don't cooperate," said Ethan, "we'll kill them."

"What about innocent people?" I inquired.

Ethan spat a glob of tobacco juice on the ground then stated, "There ain't no innocent people in a place like that."

His logic really bewildered me. I didn't even comment on his statement. Instead, I suggested we all get some sleep and start out in the morning.

During the evening I talked with Maria. She was easy to talk to, and she had some answers I needed. I was worried about how Sarah might react to me now.

"Maria," I said, "how do you feel about men now?"

She thought a moment and then answered.

"I don't like them. I hate them I guess. Not each individual one but men in general. They've degraded me, used me, and abused me. I don't think I'll ever be able to forgive that."

"Will you be able to forget it?" I asked.

"No not entirely. I've been hurt too deeply," she replied.

"Do you see what I'm getting at?" I asked.

She looked me straight in the eyes and said yes.

"Look, Kirby, Sarah hasn't been involved in this as long as I have. She doesn't have quite as much to forget as I do. And, most important of all, she has someone to help her forget."

It was what I wanted to hear. I needed reassurance and Maria was supplying it.

"It's going to take time," Maria continued, "and you must be patient. But you won't be sorry. I wish I had someone like you looking for me. Maybe then I could forget too."

She started to cry quietly, and I held her in my arms giving the shoulder she needed.

CHAPTER 28

In the morning we rode down slowly to L. Q. Tyler's place; Ethan, Maria, and I leading our pack horse.

We dismounted, tied our horses to the hitching rack and entered the barroom. The room was sparsely furnished. A few tables and chairs were scattered here and there on the sawdust floor. A makeshift bar filled one side of the room.

The man who was L.Q. Tyler's uncle was behind the bar. He was heavyset and sported a large walrus style mustache.

The boy we had seen was busy repairing one of the chairs.

Two of the three hardcases we'd seen were sitting playing cards at a corner table. Near them were two wall shelves filled with canned goods. The third man wasn't in sight.

In a situation like this it's always smart to keep yourself from getting bottled up. We did that, Maria and I moved alongside the bar while Ethan strolled toward the canned good shelves.

Two card players didn't seem particularly disturbed which was good for us.

The man behind the bar smiled at me and said, "Good morning. What can I do for you?"

I leaned forward and spoke in a whisper.

"I am here looking for a black haired girl named Sarah Owen. I've come a long way. I know she is here. I aim to take her with me. Now you'll tell me where she is so I can get on with my task."

The smile disappeared from his face and was replaced by an expression denoting fear or nervousness.

One of the men playing cards looked up. He caught the change in the expression in the bartender's face. He started to rise. That was his last move for awhile.

Ethan swung the butt of the Sharps rifle and caught the card player full in the face. I could hear the nose break and teeth crack.

The other man went for his gun and was just a split second faster than me. His bullet nicked my top, left shoulder. Mine caught him in the stomach.

If he wasn't dead when he hit the table, I knew he soon would be. Stomach wounds almost always were fatal.

I spun around, thumbed back the hammer of my Colt again and said to the bartender, "Now I want Sarah Owen. You take me to her."

He was visibly trembling as he led the way down the hall followed by the boy, me, Ethan and Maria.

He knocked on the door. There was a muffled, "What's going on out there?" from inside.

I poked my Colt into the fat man's ribs urging him to come up with a satisfactory answer.

He stammered a little as he spoke.

"Nothin Joe. Aah-a gent's gun misfired that's all. Billy wants to see you out here right quick."

We waited. There was the sound of shuffling from within the room. I could hear the bolt sliding to unlock the door.

The door swung open and I could see a man naked from the waist up standing in the opening.

My view was only momentary because there was a loud explosion behind me and the man's face seemed to erupt in front of me. I was pushed forward and fell on top of the body of the shot man.

Behind me I heard Maria screaming. "No!! No!!"

I looked up and Ethan had vaulted past me into the room. I caught the glint of his skinning knife in his hand.

On the bed was Sarah. The sheets were pulled up covering her body. On her face was a look of complete astonishment.

Ethan's voice resounded in the small room as he yelled, "Whore!!"

He sprang toward the bed, and his daughter with the knife raised.

I fired from the floor – one shot – then fanned two more. I saw all three bullets strike the big man in the back. He toppled onto the bed like falling timber and then slipped to the floor.

I quickly turned to the doorway, the bartender, and the boy. "Stay right where you are and don't move an inch," I ordered.

Maria came through the doorway and ran to comfort Sarah. The girl was sobbing uncontrollably and understandably so.

I motioned the boy and his father outside. I got them started digging graves for the dead. I didn't much like the idea of leaving Ethan, but there really wasn't any choice.

Chapter 29

We buried the two bad men and Ethan. Sarah cried and I comforted her. I can imagine how she must have felt. She had been through a lot, more than many people have to endure over a lifetime, and the death of her father seemed to be the culmination of her terrible ordeal. We took our horses and provisions and headed north toward Wichita. It was a strange looking caravan: Sarah, Maria, two other girls we freed from Elm Spring, and me.

Things had happened so fast that I had hardly had a chance to even speak to Sarah. That night when tensions had eased and the events of the morning seemed far away, we were able to talk.

I felt so awkward I really didn't know how to begin so I just said, "Sarah, I'm sorry. I'm sorry about everything."

She looked up at me and said, "I am too, Grant. Sometimes things just can't be helped."

I knew that at that moment she was forgiving me for killing her father. In fact, I think she understood that the man I killed, the instant I shot him, wasn't really her father. For that instant he was someone else; someone tortured by childhood memories and guilt.

"I never gave up hoping you'd come," she said.

"I just never gave up," I replied.

"Look," I continued, "I know it's going to take a long time, but I still think the two of us have a life to live together. What do you think?"

Sarah kissed me then, and it was as if we had never parted. I knew somehow we would make it and so did she.

The trip to Wichita was without incident. When we arrived in town I split Ethan's share of the reward for Cletus among Maria and the other two girls, Laura and Claire. They gratefully accepted. Laura and Claire made arrangements to travel back to their homes. Maria did not.

Maria went to work at a lady's dress shop. Eventually, she was able to buy the business. A position, I might add, that she holds to this day. Even at her advanced age, she can conduct her affairs precisely as she did some fifty years ago. She never married. I guess the scars were too deep to heal.

Sarah and I did marry a few months after our return to Wichita. I got an offer of a job in New Mexico and took it. I hated to leave old friends, but I thought the move would do us good. So, I bid Sam Lane a final good-bye (we did write though up until the time of his death seven years later) and Sarah and I were on our way.

The rest is history. My rise in the political world on the local, state, and national level is in the records for anyone to see. From town marshal to mayor, to congressman, to senator, my public life has been an open book. It's a life I've been proud of.

Epilogue

So, I come to the end of my story, and I swear it is all true.

In answer to Peter Anderson's accusations I must say yes. Yes, technically I was a murderer. Although, I think that the reader is now more well-equipped to make a decision on his own as to the degree of guilt. Yes, technically, my wife was a prostitute. Again, the reader now has sufficient information to make up his own mind on that score too.

I think also that people will now understand my decision not to refute these claims while my dear wife was still alive. She meant more to me than victory in any election.

My son, Ethan, and daughter, Anne, have known the story for sometime and, I think, it has made us an even more loving family as a result.

I have been in public life a long time and have always abhorred mud slinging. Politics should be issues not personalities.

When these accusations came out, I searched my brain trying to figure out how Peter Anderson could possibly have come by this information. Most everyone from those days was dead except Marie and me.

Good old Maria. I contacted her and she came up with the answer. Remember, she worked for a time for L.Q. Tyler at Elm Spring. She knew Tyler's uncle and the boy --- the boy who cleaned up and was paid off with the favors of a prostitute. That boy's name was Peter Anderson.

Noah

My riding days were ended rather quickly, when, as a younker, I took a fall on one of R.W. Clifford's colts near Ubet. I broke both legs and one never quite healed correctly. Even now, in my sixties, I still walk with a limp.

I moved into Utica which was the sight of the biggest cattle roundup in Montana in those days. I could ride, but I couldn't tolerate the long hours in the saddle necessary to keep a cowboy's job. I had had some experience and talent in leather-work, and Mr. Clifford was kind enough to bankroll my start in the saddle business. I got to doing leather repair and making equipment while I was recuperating. My hope was to parlay that skill into a money making job. I was certainly in the place for it.

The Judith Basin was almost a cattleman's paradise. Cattlemen needed horses, and good horse equipment was vital to their success. I hoped to fill that need and earn a livelihood for myself.

In my spare time I wrote stories. It was an outlet for me, a pleasure that my departed parents had fostered in me. I even sold some articles to the Helena Weekly Herald, and the Helena Independent. Little was I to know that one day I would write novels and even screen stories for the fledgling motion picture industry.

In those early days a good pal of mine was Kid Russell. We were alike in some ways. Our ages were similar and we even physically resembled one another. While I worked on leather goods, Russell toiled as a wrangler for John Cabler and spent his spare time drawing and painting for fun. I have written about him and his success several times. What a story teller he was! I remember how entertaining he could be. His art will live forever as an accurate representation of the West of our youth.

But, I don't mean to mislead you, this story is not about Charlie Russell, although he is in it. This story is about Noah Toobers.

Noah's real name was Noah Two Bears. Somehow, over the years it got altered, and I doubt if Noah cared. Maybe it helped him. Some people might've shied away from a half-breed. There were still a lot of Indians in our part of the country then, and the Indian Wars were recent history. It had only been about ten years earlier that Custer and his command had been wiped out at the Little Big Horn.

Noah Toobers didn't look like an Indian except for his skin tone which had a reddish, brown tint. There was some talk that he might've even had some Negro blood in him. I don't know. No one had the courage to inquire - certainly not me.

I believe Noah was the most dangerous man I've ever known. His appearance though was fairly common. He was short and stocky, not very imposing or frightening. He wore a hat with a Montana Peak crown atop short cropped hair the color of a raven's wing, a typical shirt and leather vest, cotton duck trousers with deerskin sewn on the seat and inner thighs tucked into stovepipe boots. Silver mounted spurs with jinglebobs hung on his boot-heels, so that every step he took made a little music.

The deadly aspect of him was due to the gunbelt strapped over the red sash at his waist. He carried two handguns, a short barreled revolver on his right hip and a longer barreled Colt in a crossdraw holster on his left. In addition, nestled in a scabbard sewn to the back of his vest was a wicked looking Bowie knife. The talk was that he could use all those weapons effectively along with the Spencer Carbine he carried across his saddle.

Kid Russell and I were seated at a table near the front window of Cray's Saloon when we saw Toobers ride up.

"Is that Noah Toobers?" Russell asked excitedly.

"It is ," I responded. "Ain't you never seen him before?"

"No, "said Russell. "What a pony he's riding!

Toobers tied his Palouse stallion to the hitch rail. The animal was a beauty. He was well muscled and a solid sorrel from head through chest. A white blanket generously splashed with spots of all sizes covered the stud's rump and hindquarters. The horse was adorned with a rawhide braided headstall, reins, and romal. A finely tooled center fire saddle with eagle beak tapaderos sat on his back.

Kid Russell and I both had something to admire. Charlie fairly loved horses and immediately took a pencil from his vest pocket and began to sketch on a piece of brown wrapping paper from Lehman's General Store. I, of course, admired Toober's rig, wondering if I could ever produce something as beautiful.

It was the end of fall works and Cray's was crowded. Whiskey was consumed as conversation ebbed and flowed. When Noah Toobers entered the room, there was a noticeable drop in the volume and amount of talking.

Toobers strode forward, approaching the bar where several cowboys stood drinking. I saw Lucky Red Donavon lean aside, shielding himself Noah's gaze.

"Red Donavon," Toobers called, his deep voice exceptionally loud in a room that had fallen silent. "You are a horse thieving son of a bitch, and I've finally caught up to you. Now you'll join you friend Stringer Jack in hell, and I can retire."

One by one men began to move away from the bar. Russell whispered to me, "What's he talking about?"

I replied, "Stringer Jack and ten other horse thieves were caught by a posse last July below the mouth of the Musselshell. Three escaped. Two were later caught and hanged. One got away. Granville Stuart wanted a full sack. I reckon Noah Toobers means to give him that last man."

"You can't prove nothing on me,"stammered Red Donavon unconvincingly. He looked like a trapped animal. His hands remained on the bar, not making any move toward the gun on his hip.

"I can and will, "said Noah Toobers. "You just step out in the street here. This saloon is too crowded. I wouldn't want innocent people hurt. Mark my words now. You either surrender or die."

That was it . Toobers stated the situation so matter of factly that it seemed there was no other possibility than what he had set forth.

Toobers backed through the batwing doors. Just as he turned to step down into the street, I saw Red Donavon frantically reach for his handgun. I guess he felt it was his only chance at remaining alive.

"Toobers!" I screamed , and then Russell and I hit the floor. Handguns were notoriously inaccurate, and I was scared of becoming a casualty of a stray bullet.

Donavon's shot splintered the saloon doors. A split second later another shot sounded. This bullet did not shatter the doors because it was fired through the open space beneath. Noah Toobers must've dropped down to make himself a smaller target and so was able to aim directly at Donavon.

Lucky Red Donavon's luck ran out as he was slammed back against the bar. A second shot struck as he slid to the floor, his eyes already wearing a deathly glaze.

Noah Toobers walked in again, his Colt still in his hand. He approached the body carefully, checked it for any signs of life, and then holstered his weapon.

He turned to our table as people began to rise from the floor. "Who yelled?" he asked.

Rather sheepishly I replied, "I did."

"Much obliged, "he responded, "I owe you."

He then grabbed Red Donavon's legs and dragged the body out, bouncing down the steps to the street.

I never regretted what I did. After all, Donavon meant to shoot Toobers in the back. People had suspected Red of wrongdoing but just hadn't been able to prove it.

Noah Toobers was true to his word. About a year later a beautiful Appaloosa colt was delivered to me in Utica with this note: "Thanks. I owed you. N Toobers".

I heard later that Noah had moved all the way to Washington and was raising Appaloosa horses.

The drawing by Charlie Russell of Toober's stallion I had framed. It now hangs on a wall in my study. Since Kid Russell has passed away, it means more to me that just a priceless piece of art. It is also a priceless memory.

My guess is that Noah Toobers has also met his Maker. I still have descendants of his colt on my place-another priceless memory.

I just may have to make old Noah a character in an upcoming screenplay. Audiences will think it is all make believe, but I'll know the truth.

Strange Medicine

John McDougal lovingly moved the bagpipes aside in the wagon bed as he reached for the toolbox. "Aye," he said, "our luck has turned a bit bad. I'd say the odds against needing to repair two wheels must be mighty high."

The other men nodded or mumbled in assent. A rough group these buffalo hunters were. Buckskin clad and bearded, they waited for instructions from the big Scotsman.

McDougal ran a huge paw through his sandy hair as he spoke. "Aye, we canna afford to let that herd get too far ahead of us. Larson, you and Hedge go on with Billy and the other wagon. You've still got light and can cover a lot of ground yet. I'll stay here with Dub and fix the wagon. We'll catch up with you tomorrow."

Larson did not speak He mounted his horse, spat a stream of tobacco juice, and moved forward, cradling his big Sharps rifle in the crook of his arm.

Young Billy, who must have been all of nineteen, slapped the reins on the back of his mule team, and the wagon creaked and groaned as it rolled across the prairie.

Hedge, all five foot two of him, followed along on his huge black mare. The two made an incongruous pair. He called back to McDougal, "John, this here's going to be a stand. I feel it in my bones. We're going to fill up both of the wagons."

McDougal smiled and waved at his men. He then turned to Dub and said, "let's get to work you old fart."

In the evening after the repairs were made, McDougal gazed at the star laden sky as he lit his pipe. "That was a bear Dub, but we got her done," he said.

The old man sitting on the other side of the small fire flashed an almost toothless grin and his voice sort of whistled as he spoke. "You figger they caught that herd today?"

"Aye," McDougal answered as he blew smoke rings to the sky. "I'd say by afternoon anyway. I bet they brought down a mess of them big shaggies already."

He reached for the bagpipes that lay next to him. As he began to pump air into the bag and the first moaning sounds escaped, Dub spoke, you better not John."

McDougal looked a little incredulous.

"Those animals are used to the sounds," he said, "and I know you kind of like my little serenades."

"I taught you better," Dub responded. "It's not the animals I'm worried about. A herd as big as the one we're followin' spells injun to me. Sooner as later them red hides'll be on 'em like flies on horse turds."

"You're probably right," the big Scotsman said as he slid down under his blankets. "Even with summer coming, it will still be chilly tonight" There was no substitute for Dub's experience and common sense, McDougal thought as he waited for sleep to overtake him.

Dub stoked the fire a bit, checked the animals and crawled under his own covers.

With the wind blowing their way McDougal and Dub smelled it before they saw it. They crested the lip of a small basin and looked down upon a dozen buffalo carcasses However, instead of meat beginning to spoil in the sun, these bison had been butchered.

McDougal turned to Dub, and it seemed like sparks of fear leapt from their eyes simultaneously. Then Dub said, "look to the west side."

What was left of the other wagon sat smoldering in the morning breeze. They saw the bodies, but not clearly.

They moved down the bill slowly. Their animals' noses twitched at the unpleasant scents.

The corpses of Billy and Hedge looked like porcupine quills, they were so filled with arrows. Their heads dripped red from the work of scalping knives, and both faces had been bashed in.

Larson was the worst though. His naked body was tied to a wagon wheel. There were knife cuts all over his torso. His private parts were burned and his eyelids slashed so he couldn't even close his eyes to what was happening.

"My God," McDougal whispered as he dismounted. Dub examined the arrows. "Look like mebbe Cheyenne," he said.

Stoically, the two men set about the task of digging makeshift graves. When they were finished, Dub said, "the Injuns must' ye come on 'em real sudden after they kilt them buff."

"Aye," McDougal answered. "The boys not only furnished them with food, but they provided the heathens with good weapons too."

Not one to show much emotion ever, even big John McDougal fought
back a tear as he spoke.

They heard the muffled report, and then a split second later the thud of a shell as it splintered wagon wood.

McDougal quickly dove for cover under the wagon. Dub moved too, but he was not swift enough as a Sharps fifty caliber bullet knocked him to the ground. McDougal called to him, but there was no answer.

John McDougal's entire crew was dead around him. It made him very sad. The men were not his friends, but they did not deserve to die this harshly. Even though the job was dangerous, this was a shocking ending.

The one that really hurt was Dub. He had been a real friend, almost like a father. They had been together since John McDougal had come to this country. Dub had saved his skin many times, had taught him about Indians, had taught him how to hunt and how to survive. Now, without so much as a good-bye or a word of any kind, the old man's body lay lifeless on the Kansas prairie.

"Dub," John McDougal spoke aloud, "I hope you're resting in God's bosom now, although, after knowing you all these years, you may be elsewhere. I could surely use your help one more time. This is a hell of a fix."

McDougal always considered himself a brave man, but bravery did not necessarily eradicate fear. He was fearful now. He could see three braves as they sat their horses on the lip of the basin. Being the excellent trackers they were, they had probably ridden larger and larger circles until they cut the buffalo hunters' trail and then followed John and Dub straight to the little basin.

The sun faded as clouds blocked it, and McDougal heard the faint growl of thunder signaling a coming spring shower.

He knew that if the Indians split up and came at him from different directions at the same time, his chances were poor. He also knew he did not have many options. He knew one thing though—he was not going to sit and wait. The only person who meant anything to him was dead only a few feet away. All of a sudden his own life did not seem to mean much.

"Dub," he said, "you always told me how superstitious the Indians were. Only fought when medicine was good. Well, I've got some strong medicine myself and nothing to lose but me miserable life. I'll not sit here like a chicken waiting to be plucked."

McDougal checked the loads in the Navy Colt in his waistband. Then he reached up into the wagon bed and felt around until be grasped his bagpipes. He pulled them up and over, wincing a bit as they clattered and clanked. They were, after all, a family heirloom handed down from his grandfather.

The sky darkened and the thunder became more ominous as the big Scotsman crawled from under the wagon with his bagpipes under his arm and his chanter to his lips. "Dub," I'll bury you soon or join you," he called.

The harsh initial squeak of the pipes, coupled with the counterpoint of rolling thunder and an occasional streak of lightning splitting the sky, filled the air as McDougal marched toward the three Indians who had not moved.

He increased the volume as he continued his steady pace and when the thunder lessened, the pipes were deafeningly shrill.

The three braves pointed, gestured and seemed definitely baffled by this odd turn of events.

McDougal was only about one hundred fifty yards away now, playing as loudly and forcefully as he could with little regard for what notes emanated from his instrument.

The Indians ponies began to jump and shy, petrified from the sounds that assaulted their ears. The braves sawed at their rawhide reins to keep the horses from running away. It seemed like they had forgotten all about their weapons. The white man's medicine was just too strong.

A massive clap of thunder accompanying a crackling lightning flash brought the rain as John McDougal cut the distance between himself and the Indians in half. He hoped to get close enough to use his Colt. So far his playing appeared to have the Cheyenne confused and rattled.

Finally, when he was close enough to see their faces clearly, the braves abruptly wheeled their ponies about, dug in their heels and galloped away. The combination of the dissonant music, thunder, lightning, and rain and a white man who was acting in a crazy fashion proved to be too much for the superstitious Cheyenne.

McDougal stopped his advance, but continued to play his ancient instrument as tears streamed down his cheeks and he smiled in relief.

That night in the Cheyenne camp stories of the strange medicine were told around the fire. The listeners shook their heads in wonder. This was something they would not soon forget.

Nor would John McDougal ever forget. Those bagpipes remained with him to his dying day and only then did he pass them on to his own grandson.

The Gun

I bought the gun because it fit my hand. My hands are small and that little revolver nestled in my palm just right. It had a 3 1/2" barrel and walnut bird's head grips. The finish was finely blued, and it was a mighty nice looking weapon. It used a large cartridge, a .44-40, the same as many rifles. It shot a little high, but that was easy to rectify. The only drawback was noise. It surely was loud when fired.

I think Bagby got a special price on that gun. It came complete with an ornately tooled shell belt and holster. I believe it was a company sample. It didn't matter to me though because I bought it right away. After all, the old timers said it was part of any real cowboy's necessary equipment, and I counted myself as the real article.

I guess I'll never forget that little gun. I can't. You see that's the gun I used to kill Price Tipton.

Even though the century had turned five years earlier, in our part of the country things hadn't changed much. Our valley was great for raising cattle. We had good grass, ample water, and a pretty favorable climate. Oh there were times we didn't get enough rain or got too much, but, all in all, it was a fine place.

As a younker, whatever I cinched my saddle to I could ride, so that's what I did. I broke horses for the ranchers in the valley. I'd ride the rough off them and put a little handle on them. The cowboys on the various ranches would then finish off those ponies' educations.

My home ranch was Sid McCarthy's. His wife, Tess, really took a liking to me. She never had children, and I was an orphan so I guess things worked out just right for all of us.

I know I was a little arrogant in those days and let my pride grow out of hand. It sort of went with the job. My work was a little more specialized and paid a little better. I never gave a thought to the future either. I spent my money freely. I rode a custom Visalia saddle and silver spurs hung on my boot heels.

I thought I cut quite a figure on Saturday nights in Shinbone. I would deck myself out in my finest duds, strap on my Colt to complete the picture, just for show, and head to town for some fun. Fun usually included consuming a good amount of bug juice, a bit of gambling, and maybe a dalliance with one of the sporting girls at Waco Lil's.

Price Tipton and his brothers ran the Triple T Saloon and Billiard Parlor. He was a big, burly fellow about fifteen years my senior. The Tipton brothers had come to the valley with reputations but had stayed on the straight and narrow. In fact they made some strong political alliances and contributed money to the right candidates. I wish I had been more aware of that then.

It was an evening in October when it happened. There was a bit of a chill in the air, but it felt good. I tied my personal horse, a dun named Cody after the great scout and showman, to the hitch rail in front of the Triple T. I loosened the cinch a little since I figured I'd be inside awhile. I thought Cody might as well be comfortable while waiting.

There were many of my acquaintances inside. I went around shaking hands and receiving slaps on the back and praiseworthy comments for my word with the young horses in the valley.

Obviously, it made me feel good and puffed me up like a peacock.

Price Tipton called me to the blackjack table. "Lane, come on over here. A man with your luck with horses is bound to be lucky at cards."

"Luck's got nothing to do with it," I replied, "pure skill."

I approached, my jingle bobs announcing my arrival with every musical foot fall.

Tipton was dressed for business. He had on a grey suit and burgundy brocade vest. A diamond ring sparkled on the small finger of his left hand. He was good at his job too. His job was winning, and he surely hated losing.

He smiled as I approached. "First hand is on the house, bronc buster," he announced.

I never liked Price Tipton. Maybe it was that too ready smile or the rumors about his light fingered card dealing. He could always get my goat without even really trying it seemed. Well, that night he tried.

"I hear you met your match with that black stud at McCarthy's place," he said. "That Midnight is a real devil I'm told! You shouldn't be ashamed. Everyone gets thrown. Even you."

Tipton stressed those last words a little more than necessary I thought.

Maybe I was a bit too sensitive, but, remember, I was a good sized fish in a little pond. In our valley I was the only horse breaker. I liked that feeling.

"That's not the whole story, Tipton," I replied. "I run that stallion through a corral fence and bailed off so as not to get busted up. The horse come out worse than me. McCarthy says it'll take a month for the stud's leg to heal. Then we'll try again."

I figured that would put Price Tipton in his place, but, being young, I just couldn't leave well enough alone.

"You still looking for a horse that can give Cody a race?" I asked, knowing this was a sore spot for the gambler. He'd already lost to my horse twice in match races which cost him considerable money in wagers.

Tipton's smile faded. "Yes, I'm still looking," he replied. "I'll find the right horse one day."

Then he let it go. He dealt cards. But, whenever I caught his stare at me, it was hard. There was hate in his eyes. My eyes, I'm sorry to say, were becoming fogged by too much coffin varnish.

As the evening passed, I made the rounds visiting different tables and was quite successful. I ended up back at Price Tipton's blackjack spread with a large bet, about two months wages, on my cards. I had a king showing and a nine for a nineteen, so I held. Tipton began with fourteen, a ten and a four, and drew three twos in a row to beat me with twenty.

To my whiskey clouded mind three consecutive twos seemed too lucky to me. The fact that Price Tipton was a professional and that he had lost to me before, made me believe that those twos didn't appear just by chance. I called him on it.

"That wasn't a fair deal, Tipton. What are the odds of three twos coming up in a row?"

"Those would be long odds," Tipton replied, "but funny things happen with cards. Maybe your luck with horses just don't apply to the blackjack table."

He smiled rather unpleasantly. His teeth shone, but that hate for me was still visible in his eyes.

I stood up and it was like scenes old timers had recounted to me about the trail driving days.

"Tipton, you're a cheating son of a bitch," I called and reached for my little Colt.

I heard chairs scrape and tables fall and saw the gambler's hand fumble under his coat.

The gun, which seemed to appear in my hand in an instant, roared, deafening in the room, and a red blossom of blood spread across Tipton's grey coat. He crumpled forward, smashing the table to the floor.

I don't remember much of the aftermath. I found out, though, that being the best horse breaker in the valley didn't count for much up against political connections.

Price Tipton's brothers made sure that I was prosecuted. Even though Tipton had a gun, I was termed the aggressor, and I was really lucky to get off with a manslaughter conviction.

I've served seven years and learned a lot in prison. I've got some book education and some people education. My parole starts in ten days.

Sid McCarthy has my saddle and possibles at his place. With no kin of my own he and Tess have been mighty good to me. I don't know how I'll repay them. I'm just happy to be getting a second chance.

When I get back, I believe I'll take that little gun back to Bagby's. Maybe he'll sell it for me or trade me for some other goods. The times have changed and now, finally, I'm more than ready to change also.

The Last Manhunt

The two riders reined their horses to a stop at the summit of a low hill. They stood under a tall pine tree. The air was heavy with moisture indicating that more rain would soon fall. Steam rose skyward from the coats of their perspiring, bone weary animals.

The taller of the two men, a young fellow in his late twenties with golden blond hair peeking from beneath the brim of a brown Stetson, spoke, "These horses are played out. If we don't get new mounts, we'll be afoot in no time. Mariposa is still a good three days ride from here. We won't be able to rest easy till we get there."

The other horseman pushed the Mexican sombrero to the back of his head, revealing a scarred, swarthy face adorned by a heavy mustache. He spat a stream of tobacco juice. A few droplets fell to his yellow slicker as he nodded his head affirmatively.

"J.T.," he said, "you are right. The old man has a couple of likely looking geldings down there in his corral. You figure he'll be in a trading mood?"

The small, dark man chuckled at his own statement and touched his spurs to his horse's flanks. The tired animal moved slowly down the hill. The blond man followed.

The two riders dismounted in front of the small log house. The blond man called out, "Hello, the house. We are in need of water."

There was a scuffle inside, the sound of a latch being lifted. The door swung open and an old man with hair like tufted cotton stepped into the doorway.

The old man opened his mouth to speak but had no chance. The roar of a shotgun split the silence. The area once filled with an aging face and white hair was vacant. In its place was a bloody stump. The body stood momentarily as if in shock then fell backward. Dust billowed from the floor as the dead weight hit the boards.

"Pete, you son of a bitch!!"

It was the blond man screaming.

"I knew this old man. We could have took those horses easy."

"Look, J.T., you can only hang once, and we got two killings behind us now. I aim to live to spend the Clements' money, and I ain't about to leave no one behind to mark my trail for the law."

The man named Pete broke open his shotgun, dropping the empty shells on the ground. He handed the reins of the horse to J.T.

"Saddle the fresh horses. I'll check the house. Might be the old man had some things of value."

The blond man stood for a moment as if undecided as to what to do. Then his shoulders slumped, and he trudged off to the corral, leading the tired horses. The musical sound of his spur rowels and jinglebobs seemed distinctly out of place.

Samuel Tyler was getting old. His eyes were not as keen; his ears not as sharp. But he was still able to rely on some thirty years of experience as a lawman. Twenty of those years he had spent here in Creed, Colorado.

He had a month to go and he would retire. In fact, he had cut back on work so much that some people thought he had already retired. His job would, no doubt, go to his deputy, Homer Cox. Sam thought Homer was a smart boy----too smart to spend his life as a law officer.

Tyler slipped his new Winchester 94 into its boot and checked the saddle cincha. Ever since he broke his arm at age ten as the result of a loose saddle, Sam always remembered to check the cincha.

Horses had that nasty habit of filling their bellies full of air so that girths wouldn't be so tight. Sam's father had taught him that. They had been close. How ironic that that closeness had not existed between Sam and his own son.

Tyler looped a bandoleer of rifle cartridges over the saddle horn along with his canteen.

"Sam, don't you think you had better take some spare cartridges for your handgun too?"

It was Homer Cox speaking. A thin young man of 28, Cox seemed to have a real love for the old lawman. Deep furrows creased his forehead as he spoke again.

"Sam, for the last time I'm askin' you. Why don't you let me come along?

You're just looking for trouble. Whoever killed Curtis took no chances.

Hell, the old man was blown apart in his own doorway. This might be more than you can handle."

Tyler's face flushed, and anger began to well up in him. To think that this young upstart, Cox, was doubting the ability of the man who taught him how to handle a gun and showed him the border shift and road agent spin was infuriating.

But Sam's anger quickly cooled as it always did. Homer had been closer to him than his own son. When James ran away, the Cox boy had filled the gap in the marshal's life. He just couldn't stay mad at the young fellow. Tyler's lined and leather-like face broke into a smile.

"Thanks Homer. I'll take those bullets but not you."

"Damn it Sam!!! You're taking too big of a risk so close to retirement. Stay here and let me go."

"No need to worry Homer. I'm not in a wheelchair yet. I've always pulled my own weight and that I'll do up to the end. Besides, this job is all I know and all I've got. I'm gonna work it up to the last minute Now, fetch me my buckskin jacket will you?"

Tyler finished filling his shell belt with bullets.

Cox stepped from the office with the jacket. It was old like the marshal.

"Homer, don't worry about me. Staying behind will get you used to some of that office work you'll be doing when you become marshal."

They smiled at each other and shook hands.

"So long," Cox said.

Tyler stepped into the stirrup, his spurs jingling as he swung into the saddle. With a wave at Homer he urged the well-muscled dun into an easy lope.

Homer thought that the old man still cut quite a figure. He was a little heavier now, and his blond hair was streaked with silver, but he was still a handsome figure astride a horse.

The marshal dressed plainly: faded jeans, a blue shield-front shirt that had seen many years, a tan cloth vest, a red bandana loosely knotted around his neck, and a grey Stetson atop his head. The only thing fancy about him was that a fringed buckskin jacket.

Homer watched Tyler until man and horse were a speck on the horizon. He shrugged and went back in the office.

Sam Tyler was at the Curtis place in an hour. He walked the dun slowly in front of the house, checking for tracks in the moist earth. He found what he needed in a surprisingly short time. One hoof print showed a U-shaped crack in the shoe. After following the tracks for a few hundred yards, Sam was quite sure he had the right trail. He thanked God for the wet earth.

Tyler's mind wandered, as it often did, back to his wife Nora, now ten years dead, and to his only son, James. Nora had been a wonder. A woman of quiet beauty but not physically strong, she found the life of a marshal's wife extremely difficult. When she heard that James had been involved in a killing in New Mexico, her heart had just given out. James was only sixteen then. Sam wondered and picked his mind trying to find a reason for the boy going bad. But there was nothing he could do now. It was just another constant hurt along with Nora's death and the loss of his life's job that was present always in his thoughts.

The marshal followed the trail all day, walking alongside his horse fifteen minutes out of every hour. He made a cold camp that night knowing now from the tracks that he was trailing two killers. He figured they were headed for a cluster of ramshackle buildings called Mariposa. It was a sort of robbers' haven that was like a blight on that beautiful Colorado country. He hoped he could catch his prey before they reached the outlaw sanctuary.

Pete and J.T. hunkered close to a small fire and sipped bitter coffee from tin cups.

"I didn't figure we'd have company so soon. It's only one man though. Shouldn't be trouble. He won't be expecting us."

Pete made the statement and then spilled the rest of his coffee on the ground.

"I wonder if he's after us for the Clement boys or the old man?" asked J.T. as he drained his cup.

"It don't really matter, does it?" answered Pete. "We'll cut him tomorrow. Too bad. If it wasn't for that damned lame horse of mine, we'd be in Mariposa now with no more worries."

They doused the fire and rolled up in their blankets. In minutes their snoring filled the air.

As the horizon turned from blue to pink in the east, Sam Tyler headed his dun in that direction. His body was stiff against the morning chill, and his mind wandered.

When the sun had burned the dew off the grass, Sam crested a hill and saw them. Puffs of smoke followed by the crack of rifle fire brought him instantly to his senses.

Tyler rolled the dun over its hocks and headed toward an outcropping of boulders some 300 yards distance that offered him some protection.

The dun stretched forward at a full gallop. When the horse hit the hole in the ground, the momentum somersaulted the animal forward catapulting Sam over its head.

Tyler felt a sharp jab in his side as he hit the ground and figured he had broken a rib or two. But he had no time to think of it. He grabbed his Winchester, as the distant fire kicked up clods of dirt around him, and scurried to safety behind the boulders.

Sam checked his weapons. The rifle contained seven shots. The bandoleer of bullets had been lost in the fall. His handgun contained five cartridges with twenty more in his belt. His Bowie knife lay secure in its sheath on his belt.

And so, the siege began.

The killers fired intermittently from various positions moving back and forth among trees, bushes, and rocks, creeping closer all the time. Sam Tyler returned their fire sparingly, trying to take only good shots.

The marshal waited. The perspiration trickled down his neck and bathed his forehead. His eyes glued to the landscape. Every movement out there was important. Suddenly, Sam felt very old and began to wonder if he would ever get any older.

The two killers were clever. They showed themselves just enough to draw the marshal's fire, and then they hurried back to cover. They kept coming closer, one on the right the other on the left.

Then Sam saw his chance. The crown of the Mexican Sombrero peeked over the top of a bush. Tyler dropped the Winchester's sights and fired twice. He heard a cry and then nothing. He levered the rifle, but it was empty.

A figure emerged from cover and ran in a zig zag fashion.

Sam threw a few shots in the direction of the moving figure. He knew the range was too far for the handgun, but he wanted to give the man something to think about.

When Tyler began to reload, his heart dropped to the pit of his stomach. His luck as a lawman seemed to have run out.

The ejecting rod of his Colt wouldn't work.

He couldn't get the spent shells out of the cylinder. He had a gun and bullets but could use neither one.

He cursed himself for not bringing another gun, but his stubbornness and will to live kept his mind clear. He could think of only one more thing to do.

Sam took off his buckskin jacket and cut a hole in the back of it with his knife. He crawled to his dead horse and slashed the hindquarters, smearing the blood heavily around the hole in the jacket. Satisfied, he put it back on.

The marshal sucked in his breath. His heart pounded as he ran from the shelter of the rocks.

Almost immediately rifle fire filled the air. Sam Tyler screamed, spun and fell face down on the ground, the Bowie knife tucked under his belly. Perhaps his luck hadn't left after all.

Sam lay as still as he could. He strained his ears. He heard footsteps coming closer and the musical sound of spinning spur rowels and jinglebobs.

A horrible thought tried to push its way into his mind, but he fought it off. No more mind wandering he told himself. His life was on the line, and he had to concentrate on the moment.

The footsteps now stopped next to his body. He could feel the toe of a boot touching his left leg. He heard the sound of a gun hammer being uncocked. Now was the time.

In one swift move, Sam grabbed the man's leg, throwing him to the ground. The Bowie knife flashed in the sun as Tyler drove it into the man's stomach. Then he looked at the killer.

J.T. gasped, moaned and looked up. His face contorted in pain. He clutched at the knife with both hands. His eyes seemed to glaze over as he whispered one word, "Pa."

Manolito

I was a boy of eight when I first met Manolito. Although I really only knew him a short time, I've never forgotten him or what he did for my family and me.

We had a small horse ranch in southern New Mexico. Even though the century was pretty new and new methods of transportation were on the rise, in our little corner of the world good horseflesh was still a valuable commodity, and my father raised some of the best.

We had two stallions: Sunset and Paint. Sunset was a bright sorrel thoroughbred who could travel all day and never seemed to tire. Paint was a horse my father bought in the Indian Nation. He was cat quick and had blazing speed over short distances. We bred our own mares and some outside horses too.

Over the years our reputation grew. "Conners" horses became synonymous with quality. John Connors was able to provide a nice living for my mother, Rose; my sisters, Ann and Jenny; and me, Jacob.

We all worked hard, but there were times when my father would hire extra help. That's how Manolito became a member of the Connor ranch.

I'm sure my father had prejudices like everyone else, but I never saw him treat anyone that way. A lot of Mexicans in our part of the country were looked down upon and treated poorly by Anglos. My father took no part in that. He even made sure that we all learned enough Spanish to become conversant. Mexicans were always impressed by our ability to communicate in their tongue.

Manolito rode up to our ranch-house on a beautiful black mare. Her sleekness and color were complimented by an ornate Mexican saddle lavishly trimmed in silver. The mare was stopped by an almost imperceptible pull on the reins. She then stood quietly while her rider dismounted.

He was a rather small man, standing about five and one half feet tall and probably not weighing in excess of one hundred forty pounds. I couldn't tell his age but his dark hair and mustache had tinges of gray in them.

(What I recount now was really spoken in Spanish, but I will translate into English to the best of my recollection).

My father stepped of f the porch of the house. "Good morning," he said smiling. Behind him my mother, sisters, and I stood and echoed his greeting.

Manolito took the sombrero off his head and bowed to my mother and the girls.

"Good morning to you all", he replied. His voice was very deep and resonant. It seemed odd such a big voice coining from such a small man.

"I was hoping I could water my horse and fill my canteen," he continued.

"Sure. Go on ahead. We got breakfast coffee and the fire's still hot if you're hungry," offered my father.

Manolito hesitated. It was clear that he wasn't used to this type of treatment from Anglos and he was distrustful. Whether it was just the offer or the aroma of frying bacon from the house, he responded, "Yes, thank you. I would enjoy a hot meal, but I would like to water my horse first."

My father's eyes brightened. This vaquero would tend to his horse first. My father liked that. "That's fine," he said, "the food will take a bit anyway. Put her in that small corral."

"Thank you. I will," replied the Mexican.

The black mare was still standing, not tied or even ground tied. As her master moved toward the trough, she followed him careful not to get too close.

Being the horseman he was, my father observed this closely.

When they reached the trough, the Mexican removed his gear, tossing his saddle on the corral rail. The mare didn't drink until he gave a slight push to her head.

When she was finished, the vaquero gestured with his hand and the mare began to follow him. He held up his hand again as a signal to stop which she did while he opened the gate. He then motioned for her to enter. The horse moved forward and immediately began to munch on some hay on the rack in the middle of the corral.

My father looked at me and smiled broadly, and I got his meaning instantly. This man was a horseman. I knew then that this Mexican was going to be offered a job.

Well, that's exactly what happened. It may seem a little foolhardy to offer a job to someone you've just met, but my father considered himself a good judge of horses and of men. A man who could handle a horse like this man couldn't be all bad John Connor said. He believed that people who were good with animals were good people too.

My father was right more often than not. Like the time in Columbus when we watched the magician at a carnival side show. My father could almost predict what was going to happen and how it was done. "Things aren't always as they appear to be," he said at the time. I was to find that that comment wasn't just restricted to a magician's tricks.

We learned that the stranger's name was Manolito and precious little else. He was pleasant and mannerly. I believe my sisters regarded him as handsome.

Manolito proved to be a diligent, talented worker. There was a small room in the barn in which he slept. He took his meals with us. After only a few weeks it seemed like he had been with us for years. He came with us to Columbus on our weekly trips and spent hours exploring the town.

This Mexican horseman was almost a miracle worker with the young colts and fillies. With his quiet manner he seemed to have those horses working in no time. Under saddle I never saw a horse try to buck with him. And, Manolito himself appeared to be enjoying his work. The nervousness he exhibited the first few days eventually passed, and he became more relaxed, although oftentimes I caught him just staring southward, seemingly in anticipation. At least that's what it appeared like to me.

One morning when my father was out moving horses to different pastures, three men rode in from the South.

Manolito saw the men approaching, he quickly dismounted, unsaddled the colt and pulled the hackamore from his head, setting the young horse free. He then turned to me and spoke more forcefully than I'd ever heard him. "Jacob," he said, "I want you to take your mother and sister into the house."

When I hesitated, he called sharply, "Do it now! Keep away from the windows!"

I moved quickly then and led my protesting female family members into the house. When they caught sight of the approaching riders, they didn't balk at ducking into the protection of their home.

Like every other child warned not to do something, I proceeded to do it anyway. I positioned myself so I could peek through a curtained window and observe the action outside.

Manolito emerged from the barn with a Winchester rifle in his hands just as the three Mexican riders arrived at the front of the house. They were heavily armed and as menacing looking as any men I had ever seen.

The man in the middle was larger and meaner looking than the other two. His face was horribly scarred and, when he spoke, his voice was so raspy it was eerie to hear.

"Amigo, the general approaches. He needs to know things."

Manolito's voice was cold when he replied, "There is no rush. I know what he needs to know."

"There are fine horses here," the big man said, smiling broadly, revealing gaps where teeth had once been. "Pretty women are here too," he added.

The other two chuckled at that comment, and the one to the left started to dismount.

"Stop." said Manolito, "there is nothing for you here."

"The hell with you, I'm getting mine early before the crowd gathers. Two of them look young and fresh," he sneered.

"I told you to stop," Manolito said, a little louder this time as he levered a shell into his rifle.

The rough looking Mexican never broke stride. He just shouted back, "Go to hell. I want a little, and I mean to have it."

His last word was clipped short by the roar of Manolito's rifle.

The bullet caught the man in the knee, shattering bone, and he went down shrieking, "You son of a bitch!"

The wounded Mexican grabbed for the handgun at his waist, and, almost nonchalantly, Manolito shot him dead.

In the house we gasped almost simultaneously. My sisters cried and I couldn't believe what I'd seen. Gentle horseman, Manolito, had just killed a man like any of us might swat a fly.

The other two Mexicans sat their horses but didn't move. Then the big man spoke, "He won't like losing Antonio."

"Antonio was a fool," said Manolito. "He's no loss. He never could take orders. How soon?"

"Later today," the big man replied.

At that moment my father galloped into the scene and my mother and sisters screamed for fear he'd be shot. I think he would've too if Manolito hadn't stopped it.

Manolito ushered my father into the house with the rest of us. We were all relieved and hugged each other not wanting to let go. We all looked incredulously with questioning eyes at our horse breaker — turned killer. Finally, my father asked, "Manolito, what is this?"

"I am sorry Senor Connors. Believe me. You and your family are in no danger. Please stay in the house."

With that he turned and left.

I don't know how much time passed, but we all heard a rumble that grew louder and louder. I rushed to the window to gaze upon a great number of riders. Mexican horsemen seemed to fill the range of my visibility. They all had rifles and pistols and bandoleers of bullets.

Manolito came into view looking entirely different than we had seen him. He had on a vaquero's jacket and matching pants in dark blue with silver trim. At his waist was a gun belt and two Colt revolvers.

A rider in the forefront dismounted and strode forward, embracing Manolito. They talked for a few minutes. I could not hear what they said, but it was a rather animated discussion. Then the rider unknown to use began to give information to other men around him, and those men moved through among the others. Manolito headed toward our house.

As he entered, he removed his sombrero, and stood gathering his thoughts. We all waited.

"I am sorry for the inconvenience and fright I've caused you all. You've been very kind to me, not like other Anglos I've known. In return I promise none of you or your property will come to harm."

Before my father could even form the question, Manolito answered it.

"I was sent ahead by General Villa to reconnoiter."

We were all dumbfounded. This was America not Mexico. Pancho Villa in America? Why?

"What do you mean?" my father asked.

"Columbus."

We were all shocked and dumbfounded.

"Senor, politics is a strange game that requires us to do unusual, distasteful things at times. There will be some men left here to make sure no one leaves. Please do not try. Adios."

With that he put on his sombrero and left. He mounted his black mare and rode out with the men, leaving dust billows to mark their passing. That was the last time we ever saw Manolito. We never learned what happened to him or even his last name.

The raid on Columbus, New Mexico by Pancho Villa took place, and we were powerless to stop it. Innocent people suffered and died. The incident resulted in the American Army being sent into Mexico to find Villa. They never did.

Today, after all these years, I still don't understand the why of it. As a family we pledged to keep the incident a family secret and we did. Until now. I've never told a single soul, and now it really doesn't matter. Everyone else has passed on. My father was right though those many years ago when he told me, "Things aren't always as they seem to be."

But, then, we only knew Manolito as a horseman, a gentle man who could communicate with dumb animals better than anyone I've ever seen. I guess he was much more than that.

I'd like to think that what we knew was the best of him, and I'm forever happy yet sad also, that he came into our lives.

Rusty

Clay Cutter was an ornery cuss who liked animals better than people, but he was one of the best hands on our family ranch and a man I really admired. I guess he tolerated me because I was just a kid. I listened to his stories and made myself helpful, but, most importantly, I was an unabashed fan of his skill with animals of all kinds and especially of his uncanny skill with horses.

Clay always looked the same to me - old. His grey hair, leathery lined skin, and missing teeth never changed. His legs were always bowed. Garcia spurs

always hung on his boots, and his black Stetson always sat atop his head at a jaunty angle.

My father told me that Clay had been a top bronc twister in his day. Then, when he was tired of breaking bones and doctoring bruises, he became an all around top hand. Now in his declining years he could still out cowboy many of the younger waddies on our place.

Clay Cutter was a loner. He preferred the company of his dogs, Ham and Eggs, to most people. He truly welcomed spring when he could get away from everyone. We moved the cattle to those high mountain meadows then so they could take advantage of that verdant, abundant grass. Clay would help move the cattle. Most of the other hands went to work on other areas of the ranch while Clay stayed the season at Cross Creek cabin. His job was just to ride big leisurely loops, checking the condition of cattle, doctoring when necessary, mending some fences, and working a couple of young horses.

My father knew that Clay could be trusted to be on the job all summer. In the fall the old timer would be ready to help gather cattle and drive them back down before snow came. By then he was even ready to talk to people again.

Now Clay was a believer in using every available method and advantage when training horses. He watched and learned from everyone he said. He told me once, "Pete, you got to use everything God gave you to work with these critters. The head comes first followed by the hands, legs, and feet, but many forget you got another help too."

That day I was surely puzzled. I didn't know what he was getting at. He saw I was stumped and finally satisfied my curiosity.

"You got a voice too," he said, "and it's a mighty fine thing to have, real useful. It can be loud or soft, mean or gentle. The key is to put all your cues together so Mr. Horse gets what you want. Then there will come a time when he'll respond to any kind of command you give him."

I watched Clay work horses in the round pen often, and he was as good as his word. He reinforced every physical command with a verbal one. Why, within what seemed to be just a few days, he had a blaze faced young bay gelding, Rusty, stopping on the word "Whoa" before he even picked up the reins. That little horse appeared to have a good vocabulary. He could walk, trot and stop at the sound of Clay Cutter's voice. At least it looked that way me. The old cowboy's hands and legs never seemed to move.

Clay used to have to break horses quick in the old days. Now he was allowed to take his time and work on fewer animals. The boys who were lucky enough to get horses he trained in their strings were always mighty thankful. Those ponies were bridlewise and could handle most anything. Clay roped and dragged bushes, tree limbs, and bags of cans up and down hills, through gullies, and across streams.

He even shot guns off around them until they would hardly flinch. He pulled enough wet saddle blankets off them to where they were pretty finished horses when he was done.

In the summer of my thirteenth year I learned that Clay Cutter really knew his work and it saved his life.

Clay began his trek to Cross Creek Cabin with his string of five horses. One was a pack animal. One was an older ranch horse that deserved some easy duty. The other three were in various stages of training. This summer Rusty was one of those three.

Ham and Eggs were always excited when these trips came about. They dearly loved home and all the tasty leftovers, but those hounds did enjoy getting on the trail. There was always plenty to look at and sniff at, and they knew the way as well as Clay. They would bound off ahead of him chasing each other in the grass like a blur of red and yellow.

It was some weeks later when I saw those dogs again. They came running to me with tails wagging and I became awful worried. Those hounds never went anywhere without Clay.

As I searched the horizon, I spotted a riderless horse approaching. I started to run, and then Ham and Eggs sprinted out ahead of me.

As I drew closer, I could see the form clutching the near side stirrup. It was Clay! That little bay pony was walking softly and quietly, pulling the old man's body along the ground. The miracle was that he was alive.

Rusty stood still as we got Clay unhooked and inside. He was cleaned, fed and doctored. Rusty was unsaddled, turned into the big corral and watered and fed.

When Clay was on the mend, he told me the whole story.

"Pete," he said, "It was the damnedest thing. I was just riding along easy on Rusty, just walking, trotting, and loping over some broken ground. I wanted to get him to looking where he put his feet. We come down a gully that was steeper than I remember. It was a little muddy and the pony slipped. I ain't proud to say it, but I ain't the hand I once was. I come off like bacon sliding out of a pan. I knew right away when I hit the ground that my left leg was hurt. I been hurt enough times so I had no doubts.

"Now Rusty shied a bit, but when he felt the pull on the mecate as it was jerked from my belt and heard me yell 'Whoa', he stopped dead.

"I was in a bad way, and I figured I wasn't going to be able to remount, so I drug myself over next to that little bay horse and grabbed a hold of the stirrup so I wouldn't lose my grip so easy, and I told Ham and Eggs to head for home. I knew they'd lead me right there.

"I told Rusty to walk and he started after his pals nice and easy. I didn't have to talk to him much. Once in a while I'd have him stop so he could graze a little. I could rest then too and shift my body or adjust my hand or arm then we'd start again.

"I figured steady going might get me here by nightfall and I was right. I'm mighty sore and scraped, but I thank the Lord I'm alive. Had it been another horse I could've been kicked in the head and dragged to death."

Even as a boy I recognized that his incident was something special. If I hadn't seen it with my own eyes, I would have found it hard to believe.

In this ranching business you depend a lot on animals, and a lot of strange things happen. This one, however, was one to remember.

My father was absolutely convinced that it was Clay's training that did it. That the little bay horse, as young as it was, knew to respond not only to touch but to voice as well. Pa made sure that the rest of the hands were well aware of that fact.

When Clay healed up, my father gave Rusty to him as his personal horse, and the old man rode that bay gelding until he couldn't ride anymore.

Now Clay has long since passed on, and Rusty has retired to the easy pasture life. Every once in awhile I'll stop by to see him, and, as old as he is, he still listens. That always brings a smile to my face and gives me pleasant thoughts.

The Hat

There was a nice turnout at Harley Burke's funeral. The horses grazing around the small cemetery fence bore brands from the Rocker R, Box L, and the Slash T, all neighboring ranches in the valley. Their riders held hats in hand as they watched Harley's casket being lowered into the ground.

Reverend Price put an Amen to the last prayer and announced that everyone should stop at the Kane spread for some food and reminiscing. Harley had worked for Bryce Kane for the last fifteen years, and the Kane family had come to look on the old puncher as one of their own.

Harley Burke, like many of his brethren was a loner. He had no kin near at hand. There was some talk of a brother up in Canada, but there had been a falling out between the two of them many years before. Bryce Kane had sent word to him about Harley's passing but had heard nothing back.

Afternoon passed into early evening as guests ate and drank and shared tales of their experiences with Harley. Nancy Kane and her daughters, Melissa and Rebecca, kept platters filled and coffee on the boil.

After generous pieces of Harley's favorite apple pie with cinnamon and raisins, the guests bid their goodbyes, snugged cinches, mounted up and rode off to the four winds.

The Kanes then began to process of cleaning up.

Nancy Kane motioned to her husband as the girls cleared the table. In a
low voice she said, "Melissa's taking this real hard."

Bryce nodded. "Yes. I've seen. She's been teary eyed much of the day. I know she was mighty fond of old Harley."

"She's only thirteen Bryce, and this is the first person close to her to pass on. I sure wish I could make it easier on her."

Bryce observed his wife's furrowed brow. "Sometimes it can't be," he replied.

Nancy looked deeply into her husband's eyes. "Becky's easier for me to talk to. You've always had a good touch with Melissa. I know you can figure a way to help her through this."

There was a special stress on the word <u>know</u>. She kissed him on the cheek, flashed that smile that always melted his heart, turned with a swirl of petticoats, and went about her work.

Bryce took his pipe off the fireplace mantle and filled it with tobacco from his pouch. He scratched a match on a stone and put a flame to his bowl, puffing until grey smoke rose.

As Bryce Kane looked out of his window into the purple dusk, he saw Ned Turner carrying his saddle, bridle, and blankets into the tack shed.

"Tools of the trade," he thought to himself. Kane watched as Ned entered the log bunk house, his figure silhouetted in lamplight when he opened the door. It was then that the thought came to him, a way maybe to help his daughter cope with the loss of someone she loved.

"Missy," he called to Melissa. "When you're finished, come with me to the bunkhouse. I want to go through some of Harley's things."

The young girl paused in her work for a moment to wipe her eyes. Bryce caught the hint of a smile on his wife's face and the almost imperceptible nod of her head.

The moon had risen when the father and daughter stepped outside. As they walked, Melissa spoke, "I just can't believe he's gone, Papa. I'll never get to see him or talk to him again. It's so unfair. I don't want to, but I'm afraid I'll forget him. We don't even have a picture of him."

With that the girl began crying quietly again.

Bryce spoke quickly trying to head off what he feared would be a long period of sobbing for his daughter. Like most men of his time, tears made him uncomfortable.

"Now, you know Missy," he said, "Harley wasn't one for pictures. You couldn't get him into Sullivan's studio for love or money. He claimed a face like his would break the camera. I think it was that Indian blood in him though. He didn't want his spirit stolen."

"Really," replied Melissa almost incredulously, the tears seemingly halted.

Bryce Kane nodded. "Besides, we don't need pictures to remember

Harley. He'll be in here and here." He pointed to his head and chest as he spoke.

"Honey, people leave pieces of themselves behind to help us remember them. We don't need a picture of them. We can conjure that in our own minds."

Melissa listened attentively as they crossed to the tack shed.

"Look here at Harley's saddle, "he said as he lit a lamp and held it over the deceased cowboy's rig. It was a beautiful Visalia that had cost Harley several month's wages. Bryce pointed to the back of the cantle where the initials H.B. were carved.

"See Missy," he pointed. "Harley gave me this saddle before he passed on. Why, whenever I ride it or even see it, I can't help but think of him."

Melissa smiled at that and ran her hand over the saddle's fine hand carving.

"Papa, did Harley leave me anything?" she asked timidly.

"Yes he did. He said he had something that wouldn't mean much to anyone but you. You wait here and I'll go fetch it."

Bryce Kane left his daughter in the tack shed while he strode to the bunkhouse. Minutes later he returned with something in his hand. When he entered the dimly lit area, Melissa could see that it was Harley's hat. Kane handed it to his daughter.

Melissa smiled broadly when she took the battered grey Stetson into her hands.

"You know Harley was like most punchers," said Bryce Kane. "He didn't have lots of value except his equipment. In fact, except for his saddle and hat he told me to give the rest of his possibles to the agent at the reservation. He figured Connors was a religious man and would see to it that the things went where they were needed.

"How come he gave that old bonnet to you?"

Melissa cradled the hat in her hands as she answered. "I picked this out for him myself over at Bagby's when I was just a little girl. Harley made me feel pretty special taking my advice and all." The smile on her face broadened and her voice became more animated.

"See this hatband, Papa?" she asked.

Bryce tilted his head forward.

"Harley taught me how to braid horsehair," she continued. "This is the first thing I ever completed without making a mistake. Harley used to laugh and tell me that our horses wouldn't have tails enough left to swat flies in the summer with me around pulling hair."

They both chuckled a little as Melissa turned the hat in her hand. She fingered the leather stampede string, and it jogged yet another memory.

"When Harley was teaching me to ride, I got old Buck to loping. Buck never moved faster than a trot for anybody. I think Harley was worried about me because he took after me so fast his hat flew back like someone had just knocked it off his head. I thought it was so funny seeing his bald head in the sunlight I couldn't stop laughing."

Melissa laughed now, and her father joined in.

"Yes, Harley was a little scarce when it comes to hair. He used to say he never feared being scalped. There was nothing on his head an Indian could grab ahold of."

"That's when he made this stampede string," continued Melissa. "He told me he couldn't have little girls laughing at him like that. It would set a bad example for the other hands."

She fingered the matchsticks in the hatband and spoke again. "Harley used to let me roll cigarettes for him. He said I had the touch. They were always filled right, and I never spilled the makings. He even let me try one once."

Melissa stopped abruptly, realizing what she had said. Bryce feigned a gasp and then reached out to hug his daughter.

"You feel better now?" he asked.

Melissa nodded.

"You see, honey, Harley's really still here on this ranch. His body is up under the oaks, but his spirit is all around. We can see it in every colt he broke and in the tools he used to get the job done. He won't be forgotten because you can hold a part of him in your hands anytime you want. I can too everytime I ride his saddle or even look at it in the shed here.

"Harley was a lucky man, Missy. He was satisfied with his life. Not many are you know.

"We were mighty lucky also - lucky that he was a part of all of our lives.

He looked into his daughter's eyes and saw that the pain was gone. It had been replaced by a sort of calm acceptance.

"Missy, I believe Harley's saddle could do with a cleaning. He did love to have a shiny rig to ride. What say you tend to that first thing in the morning?"

"It'll be a pleasure," Melissa replied.

Bryce blew out the lamp and they turned to walk back to the house. Melissa clutched Harley's hat to her breast and leaned her head on her father's shoulder. He put his arm around her and sighed.

The Blue Devil

Josh Barnet was the best bronc peeler in our valley. Just in his early twenties, he was wiry and strong and stuck in the saddle like a magnet to metal. Much to my disappointment, the few single girls around also thought Josh was mighty handsome. It made it tough on the rest of us bachelors.

In those days horses weren't broken to ride until they were pretty mature. They were strong and used to freedom on the open range. They had been handled but not ridden.

There wasn't time to be slow and gentle if a breaker was to make money. They had to be broken in as short a time as possible. That usually meant some wild rides in a round pen with spurring and quirting on every jump.

Josh Barnet's strength was also his weakness. He was so good at what he did that he developed an arrogance about his work. He believed he could ride anything that came his way. The trouble was, he did, and his reputation grew.

I worked on the Slash R those days and fancied myself a good rider. I could fork most broncs, but, even as a younker, I had a good dose of common sense. I knew when to quit.

I watched Josh Barnet many a time and marveled at his skill. To be honest, I was probably a little jealous. He seemed to have no fear and put the rest of us to shame.

I'm not proud of what I did. I've learned to accept it, but I'll regret and remember it till my dying day. I've had many sleepless nights and have done a lot of praying over it in these last fifty years.

We had out share of rank horses on the ranch, but that was nothing unusual. Sometimes those salty ponies turned out to be the best working animals. They had a lot of bottom and wouldn't let you down when the going got tough.

There were still some wild horses in the valley then which we pretty much left alone. Their leader was a blue roan stud that looked mighty fine from a distance. We never could get close enough to get a rope on him. Somehow that stud got to one of our brood mares. Come foaling time that mare dropped a blue roan filly that was the spitting image of that wild stallion. It didn't matter to our ramrod, Enos Miller. To him the filly was just another horse to break.

When the time came, nearly every hand took his turn with her but to no avail. I have never seen a horse buck, kick, spin or fishtail like she did. There wasn't a rider could stay aboard.

On the top of things little Blue Devil, as we called her, would also try to take a bite out of you if she got a chance.

One Saturday night Enos, myself and Lee Ellis were oiling up our insides at the Longhorn Saloon and Billiard Parlor in Shinbone. We had had a healthy supply of bug juice already when Josh Barnet sauntered in. He was decked out with silver spurs and conchos on his vest, and his superior attitude just rankled me.

"Barnet," I called to him, "I hear your saddle sprung a leak." I just made it up to get under his skin a little. He wasn't known for his sense of humor, so I hoped for a response.

"Curtis," he called to me, "that'll be the day. You must've been misinformed. My saddle don't leak."

There was almost a sneer on his face when he spoke those words.

A thought entered my mind. Enos was about to give up on the Blue Devil. He figured her for a real outlaw horse, and it wasn't worth getting a rider busted up for no good reason. The Slash R had lots of horses.

"Barnet's due our way soon. Let's have him give Blue Devil a try," I said to my compadre.

"Nobody can ride her," replied Enos. "She's a hell bitch if I've ever seen one."

I smiled and Lee Ellis caught my drift. "It'd be nice to see Barnet eat crow for a change, said Ellis. "Maybe we could make a little money on this," he continued.

That sounded good to me - so good in fact that I offered the challenge to Josh Barnet that night.

Come Monday Josh was to meet us at the Slash R. I bet him a week's wages he couldn't stay aboard the Blue Devil. There were other bets too. I don't know how many.

Josh's answer was a curt, "You must not need that pay." He walked away chuckling deep in his throat.

That Monday dawned clear and bright, as fine a day as we'd seen in a while. Even Carl Rasmussen, owner of the Slash R, found himself a spot on the corral fence to view the proceedings.

The Blue Devil stood stock still in the corral to be saddled and bridled. Her eyes and ears worked and her nostrils flared but she didn't move. Maybe she was just trying to fool the human about to climb on her back.

Josh Barnet looked her all over, walked around rubbing his hands on her neck and flank, sensing the tenseness in her. He eased his foot in the stirrup while Lee Ellis and Cal Ransey held her head and Cal took a bite of her ear. In one smooth motion Barnet was in the saddle. The boys turned her loose and stepped away fast.

Blue Devil didn't move. She just stood. Josh was poised, waiting. Some seconds passed and a little grin rippled across Barnet's face. When he shifted his weight in the seat slightly, the mare exploded. She leapt high, kicking with her back legs, spinning left then right, squealing all the while.

It was a hell of a show for a time. The bronc peeler stuck with every jump and twist, taking a fearful pounding. Barnet punished her with spurs and quirt but it didn't slow her down at all. Finally, Blue Devil jolted to a stop and reared on her hind legs, pawing the air with her forelegs.

There was a gasp from among us at the realization of what might happen, and an almost simultaneous shout, "Get off" I know I screamed the words.

Josh Barnet paid us no heed. In fact he took off his hat and slapped the roan mare on the rump.

She reared again. This time when she reached the apex, she fell over backward, her full weight crushing Josh Barnet into the ground.

We were all stunned. It happened so fast. Blue Devil rolled to the right and gained her footing.

Josh Barnet's right foot remained in the stirrup, but his body just dangled at the side. The mare shied but didn't bolt. She seemed satisfied that she had gotten him off her back. We were able to approach her and dislodge the body without a problem.

Words can't describe how I felt. What had once been a vital young fellow was now a mangled shell. It's funny how the things that had seemed so important just days ago meant nothing at that moment.

The old saying goes, "There was never a horse that couldn't be rode –

never a rider that couldn't be throwed" and it's mighty true. I felt awful bad about prodding Josh Barnet into riding that outlaw, and I learned a bitter lesson about life that day.

In all the years since I've never bet on a ride or a race, and I've always let people make up their own minds. I've never offered advice unless asked.

What happened to the Blue Devil? Some wanted to shoot her, but what purpose would that have served? She was just an animal acting out of instinct. We turned her loose to run with the wild ones. I never did see her again and I'm glad. She would've just been a reminder of a sad memory.

Wolf Mountain

The two boys rolled in the dust, kicking, biting and punching with gusto. Their curses and oaths were shocking to the young ladies in the crowd that surrounded them.

It was a bright New Mexican Sunday morning and people had just exited Church following Mass. As they stepped into the sunlight, the noise and the movement of the conflict caught their attention.

As often happens with fights, especially ones involving youngsters, the observers really added fuel to the fire by egging the fighters on. They sometimes chose sides and cheered every blow. A particularly forceful strike evoked a loud verbal response. Not one person in the audience made a move to separate the participants or to stop the battle.

One boy was tall and lanky with sandy blond hair. The other was shorter and stocky with an unruly shock of hair the color of adobe bricks. They were both about thirteen or "between hay and grass" as the old timers used to say.

From just inside the door of the Church a voice thundered, "Stop it! Stop it now!"

The voice was huge and ominous like the man to whom it belong

Father Thomas Patrick O'Hara, all two hundred fifty pounds of him and as Irish as his name, strode forward, his vestments tailing behind him like a cavalry guidon in the wind.

The crowd parted to let the priest through. Father O'Hara reached out his massive hands and grabbed one boy in each, lifting and pulling in one stroke.

The youngsters who were so intent on doing serious physical harm to one another suddenly found themselves being shaken like rag dolls.

"That'll be enough from you two," bellowed the huge cleric. "Every week it's the same thing. Bad enough you two fight, but on the Lord's day and outside the door of his home. This cannot be tolerated any longer."

With that the priest literally dragged the two young fellows with him toward the sacristy. If the parents of the two were in the crowd, they made no effort to stop proceedings or to identify themselves.

Father O'Hara placed each boy on a stool in the sacristy while he took of f his vestments. He gave them towels to clean their faces. Both had been bloodied and sparks of hatred burned in their eyes.

When O'Hara was finished, he lowered his six feet five inch frame into a chair and faced the two.

"Well," he said, "If you don't stop this behavior, one day you'll do serious harm to one another — maybe one of you might even end up dead. Is that what you want?"

The tall, blond boy, John, spoke first. "He started it", and nodded toward the shorter boy.

"Bullshit!" screamed the stocky youngster. Then realizing what he'd said, his face colored and he whispered, "Sorry, Father."

"You should be sorry," O'Hara bellowed.

John made the mistake of allowing a trace of a smile to cross his lips which didn't escape Father O'Hara.

"You too John," he yelled at the blond boy.

Father then lowered his voice to a normal level and continued.

"It doesn't matter who started what. It's the outcome that I'm worried about. I've seen too many fights and too much hatred turn into tragedy."

The boys sat still while the priest thought. He rose and walked to the window that faced the mountains. It was a view he enjoyed a lot for its natural beauty, especially at sunset when the snow—capped peaks turned crimson.

As he stared, an idea began to take root. He mulled it over a bit then turned to the boys.

"What is that out the window?" he asked.

The boys responded almost in unison. "Wolf Mountain."

"I'm going to tell you a story not many know these days. It happened in this country when I was a youngster."

John and Will perked their ears. No youngster could resist a good story, and Father O'Hara knew a lot of good ones. Churchgoers never fell asleep during his sermons either.

"This country was wild when I was young," he continued. "There were still a few unfriendly Indians and bandits around. Most everyone carried a weapon for protection and deadly violence was not uncommon.

"Two of the wildest characters were Nate Cardwell and Luke Lassiter. They were friends as youngsters and later became bitter enemies, fighting and feuding all the time. No one really knew why.

"Cardwell owned a big ranch at the base of the foot hills of Wolf Mountain. He had a strange fondness for wolves. He never let his cowboys shoot or trap them. In fact that's how the mountain got its name.

"Lassiter had an adjoining ranch in the valley so the two men were neighbors even though they couldn't stand one another.

"Well, as the story goes, some of Lassiter's calves were being preyed upon by wolves. The packs would hunt in the valley then return to the foothills. It seems that Cardwell's cattle weren't bothered — only Lassiter's."

The priest shifted in his seat and reached for his pipe, filling and lighting it deliberately. He knew that he had his tiny audience sufficiently captivated. He puffed silently for a few moments before forging ahead.

"Mr. Lassiter made it known that he would not tolerate this. He also said he would hunt down those wolves and kill them one and all.

"Mr. Cardwell warned his enemy, saying that there would be no hunting on his property. Both of these men were old timers who had never learned to back down gracefully so they stuck to their words. Many people in town predicted it would end in bloodshed and they were right.

"Mr. Lassiter rode off armed to the teeth and all knew he wasn't really hunting wolves. He was hunting Mr. Cardwell. Cardwell willingly obliged by meeting him in the foothills to settle their differences once and for all.

"Since there weren't any witnesses to the battle, we can only guess as to how it actually occurred, however, I was there at the end. My father took me and we accompanied several townspeople up into the foothills."

Father O'Hara paused to relight his pipe and to check his audience's attention level. John and Will were riveted.

"It wasn't a pretty sight boys. Mr. Cardwell was at the base of a tree with a huge hole in his chest. You see Mr. Lassiter had been a buffalo hunter and he favored the Sharps rifle. A fifty caliber bullet does unbelievable damage, especially at close range.

"Believe it or not, Mr. Lassiter was in worse shape. His body was across the little clearing. His right arm and leg had been shattered by bullets from Cardwell's Winchester, but that's not what killed him."

O'Hara paused again for dramatic effect. John and Will's eyes were opened wide.

"I had seen Mr. Lassiter many times, but could hardly recognize him. The wolf pack had been there. Maybe the sound of Lassiter's cries when he was wounded brought them or maybe it was the smell of blood. It doesn't really matter. He had died a horrible death. Because of his wounds he couldn't use his gun or get away. Lassiter's body was chewed to shreds while Cardwell's was untouched by the wolves.

"Even though it happened many years ago, it's still fresh in my mind and I'll never forget it.

"Isn't it horrible what hate can do?"

John and Will looked at one another then back at Father O'Hara.

"Think about it boys," he said. "Now go home and let's stop this fighting."

The two young fellows rose and left the sacristy. O'Hara watched as they moved out into the sun. They seemed to actually be talking.

Father Thomas Patrick O'Hara smiled to himself and then turned his attention to the grumbling in his stomach. It was time for a well deserved breakfast.

Elijah and the Demise of Eldon Crow

Elijah Edwards retired from his job as a lawman in 1892. He was fifty-six years old. His whole adult life had been spent on one side of the law or the other with a gun in his hand. He earned a considerable amount of money, especially in his years as a gunman for hire. He had invested wisely and now really no longer needed the salary or the headaches of a peace officer. He wished rather to pursue other interests like reading.

In his rooms at the Menger Hotel in San Antonio where he had recently moved, he had bookshelves filled with classic novels and works of non-fiction. He even subscribed to several magazines including The British publication <u>Strand</u> so he could follow the exploits of his new, favorite fictional character, Sherlock Holmes.

The Menger furnished his living quarters for a nominal amount because his mere presence deterred undesirables like con men and card sharps from even considering applying their skills at the Menger. Elijah Edwards was sort of a southwestern legend.

Elijah was not a tall man, but he was bulky, barrel chested and stocky. Over the years his fondness for good food tended to expand his already large girth.

He gazed across the table at his friends: Captain James A. Siesse of the San Antonio police, his wife, Hallie, and their children, Jimmy and Jessica. They were dining in San Antonio's only Chinese restaurant, Chen's.

Each of them was trying hard to manipulate chopsticks as Elijah demonstrated. After much laughter they all seemed to get the hang of it.

"Now, you've got to try all of these dishes," Elijah said. "They may seem unusual to you, but you may be pleasantly surprised."

Edwards had ordered several dishes, including: green pepper beef, mooshu pork, Szechwan chicken, and Peking duck.

"I don't know how Joe does it. He's got to import an awful lot of these ingredients," Elijah said.

"Trains," replied Captain Siesse. "They move things very quickly these days."

"Everything is delicious," Hallie commented. "The chicken's a little spicy for me though."

"I like the peanuts," interjected Jimmy. Jessica just smiled as she guided fried rice into her mouth.

Joseph Chen approached and asked if everything was satisfactory.

He was a small man, not much over five feet tall and couldn't have weighed more than one hundred pounds, but he had become a pretty big man in business in San Antonio. JoChen, as he was called, had come to this country to work on the railroad. He had never stopped working hard. He owned a laundry, this restaurant, and also ran a small opium den in the red light district. He had provided jobs for many relatives.

The diners all told JoChen how good everything was and he beamed. His daughter, Suzy, brought fresh tea. She was truly an oriental beauty and JoChen guarded her jealously.

Elijah saw Max Evans, a cowboy from the Slash R, admiring her beauty too. Evans was a happy-go-lucky fellow who had migrated down from Montana. You could tell when he was around, his jinglebob spurs made music whenever he walked.

Evans had made some overtures about coming to call on Suzy Chen, but her father refused. He knew Suzy was attracted to the young man, but he knew about prejudice too. Right now it didn't seem smart to upset things. Business was good.

It was a week later that the trouble started. Eldon Crow a big, burly brakeman from the railroad and a real hell-raiser when drinking, was accused of attacking Suzy Chen. She identified him.

He was arrested, jailed, tried, and promptly acquitted. His friends were loud and vocal and it seems that San Antonians chose not to believe the word of a lone Chinese girl. Prejudice was certainly alive in San Antonio. Many Mexicans could've attested to that fact.

Elijah Edwards followed these events sadly because he liked and respected the Chens. He was sorry he couldn't help. It was hard to open closed minds he knew.

Captain Siesse summoned Elijah one night as he often did when he thought a particular case might warrant Edwards' special talent.

The body was found in the red light district in an alley behind Big Alice's, a bordello. Eldon Crow, all six feet four of him lay in the dirt still grasping at the rope around his neck.

Elijah and Captain Siesse looked down at the body. "Did you find anything, Jim?" asked Edwards.

"Not much," replied Siesse. "Of course in this part of town no one saw anything at least not yet anyway. We did find powder on his vest."

Edwards bent down to look at the body.

"It's opium, Elijah".

Elijah looked up at him.

"You know JoChen's place is right around the corner."

Elijah nodded.

"The man attacked Suzy Chen. We all know it. The good citizens of this town are prejudiced so he went free."

"Think again, Jim," Elijah said. "Look at the size of this fellow. I don't care how angry JoChen was. How could he have reached up to get a rope around Crow's neck and then had the strength and leverage to strangle him?"

Captain Siesse smiled, "Not likely."

Elijah continued to examine the body. The rope was ordinary, cut from a lariat. There were no unique footprints around.

"I better get to questioning again, Elijah," said Siesse. "I sent for the wagon. It'll be here presently."

With that Siesse spun on his heel and went to continue his interrogations.

Elijah struck a match and began to examine the ground around the body. As he moved farther out from the corpse, he saw the glint of something in the moonlight. He bent down and picked up a small, elongated, tear drop shaped piece of metal. He held it up, smiled, and blew out the match.

Some days later Elijah Edwards was dining at Jo Chen's again. Suzy was working as if nothing had happened. Many regular customers filled the tables, Max Evans among them. The young fellow's eyes rarely left Suzy Chen. He was certainly smitten with her even after what had happened.

Elijah waved to JoChen and asked him to sit down. "Joe, I'm awful sorry about what happened."

"I know Mr. Edwards," the little man replied. "I appreciate what you did to keep me from being arrested for that man Crow's murder. Captain Siesse told me."

"It was nothing."

"I wish I had done it. A father should avenge hurt to his daughter."

Elijah could see the veins in JoChen's forehead bulging.

"Well, it's over now Joe. You've got to put it behind you."

"How! Everyone knows. People are not very forgiving. My little girl is forever damaged. No one will have her now."

"I don't know if you can say that. There's a young fellow over there who seems mighty interested.'~ Edwards motioned toward Max Evans.

"Ah-Ya-Lofan," said JoChen.

"What?" replied Edwards.

"Nothing, nothing. Maybe you're right. I have to think about that. Pleasant evening Mr. Edwards."

JoChen then got up to attend to other guests.

Max Evans rose to leave, the jingle of his spurs somewhat diminished Elijah thought. Edwards followed him out to the street.

"Hold up young man," he said.

The cowboy halted in the street.

"How do you feel about Suzy Chen?" Elijah asked.

Evans was a bit embarrassed. His face turned pink and he stammered, "I-uh-I can't stop thinking about her."

"Do you think you'd like to marry her? You know how hard that would be - the way people think around here."

"I would," he answered defiantly," but her Pa won't have me."

"He might if he knew the truth."

The color drained from Max Evans' face.

"What do you mean?" he asked.

"JoChen might think more highly of you if he knew you had avenged his daughter, if he knew you killed Eldon Crow."

Evans looked as if he might faint. Elijah reached out and grabbed his arm with is right hand. In his left he held up a small piece of metal.

"This jinglebob came off your spur. I found it not far from Eldon Crow's body. You're the only cowboy I know of that hails from that north country where punchers are partial to jinglebobs. My ears tell me you're half a tune off when you walk."

He placed the piece of metal in the young man's hands.

"You made a bad decision by killing that man. You've got to live with that. Now, I've got to make one I can live with. I'm not going to turn you in. I think you've got a life ahead of you that includes Suzy Chen. I don't want to ruin that."

With that he turned and headed back toward the Menger. Arthur Conan Doyle's newest story, <u>The</u> <u>Adventure</u> <u>of</u> <u>the</u> <u>Speckled</u> <u>Band</u>, awaited him.

Elijah and the Cardsharps Corpse

Not long after his retirement Elijah Edwards acquired a romantic interest, one Constance Mooney, librarian. She was a small woman, attractive in a severe sort of way. Suitors had been scared away by her intellect. She was equal or superior to all, and their frail male egos could not accept that fact. But, this is exactly what made her appealing to Elijah Edwards.

Edwards' dear friends: Captain James A. Siesse of the San Antonio Police; his wife, Hallie; and their children,

Jimmy and Jessica were thrilled. Elijah had spurned steady, female companionship ever since his wife, Carmen had been brutally murdered when he was a young man.

Now at age fifty-six he was seeing a woman several years his junior.

Constance and Elijah shared one burning interest; reading. The rugged, bearded, barrel chested former lawbreaker, gunman, and law officer had quite an extensive library in his rooms at the Menger Hotel. She also encouraged him to begin writing his memoirs. She said a life like his deserved to be in print.

This new relationship made Elijah more aware of women's issues and fashions and brought him into contact with many lady's shops in San Antonio. Constance Mooney was especially fond of scents; perfumes, powders, soaps. Elijah kept all these items in mind as gifts for appropriate times and became quite familiar with them also.

Elijah Edwards lived quite comfortably on investments, and his reputation was still alive and well. He often assisted Captain Siesse and the police in criminal investigations. He once told his friends, "I'm becoming a poor imitation of my new favorite fictional character, that British detective Sherlock Holmes."

In fact, he was reading his latest copy of Strand magazine which contained the new Holmes' story <u>The</u> <u>Adventure</u> <u>of</u> <u>the</u> <u>Engineer's</u> <u>Thumb</u> when he received a message from Captain Siesse.

A local cardsharp, Alvin Hardy, had been found stabbed to death in Ord's livery stable. The player, known to be less than honest at times, had been a heavy winner at a game earlier in the evening.

"I'm detaining the other four players until we have time to investigate," said Siesse.

Elijah examined the body in his normal, meticulous fashion. The knife blade protruded from between the victim's shoulder blades. The body had been rolled over on its side. There was nothing in the pockets except a handkerchief and an empty wallet.

Elijah struck his hands in the pockets and held the wallet to his nose, sniffing. He rubbed his fingers together and sniffed again.

"Anything?" queried Siesse.

"I don't know," replied Edwards. "Let's talk to those card players."

Siesse's men were holding the card players at the site of the game, the Cattleman's Bar. They sat at one table smoking, drinking, complaining and playing solitaire.

The first man questioned was Cal Daniels, a tall, gangly, extremely wealthy local rancher. Both Siesse and Edwards knew him. He loved cards but couldn't play a lick. He always lost but not excessively and was good natured about it.

"What do you know about Alvin Hardy, Cal?" asked Siesse.

"Only that I never could catch him cheating, but I think he did," answered the rancher.

"Did you see him after the game?"

"No we all went our separate ways. The first I heard was when an officer came and got me and brought me back here."

They excused Cal Daniels and called the next man to be interviewed, J.P. Harrah. Harrah was a salesman for the Curtis Corset Company. He was a pale-faced man of medium height. He wore a plaid suit and a bowler hat and was obviously nervous.

"Gentlemen, I had nothing to do with this," he sputtered. "I abhor violence."

"How much did you lose?" asked Siesse.

"Oh, maybe fifty dollars," Harrah replied.

"That'd buy a lot of lady's corsets and such," Elijah commented.

Harrah half smiled then frowned again, realizing the seriousness of the situation.

"I didn't do it," Harrah stammered. He paused then, thinking with furrows deeply creasing his brow. "I can prove it," he said.

"How?" asked Siesse.

Harrah's face began to turn red.

"Gentlemen, how can I say this delicately? I have a wife and family. I was-uh-visiting a lady friend at Big Alice's."

Siesse and Edwards almost laughed, and the captain sent a man to check the alibi while they ushered Harrah into the next room.

The next player was a salesman also. He worked for Lady Lee Feminine Scents. He was a thin wiry fellow with pomaded hair and polished fingernails. His suit was black and threadbare. His name was Lawrence T. Lawrence.

"Mr. Lawrence, where did you go after the card game?" asked Captain Siesse.

Lawrence sighed theatrically and responded with great effort, "I went to my room. I have to be up early tomorrow to catch a train."

"Was anyone with you?"

"Heavens No!" the fragrance salesman retorted.

Elijah and Captain Siesse looked at each other a bit surprised at the forcefulness of the denial.

"Does your company manufacture Passion Rose perfume, Mr. Lawrence?" inquired Elijah Edwards. "I have a lady friend who is very fond of that scent."

"Why yes," Lawrence answered not knowing whether to be pleased or remain cautious. "It's one of our best sellers."

"How much did you lose?"

"About forty dollars."

They excused Mr. Lawrence and directed him to the other room and called J.T. Slocum, the last player.

Slocum was a known miscreant in San Antonio. His black, tangled hair and beard were positively frightening to look upon. He had been involved in several altercations using fists, knives, and guns.

"I suppose you have an alibi?" asked Captain Siesse.

"Yes, sir. I got several people who was with me when that miserable, cheating, Tin horn Hardy got his," he sneered.

"And I bet they're all stalwart citizens," Elijah whispered in Siesse's ear.

"I was cheated out of thirty-five dollars," Slocum continued, puffing on the huge cigar clenched between his teeth.

They sent him into the other room also and sat drinking coffee.

"I don't want to make a bad decision here, Jim, but I'll tell you what I think. Your man is one of those four."

"Tell me Elijah," Siesse said.

"You can count out Cal Daniels. He could lose as much as all the rest put together every night for a month and not miss it.

"Mr. Harrah has an alibi but we know alibis can be bought. Big Alice's girls would do anything for money. I don't think he did it. He's too scared about his wife finding out about his dalliance with a Lady of the evening. He surely couldn't stab a man to death.

"You know Slocum better than me. He could've done it easily and has probably done similar things many times over, but he's too smart. He knows he'd be a prime suspect. Why chance it? He could rob someone else just as easy and not be connected to the crime in any way.

"That leaves us with Mr. Lawrence. From the looks of his suit, he can't afford to lose money. He's fairly sure there were no witnesses, and I bet he feels good about that. I believe I have a little piece of information that could help to break him down though. You see, there was the scent of Lee's Passion Rose on the corpse."

Captain Siesse smiled. Elijah Edwards rarely disappointed him.

"In fact, Elijah said, "I bought some of that very fragrance yesterday as a gift for Constance. The scent does linger on for the longest time."

Lawrence T. Lawrence did finally confess. His hanging was rather noteworthy as the wiry man put up an astounding struggle. He finally had to be tied hand and foot and dragged screaming to the gallows.

Elijah Edwards surprised Constance Mooney with Lee's Passion Rose perfume and she blushed with pleasure planting a demure kiss on Elijah's cheek.

The barrel chested ex-lawman and the rather severe, spinsterish librarian then sat down to one of Elijah's favorite pastimes – dinner at the Menger.

Elijah and the Murder at the Alamo

To Elijah Edwards the Alamo held a special fascination. He had nothing but respect for the men who stayed in the old mission, facing certain death. He often wondered if he would've had the courage to do that. Another unusual factor that kept the Alamo alive in his mind and heart was that the final battle had been fought the day and year he'd been born.

Elijah had led a wild life on both sides of the law. He was regarded as a legend throughout the Southwest. Now, because of some wise investments, Edwards was enjoying an early retirement. He filled his time engaged in his favorite pastime, reading. He especially loved discussing current literature with Constance Mooney, librarian. The two were an incongruous pair. She was small and attractive in a severe sort of way. He was a barrel chested, bearded man who could certainly be mistaken for a ruffian if it weren't for his fine clothes.

Elijah also assisted his good friend Captain James A. Siesse of the San Antonio police force whenever the Captain requested help. The two men stood staring at the body that lay behind the long barracks at the Alamo. Edwards crouched down to examine the body more closely.

The corpse had knife slashes in his right arm and a fatal gash in the right side of his neck. The man was probably in his late fifties.

Elijah looked carefully at the wounds and the man's hands.

"There was no identification on the man's body?" asked Edwards.

"No nothing," replied Siesse. "No witnesses either."

"Let me think about this, Jim. I must meet Constance for dinner at the Menger later. I'll talk to her about coming to visit you and Hallie and the kids."

They bid each other goodbye. Siesse left and Edwards spent some time examining the old, crumbling mission as he had so many times before.

That evening the Menger dining room was especially crowded. Elijah and Constance agreed to share their table with a tall fair-haired man who was alone.

Elijah introduced Constance and himself. The man said he was H. Robert Bonham from Austin.

Elijah's eyes lit up when he heard the name. "What a pleasant surprise!" he exclaimed. "I, or should I say we, were looking forward to your presentation tomorrow."

"Is this the gentleman who is to give the lecture on the battle of the Alamo tomorrow?" asked Constance Mooney.

"Yes," responded Elijah. "He's a noted historian from Austin. "

"Pardon me," interjected Mr. Bonham with a positively pained expression on his face. "You see I'm going to have to cancel. Urgent business. I'm leaving tomorrow morning."

The excitement drained from Elijah's face. Constance noticed immediately and responded, "That is too bad. Perhaps we can discuss some things at dinner," she suggested.

Bonham hesitated then replied unconvincingly, "Surely".

Elijah smiled and the waiter arrived so they busied themselves ordering dinner.

During dinner Elijah Edwards was quite animated asking about Bowie, Crockett and Travis trying to add to his storehouse of historical knowledge. Constance Mooney observed that Bonham tried to answer, eat and change the subject of discussion. She felt sorry for the man who had just come for a pleasant dinner not to teach a class in Texas history.

"What a battle that final assault must've been under the blazing June sun, cannons firing, hand to hand combat to the last man!" exclaimed Elijah, excitement evident in his voice. Constance looked at him strangely and was about to speak when an almost imperceptible shake of Edwards' head stopped her.

"Yes it must've been," agreed Mr. Bonham, "a brutal but important page in Texas history."

"Care for a nightcap Mr. Bonham?" Elijah asked. "My treat. No more Alamo talk."

Bonham looked relieved and responded, "How can I say no?"

During after dinner drinks Elijah produced a notepad and a pencil and asked Mr. Bonham to write down his address in Austin which he did in an almost illegible left-handed scrawl.

They bid each other good night. Bonham retreated upstairs to his room. Constance and Elijah went for a stroll after he fist sent a message to Captain Siesse.

"Elijah," said Constance as they walked. "What was that all about this evening?"

He proceeded to tell her about the corpse at the Alamo.

"I've instructed Jim Siesse to telegraph Austin for information on H. Robert Bonham, and I've suggested that he somehow detain our dinner companion."

Constance looked a little puzzled.

"I think the dead man was Mr. Bonham," Elijah continued. "I believe we just dined with his killer."

Constance Mooney let out a little gasp.

"Are you trying to play Sherlock Holmes again?" she asked smiling.

"No," he answered. "I'd be a poor imitation."

"I believe from the placement of the wounds on the dead body, the killer was left handed. Our Mr. Bonham is left handed."

"A lot of people are left handed, Elijah," Constance responded.

"True. But H. Robert Bonham is supposed to be an expert on Texas history. I purposely gave him the wrong date of the final assault on the Alamo. He never corrected me. Every Texan proud of his heritage knows the battle was fought on March 6, 1836 not in June. The real H. Robert Bonham wouldn't have made that mistake."

They came to find out later that their dining companion was indeed not H. Robert Bonham. Rather, he was one Charles Goodman. Goodman had been hired by Bonham's wife to kill the professor. She was never charged, however, because Goodman under the less than watchful eyes of the San Antonio jailers was able to commit suicide by hanging himself. There was some speculation that Goodman was in love with Mrs. Bonham.

Elijah Edwards did take Constance Mooney to visit his good friend Jim Siesse, Hallie Siesse and their children Jimmy and Jessica. It was a very pleasant day. Elijah introduced Jimmy and Jessica to one of his and of Constance's favorite new authors when he read them, The Sign of the Four by Arthur Conan Doyle.

The children enjoyed the story and Elijah's dramatic reading. They had only one question, "What kind of name is Sherlock?"

Elijah and the Satin Lady

Elijah Edwards had been a city dweller for a few years, but he still enjoyed riding, especially now that he rode for pleasure rather than tracking down criminals. His companion, Constance Mooney, enjoyed riding also. She was a ranch daughter even though she currently worked as a librarian in San Antonio.

They were an interesting pair, brought together by mutual friends Captain James Siesse of the San Antonio police and his wife, Hallie. Edwards was stocky, bearded and several years older than Miss Mooney. In fact he had retired from his life as a lawman and was living on investments. The Menger Hotel furnished him living quarters in exchange for his presence. Elijah's reputation kept nere do wells away from the Menger. Mooney, considered a spinster by some, was simply a woman far ahead of her time. Striking in appearance though not beautiful, she was extremely independent and outspoken, an aspect of her character that had chased off many a suitor when she was a girl.

These same qualities had attracted Elijah who had lost his beloved Carmen when he was a young outlaw. In fact, tracking her killer had put him on the right side of the law which he continued to enforce for almost forty years.

Both the ex lawman and the librarian were avid readers. She had access to many volumes, and he had his own small library in his rooms at the Menger. Elijah was especially fond of British author Arthur Conan Doyle and Doyle's fictional detective, Sherlock Holmes.

It was late fall as Constance and Elijah rode on the outskirts of the Alamo City, enjoying the pleasant autumn weather. Elijah's big bay gelding stepped briskly and Constance's paint pony had no trouble keeping up. In fact, it seemed that the horses were taking pleasure in the outing too.

Sometimes the two talked about all sorts of things, including books they had read. Sometimes they were silent, holding hands like youngsters. This time it was the dead man under the tree that held their attention.

The corpse lay beneath an oak off to the side of the road. It could've been just a man resting in the shade. Instead it was a man not long dead.

Elijah and Constance dismounted. Constance held the horses as they started to fidget from the scent of blood in the air. Elijah went to examine the body.

The fellow was a young man of Mexican descent. He was dressed as a vaquero, wearing a short jacket with intricate stitching. A pair of engraved silver spurs adorned his fine calfskin boots. There was no wallet or purse - no identification. His shirt front was matted with dried blood; his face a death mask of pain. Whoever he was, he had died a long, painful death.

Elijah spoke, "He was gut shot and probably crawled here to die. We better ride in and notify Jim."

"I'll go," replied Constance, "you wait here and continue your examination."

She knew him well enough by now.

Elijah often helped unofficially when Captain Siesse had an unusual or difficult case. Constance left Elijah's bay horse ground tied and rode on to tell Jim Siesse.

Elijah was glad she had left. He didn't want her to see him handling the corpse like he knew he had to.

The barrel chested ex-lawman began by looking intently at the man's face. Trying not to look directly into the vacant eyes, he noticed some scratches on the face and what looked like a tiny piece of red material stuck in his teeth.

Elijah then moved to the hands. The left was open - the hand of a gentleman - smooth, no calluses. With some difficulty he pried open the right hand to find a tiny green satin button within. A grimace crossed his face as he examined the button, sighed, and then deposited it in his own vest pocket.

Under the man's left arm he found an empty shoulder holster. In an inside jacket pocket he found a deck of cards. He looked at them carefully. They were very delicately shaved and expertly marked.

The wound from which the man had died was not very large but had bled profusely. It looked like it had come from a gun fired at close range.

Elijah began to walk around the body, continually moving outward, looking over the ground carefully, pausing periodically to squat down and stare closely. When he reached out as far as his bay gelding, he stopped, a satisfied smile on his face.

He loosened his saddle cinches and took the bridle off his horse.

He knew old Sam wouldn't wander. He'd just crop the grass. Elijah leaned against a tree and waited.

Captain James Siesse arrived on horseback with two men on the morgue wagon. He was a small man and somewhat younger than Elijah, but he had the air of authority about him. When he gave orders, they were followed. Siesse and Edwards had been friends for years. The Captain looked as he had fifteen years ago. Only now were strands of hair graying. The ex lawman, on the other hand, was bulkier than he used to be and his hair and beard had turned almost completely silver.

"My God, what have you found, Elijah?", Siesse announced as he dismounted.

"Some bad doings here, Jim", replied Elijah.

"Have you solved it yet?" the captain laughed. "You've got Jimmy and Jenna reading about that Sherlock Holmes character. That fellow can solve a case from some cigar ashes. I expect they think I should be able to do the same. It's a shame to disappoint them. It's sure as hell easier in a story than real life."

He paused as he came nearer to the body and then gasped, "That's Raul Escobedo!"

There was no recognition on Elijah's face so Siesse continued, "His family has big holding3below the border. His Pa is some kind of politician too, one of many who thinks he ought to be running the Mexican government.

"I'll get pressure from above to solve this. Have you got anything to tell me?"

Elijah stepped forward nodding.

"Knowing who he is helps some. I believe Raul here comes across the border to sow his oats. His looks would surely attract women. He's a gambler but he cheats."

Edwards tossed the cards to the captain.

"He was shot at close range. He wasn't killed here. He was hauled here then dragged and propped against the tree. There are wagon tracks around from a two wheel cart one set deeper than the other. He was gagged. I found a small piece of kerchief in his mouth.

"I believe there were two who watched until he died. I found a cigar butt and two sets of boot tracks. When he was dead, they took the kerchief and lit out."

Siesse smiled, "Is that all you found?"

Elijah grinned back, "That's about it except for the scratches on his face. They could be from the tree, his struggles, his trip here, whatever."

The big man then turned away moving toward his horse as if he just wanted to end the conversation.

"Thank you, Sherlock," Siesse replied.

"Why don't you stop by the house for coffee? Constance is there with Hallie and the children. I should be there too. After all, it is Sunday. I'll have the body taken to the morgue, and I'll be home directly."

Siesse gave orders to the men on the morgue wagon while Elijah snugged cinches, bridled Sam, and mounted, hauling his bulky frame aboard with some difficulty as the horse stood patiently. He moved out without saying another word, his mind occupied with other thoughts Jim Siesse couldn't know.

Captain Siesse was correct about the pressure. Raul Escobedo's father, Edwardo, was a rich and powerful man, who had no lost love for Anglos. He vented his anger in letters to the San Antonio City government which in turn filtered down to Captain Siesse. Maybe it made Escobedo feel better. He charged that it was just another Mexican death in prejudiced San Antonio and would be treated as such. Papers would be shuffled but nothing would end up happening. The death would be attributed to person or persons unknown.

Siesse was not hurt professionally by this only personally. He prided himself on doing his job properly. He'd arrested Anglos, Mexicans, Negroes, Indians and Asians. he didn't work harder or less because of race.

The case proved to be difficult. The Captain shared his findings with Elijah one evening over dinner at JoChen's. They drank tea and munched almond cookies as Siesse talked.

"I've learned some things about Raul Escobedo his Pa wouldn't be too happy to hear," he said.

"This fellow was a gambler and a cheat like you figured and a womanizer. Whatever he won he just ended up spending on liquor or women. He had a special liking for Anglo whores and young girls. Most of the houses I visited in the city knew him or of him. They said he was a mean one too. He liked to hurt the girls. Sometimes he got rough but was always able to buy his way out. Belle Wade told me."

Elijah seemed flustered momentarily then responded, "Well, you can figure that for truth. I owned part of Belle's place for a while. If she counts you a friend, she'd never stretch the blanket."

"Do you think a girl did him in?"

"It could be," replied Edwards, "but you'll never be able to find out who."

"Yes, it's unlikely," said Siesse.

"You did your best, Jim. I know you really wanted to solve this case. Judging from what we know about Raul Escobedo, he wasn't worth your effort. You might've missed this one but you'll make up for it."

They went their separate ways. Elijah knew what he had to do even though the mere thought caused him pain.

The Satin Lady was a saloon/bordello in San Antonio with the highest reputation. It didn't cater to cowboys. They couldn't afford it. Its clientele was made up of cattle ranchers, bankers, businessmen of all kinds from all over the Southwest; Its proprietress, Belle Wade, provided young ladies with an air of refinement. She specialized in exotic girls; Asians, Indians, Negresses. Belle was always discreet. She had to be trusted or these high rollers would stay away.

Elijah had felt uncomfortable, squiring Constance Mooney about and retaining an interest in such an elegant whorehouse, so he had sold out to Belle Wade.

Now he felt uncomfortable again as he mounted the steps of the Satin Lady. He was greeted by barman Clint Yost who flicked his cigar ashes off the bar with his ever present towel and by the swamper, a negro named Bob. He was passed through to the living quarters in back.

Unexpectedly, for him, he was nervous as he rapped on the door. His knock was answered as the door swung open. He saw the smiling face of Black Annie, Belle Wade's maid.

"Mr. Elijah," she said excitedly, "so nice to see you. You don't come around near enough anymore.

The feeling was genuine Elijah knew.

"Annie, you know I can't afford to make Constance jealous. She'll think I'm dallying with you. She knows I consider you an African princess."

Annie swatted the air with her hand and laughed deeply. "Mister Elijah," she said, "you can tell whoppers with the best of 'em, but I don't mind at all."

"Is Belle up?" asked Elijah.

"Yes sir. You wait here in the parlor and I'll go fetch her and some coffee."

With a swish of skirts she was gone, leaving Edwards to recline on one of the richly upholstered chairs.

A few minutes later Belle Wade entered. She was still a handsome woman even after years in a rough business.

She was short and buxom with a complexion that still seemed creamy. Her red hair hung in curls to her shoulders, and wrapped around her ample frame was an emerald green satin robe.

"Good to see you, Elijah," she said unconvincingly as the ex lawman rose to hug her in greeting.

"You still look good in green," he said. "Don't you ever run out of those things?"

"Never," she replied.

"Belle," Elijah continued. "You know I'm not one for talking around a thing so I'll come right to it. I don't think you were honest with Jim Siesse about that Escobedo murder. He's had a lot of pressure and feels bad about his lack of success. He's my friend but so are you. I would like to help him, but I don't want to hurt you. I've got to know the truth."

He then reached in his pocket. When he extended his open hand, in the palm was a small green satin button. "I found this clutched in Escobedo's hand."

Belle gasped slightly, wringing her hands but remained silent.

Elijah continued, "Escobedo was rich and free with his money of which there was plenty. He was a crooked gambler and fancied himself a lady's man. In this whole city this is the place I figure he'd hook his spurs.

"When Jim said he talked to you, and you couldn't offer much help, my suspicions were confirmed.

"We go back a long way Belle. You saved my skin and helped me through some tough times and I'll never forget it. But, you've got to remember, Jim and I partnered for many years. I couldn't count the times that our very lives depended on one another. We couldn't be closer if we were kin. I've got to know the truth of it."

Belle paused to wipe away tears and waited until Annie brought the coffee. After the coffee was served, Belle instructed Annie that there were to be no disturbances. She sat down and asked Elijah to do the same.

"This is hard for me Elijah, so just let me tell it all before you say anything,"

Elijah nodded his head and sat back in his chair, training all his attention on the lady across from him.

"It happened here Elijah. Escobedo was mean drunk that night. He beat one of the girls. Somehow she got hold of one of the derringers I keep for protection.

"I recognized him as soon as I saw him. I was scared and worried. I thought if we could just get him out I'd be clear of trouble. I had Clint and Bob roll him up in a rug. They stuffed a neckerchief in his mouth to keep him quieter. We took anything off him that might serve as identification and burned it. The boys took him out of town so that it might look like he was shot there. They burned the rug and even the cart. There were no witnesses. He was hated by many in San Antonio so it wasn't hard to keep mouths closed. I sent the girl away the next day. There you have it."

Elijah remained silent for awhile his piercing eyes unforgiving in their intensity.

Finally he spoke, "Belle this won't wash. You have too many friends in high places in this city, or you know too much that people want kept quiet. This could've been handled quietly even if it was Edwardo Edcobedo's son. There's something more you haven't told me."

The tears welled up in Belle's eyes. She shuddered as sobs broke forth.

Elijah moved towards her and put his arm around her shoulder.

"What is it?" he whispered.

In a few seconds Belle's crying ceased. With great effort she pulled herself together.

"All right," she said finally. "I guess it's time you knew. Your daughter shot Raul Escobedo."

Elijah stumbled back to his chair, dazed as if someone had slapped his face.

"Take it easy," smiled Belle. "I'm sorry I never told you, but I had my reasons."

She took a crystal decanter of brandy and poured a stiff shot in Elijah's coffee cup.

"Drink that," she said.

Elijah took the cup and drained it. Color returned to his face and he appeared visibly calmer. Belle began her tale.

"We met after you lost Carmen. You were different and troubled and tried to drown yourself in drink. You talked to me rather than just used me. That kind of treatment I considered rare. I grew fond of you which is unwise in my business.

"On one of those nights you were so upset and drunk that we did more than talk. You were so sad that my heart almost broke. I doubt that you would remember it, but I'll never forget it. That night I became pregnant with your child.

"You were still so torn up about Carmen I didn't want to add to that pain. We went our different ways. I had the baby, a girl, Penny. I sent her East when she was old enough. I have family in Chicago. They took care of her. I furnished her support.

Belle blushed at that, her face turning bright pink. It flustered Elijah who had never seen such a reaction on her part.

'You see," Belle continued, "Penny visits once a year. She's a smart girl and knows what I do but doesn't hold it against me.

"Escobedo stumbled, roaring drunk, into my private rooms after roughing up one of my girls. Penny was wearing one of my green robes, and she does resemble me quite a bit. Escobedo and I never got along. Maybe he thought she was me. Anyway, he came at her. She fought him off until she could reach a gun. Then she shot him. She never flinched or cried. She must get that from you. The rest of the story is exactly like I told you."

"I never knew," Elijah said. "I never even suspected."

"That's because most men are emotionally dense," Belle chuckled. There was a sense of relief on her face.

"I can't change the past," Elijah responded. "I can't change the present. My feelings for Constance are deep. What I can do is try to make sure of the future and that includes protecting you and my," he hesitated for a moment as if saying the word took supreme effort. Finally, he uttered "daughter" followed by a broad smile.

"Like I told you Jim Siesse is as close to me as anyone. I'd ride to hell if he needed me. But, in this situation you need me more. You need me to let this go. It would serve no good purpose to do otherwise."

They spent the next hour looking at photographs of Penny. Belle told Elijah all about his girl. He seemed fascinated by everything.

When he left the Satin Lady that day, Elijah Edwards was emotionally spent, but he felt closer to all the important people in his life. He was aware of what he should do legally, but he had been in this position before. He had made his decision, and, somehow, he figured if there was a reckoning at the end of his life as the preachers believed, the Almighty would understand.

Elijah and the Highlander

The year 1900 was memorable for Elijah Edwards in more ways than one. It was the year he and Constance Mooney finally married after "keeping company" for several years. The difference in their ages bothered neither of them. He was a quite robust 64, and she demurely admitted to being forty something! They were true soul-mates though, and while San Antonio society might have looked askance at their nuptials, they cared not a whit for the opinions of others.

Elijah's reputation as a fearless Texas Ranger had grown over the years to almost legendary proportions. That assured no wagging tongues when he was around. He hadn't shot a man in years, but no one wanted to tempt fate.

Constance had inherited her family's large ranch holdings, so she was independent woman of wealth and power. That helped insulate her from criticism.

The two of them split their time among residences. Sometimes they lived in Elijah's rooms at the Menger Hotel. Other times they could be found on the vast Mooney ranch west of San Antonio. In the heat of summer they could travel to another Mooney ranch property in the mountains of New Mexico.

Elijah had prepared for retirement by investing wisely. His time was spent pursuing other interests like reading. He had become enamored of British author Arthur Conan Doyle' fictional detective, Sherlock Holmes. He waited anxiously for each new story to reach America. Edwards also now helped Constance in overseeing the Mooney properties. Constance had given up her position at the library to look after the family holdings when her Father passed away.

Elijah had also become sort of an unofficial consultant to the San Antonio police force. His good friend, Captain James Seisse, had called upon him several times to assist on cases. The year 1900 was memorable also because of one those cases and the ex-ranger's part in it.

Edwards and Seisse were dining alone at their favorite restaurant, Jo Chen's. Constance had returned to the ranch. The Captain's wife and children were visiting relatives in Houston.

Seisse munched an almond cookie and sipped tea as he spoke, "Joe Chen has certainly done well for himself here".

"That's because he's good at what he does and has worked hard at it, replied Edwards. "You've helped him along the way, "said the Captain. "Oh, I did at first, but that was along time ago. I just helped him get started. The success is his alone".

Elijah, paused momentarily, then continued, "Jim you didn't bring me here to discuss Jo Chen. Something is bothering you".

Seisse grinned, "We know each other too well, Elijah. I didn't want to bother you, I mean you and Constance have your lives to live, and I don't have the right to impose on you".

"The things we've been through together give you every right, Jim. You know how much Constance loves you and your family. You're the closest people to us both. She'd be upset if you didn't impose on me".

It seemed as if Seisse breathed a sigh of relief then "Thanks, I just feel different now that you're married".

"That doesn't change our friendship, "replied Elijah. "What is it?"

Jim, Seisse shifted in his seat, poured some more tea, and continued. "I'm worried about the upcoming visit of John Taggert".

A frown crossed Elijah's face at the mention of the name. "Why are you worried about that carpet bagging son of a bitch?"

"I guess I'm worried about what might happen to him. Did you know Ian MacGregor is out at Rangers Rest?"

Edwards was genuinely surprised at that bit of information. "No, I didn't know, I'm glad though. He's getting up in years. He deserves a place like that to live out his days."

His feature turned soft as he thought about the man. "That old Scotsman is a hell of a character. He's tough as oak-a man you could always count on. If he gave his word, hell would freeze over before he broke it."

"You know that he promised to kill John Taggert."

"Taggart will be here for the doings on March 6. Will Ian still keep his word?"

Elijah's brown furrowed, "That bastard Taggart would deserve it after what he did to MacGregor's family while Ian was off chasing Comanches. He only saved his skin by moving back East."

"You haven't answered my question, Elijah," said Jim Seisse.

"Why is Taggart coming?" asked the ex-lawman.

"I think he has political aspirations. Besides he probably thinks MacGregor is dead or far away. What about Ian?"

Elijah sighed, sipped some tea and then said, "You can bet on it. He's not going to let this chance go. It may be his last."

"I don't want to have to see a man like MacGregor hang for killing trash like Taggart. It will be murder because Taggart will not stand up in a fair fight. There will be no self defense, and I'll have to arrest a man who has literally given his whole life to Texas. I don't want to see him dangling from a hangman's rope."

"Neither do I Jim. I know Ian. Let me ride out and talk to him. See what I can learn. Maybe he's mellowed. Maybe he's become forgiving. People do change with age. Look at me."

Elijah patted his stomach and the two men laughed then. It was a good release of tension.

In his mind though Elijah knew Ian MacGregor would not change. How could he prevent McGregor from committing a crime that could send him to the gallows. That he did not know.

Elijah didn't ride as much as he used to when he has a lawman. He liked to rationalize and blame his expanding girth on that. The truth was that the facts really didn't support his theory. He had always been a stocky man from his days as a younker to now. His more sedentary life since his retirement and his fondness for good food helped add the extra poundage. He really welcomed the opportunity to help Constance on the ranch. It got him back in the saddle, and the exercise was truly good for him. He wasn't chasing bandits or Indians, so he could travel leisurely and enjoy it.

He rode a new horse that had been a wedding gift from Constance. The animal was a stout, dappled grey gelding that Elijah had named Jack Hays after the famous ranger. Jack had smooth gaits that included a fast walk almost like a single foot. The horse could cover lots of ground and seemed never to tire.

Elijah was riding a new Concho saddle too. He had been on a trip to San Angelo the previous year and had ordered two, one for himself and one for his wife. Constance never rode sidesaddle as was common with many ladies of the day. It was hard to work cattle and use a rope that way, so she rode astraddle as well as most vaqueros on the ranch.

Elijah set out for Ranger's Rest after a good breakfast. It was early February so mornings were pretty chilly. By midday the sun would warm up the temperature to comfortable degree. He figured it was about a three hour ride on Jack, so he relaxed in the saddle and marveled at the horse's ground covering pace.

Ranger's Rest was really the brainchild of rancher. Cleve Schreiner. He had great respect for what the Texas Rangers had done to protect the citizens of the lone star state and he sought to pay back a little by establishing Rangers Rest. He had a built a new house on the ranch.

He then made the family's old living quarters available as a retirement home for rangers with no families. They lived there free of charge and took meals with the working cowboys. Sometimes, if they were able, they would help out with ranch work, but it wasn't required. Right now there were only two men in residence, Ian MacGregor and Terrell Bucks.

Elijah heard the strains of "Amazing Grace" as he approached. The sounds of Ian MacGregor's bagpipes were unmistakable. Jack Hay's ears were working on that sound too. It was new to him and he tensed up a little. Edwards patted the grey's neck, and the horse calmed down, but those ears remained perked at attention.

The ex-ranger waved to MacGregor and dismounted, always an easier thing for him than mounting these days. He loosened the cinch on his saddle, took off the bridle, and turned Jack Hays into the nearby corral where water and hay was available. Jack made himself right at home.

"Elijah, how the hell are you? "Was the greeting from Ian MacGregor as he extended his hand. MacGregor was as tall as Edwards, but much thinner. He stood ramrod straight though, and the hand shake was firm. He was clean shaven with angular features, piercing blue eyes, and a thick shock of pure white hair.

"Congratulations on your marriage. I got to admire an old man like you getting hitched. I respect anyone who accepts that responsibility. Never could do it myself, "he grinned.

"That's because no one would have you", replied Elijah. "You are just too hard headed to share your life. You could never compromise."

"You are probably right. I guess that's why I'm living here. But, I got Terrell and the cowboys for company. Sometimes I even see Cleve and his family. They are mighty nice folks."

"You'll get no argument from me, "said Elijah. "The Schreiners are fine people. Where is Terrell anyway?"

"He went out with the boys at first light. I think my pipe playing is getting to him, but I've got to keep practicing."

"Why?" inquired Edwards.

"I'm taking part in the parade in San Antonio on March 6. Some elements of the old 79th New York Cameron Highlanders have been asked to participate, and I'm going to tag along. My brother was in that outfit.

"How did that happen-I mean-you wearing the grey and him the blue?"

"We never did see eye to eye. James had his own view. It hurt Ma and Pa, but before the war he moved North to live with relatives in New York.

"Thank God we never had to meet in battle. We wrote to one another though. The letters stopped after the battle of Secessionville, South Carolina."

Elijah thought he saw moisture creeping into those vibrant blue eyes and took the opportunity to get to the real reason for his visit.

"You know John Taggart will be a speaker at the celebration, "he said.

MacGregor returned from his momentary reverie and responded, "Sure I know. It's a dammed shame they allow someone like him to speak on the anniversary of the Alamo."

Elijah tried to read the older man's demeanor, but he couldn't. Ian MacGregor spoke matter of factly. There was no edge in his voice or glint in his eyes.

"Taggart is testing political waters, "continued MacGregor." Ever since he moved back to Texas, he's had his eye on public office. He's surely got money, so it must be the power that attracts him. He'll not get my vote I can tell you that."

They spent the next hour drinking coffee and talking about old times, swapping stories about their days as rangers. Elijah was impressed by Ian MacGregor. The older man moved a little stiffly, but he seemed to be in good physical shape and his mind was as sharp as ever.

"Well, old friend, "Elijah said, "it's time for me to be moving on. I believe on my good grey horse I can make the circle by nightfall. There I will be greeted by my wonderful wife and a hot meal."

"You are a lucky man, "said Ian.

"I know. These days I think about it often. Luck has been with me from my days as a wayward youth to now. As many dangerous spots as I've been in, I just can't figure it. There must be someone up there looking out for me."

"Could be," said MacGregor. "Sometimes it's hard to figure why some of us are allowed to live on and other lives are snuffed out when they've just begun.'

Elijah knew MacGregor was thinking about members of his own family who were turned off their land when Taggart bought up the note from the bank. They were on the road toward town and temporary quarters when a small band of Comanche caught them in the open, leaving no one alive.

"I've got to ask you straight out Ian, "said Elijah. "You promised to kill John Taggart. Are you going to keep that promise?"

Mac Gregor sighed, "That was a long time ago. I'm an old man now. Sometimes we just can't keep promises no matter how hard we try."

With that they shook hands, and Elijah headed Jack Hays toward home. He listened to the strains of bag pipes fade as he rode away. Elijah felt a little better after his meeting with Ian, but something still bothered him. MacGregor had never said he wouldn't keep his promise to kill John Taggert.

John Taggart sat in his private rail car surrounded by luxuries his wealth could provide: polished wood, red velour, shiny brass trimmings, hard cut crystal, custom hand rolled cigars. They were all trappings of an extremely successful man. Most would say that these things would make him a contented, happy man, but at this time he was neither of those things.

Taggart chewed on his cigar as beads of perspiration formed on his balding head. He habitually scratched at his mutton chop sideburns as he read and reread the telegram just handed to him by his secretary.

The wealthy business man was dressed in a custom tailored suit which cleverly masked a body that had gone soft over the years. He always wore generously cut clothes in dark colors. That helped minimize his expanding girth in appearance anyway.

"This is distressing," Taggart said, "I was sure that old bastard was long dead. In his line of work longevity is the exception to the rule. How did he survive all these years?"

His secretary, Arnold Bishop, a small middle aged man with thick spectacles responded, "We had word three years ago that MacGregor was dead. Obviously, the informant is not someone we can trust. I will consult my records, find out who it was, and make sure he will never work for any Taggart companies now or in the future."

Bishop's voice was cold and unemotional, very businesslike. It was a voice that exuded confidence.

"Why do you worry about an old man like that?" Bishop asked.

"He was quite a man in his day. In his business he was ruthless, much like me. MacGregor put a lot of men in their graves. When he went after bandit, he always brought them back, dead, or alive, usually dead. He had quite a reputation.

"He always blamed me for the deaths of his family members- unfairly I might add. After the war I bought up notes from banks or ranchers and farms.

If people couldn't pay, I took their property. It was just good business. MacGregor's family lost their land. It's not my fault they lost their lives to Indian attack. The country was wild and unsafe then."

Bishop mulled over the information he has just been given then spoke. "I doubt there is much he can do now after all these years."

"That son of a bitch promised to kill me if I ever came back to Texas, "Taggart replied angrily. "I've been back here a few years, but this is my first time back to San Antonio. I had really forgotten about him. It's been so long. I don't like this."

The secretary responded, "I'm sure it's a problem that can be eliminated. I have contacts in San Antonio. Do you want me to take care of it?"

John Taggart admired Bishop's ability to solve any situation, so he felt confident as he nodded. The little man never bothered him with details. After all, as a busy important man, the businessman didn't really need to know how things were accomplished. Only that they had been accomplished. Arnold Bishop was valuable man in business and would be indispensable in Taggart's political future. Ian MacGregor was like a bothersome fly and needed to be swatted away. Bishop would have no trouble in carrying out his bosses wishes.

Every Monday Ian Mac Gregor and Terrell Bucks went hunting. It was routine and no secret. The Texas hill country abounded with mule deer, and, even though both men moved slower, they had been blessed with good eyesight. If they had success, they Schreiner ranch hands could dine on venison instead of beef for a change.

The terrain was a little rugged, but the men weren't in a hurry. Bucks rode his sure footed mule, Sally. MacGregor was putting some miles on a young bay colt. Luckily, they were dismounting when gunshots shattered the serenity. The bay colt crumpled to the ground while Sally squealed and bolted as a bullet creased her rump. MacGregor and Bucks dove for cover flattening out under the shielding mesquite.

"Did you see where the shots came from?" asked MacGregor.

Bucks, a slight man barely over five feet tall and easily shrouded by the vegetation responded, "Up to the left". He levered a shell into his rifle and waited.

Their positions were uncomfortable and their bodies ached, but the old rangers knew better than to leave cover. They waited and watched for movement. After about an hour they were rewarded. Someone up the hill was visible for a split second, just long enough for Terrell Bucks to get a shot. Minutes later MacGregor saw a horseman riding far out of rifle range and leading a riderless horse. "Looks you had some luck, Terrell", he said.

Bucks spat a stream of tobacco juice, "No luck to it," he said. "All skill." He smiled, revealing an absence of teeth.

"We better move careful. I don't know if our man is dead or just down. I believe there were only two though".

It took them almost an hour to move, slowly, always keeping under cover, to reach their quarry. He was a young man with sandy colored hair and a baby face slumped in the Texas dust, but he was still alive.

As the two old ex-rangers continued to approach, they saw the man's rifle on the ground. He was too busy trying to stop the blood flowing from his side. He was young but hardened as he watched the two men draw nearer. He said nothing, but his eyes didn't indicate surrender. He was just too hurt to reach his gun.

"It looks like my bullet hit home, bushwhacker", said Terrell Bucks, "You better let me look at that wound."

There was no response, so Bucks left his rifle with MacGregor. Ian kept his Winchester trained on the man as Bucks moved toward the wounded fellow. When Terrell reached him, the man moved his bloodied hand to reveal a large hole.

"Not much we can do for you fella," said Buck. "We're too far from town to get any help soon enough. Why did you do it?"

The young man didn't respond. Ian MacGregor walked forward, leveled a shell into his rifle, and shot the young man in the foot.

The wounded man screamed at the new pain.

"Who were you after and why?" asked MacGregor as he levered another shell into his Winchester.

All color had drained from the boy's face and the tough facade shattered. He was now just a frightened youth facing a painful bitter end.

"I know you're gut shot and suffering the tortures of hell. Tell me what I want to know, and it may end quick. Otherwise, we'll let you bleed out here as long as it takes."

The young man was actually writhing in pain now, but he wasn't crying. He finally spoke in a high pitched almost female sounding voice, "We were supposed to get MacGregor, "he gasped." An old man we were told."

"Not too old yet," responded MacGregor.

The young man caught his breath and continued, "Man named Bishop came to us, he pays good."

Bucks and MacGregor looked at each other puzzled. The name didn't mean anything to them.

"Whatever it was, it wasn't enough, "said Bucks.

"Your hand gun here has one cartridge left in it."

He tossed the gun on the ground next to the dying man. Then Bucks and MacGregor turned and walked away, not even flinching when they heard discharge of the pistol.

"Hell, I don't know anyone named Bishop who has grudge against you. I guess I was unlucky enough to be with you today," said Bucks.

"I'm glad you were here. You saved our bacon today. Somehow this has got to be tied to John Taggart."

Buck's face showed recognition then.

"I thought that was over long ago when he moved away," he said.

"I thought so too," MacGregor responded." It rankled me to let it go, but I did. I guess that was my mistake. I should've followed that bastard East and kept my promise."

He looked straight at Terrell Bucks then and said, "I don't believe it's too late to set things straight."

The dead fellow's name was Will Barrett. Even as a young man he had already gained quite a reputation with law enforcement officers in Texas. He had been suspected of all sorts of nefarious activities from armed robbery to cattle theft, but no charges had stuck. Witnesses conveniently had memory loss, left the country or turned up dead. The investigation into Barrett's death at the hands of Terrell Bucks and Ian MacGregor was swift and categorized the man's demise as self defense.

Since Bucks and MacGregor had spent their lifetime in law enforcement, they were bound to have people angry at them and anxious for revenge.

This was the theory they presented to the police. They never mentioned Arnold Bishop or the connection to John Taggert.

Elijah had earlier reported his discussion with Ian MacGregor to Jim Seisee. There was nothing to say really. It seemed as if the old man had set his grudge to rest. Elijah and Jim both felt they had done what they could. Now they would just wait, watch, and listen. It was only ten days to the celebration. John Taggert would be gone after that and both men could then relax a little.

Texans look upon the Alamo as a shrine to heroism and independence which is easily understandable. The defenders of the old mission faced overwhelming odds and certain death, yet all but one, a man named Rose, remained to die at the hands of Santa Anna's troops. The cry "Remember the Alamo" had been on the lips of many Texans weeks later at San Jacinto and helped fuel the victory that made Texas the Lone Star Republic.

Elijah had been born on March 6, 1836 and always felt a special kinship to that place and that event. He was pleased that efforts to preserve the Alamo were being spearheaded by the Daughters of Texas. They had arranged the day of celebration to help keep the preservation of the Alamo in the public eye.

The day was beautiful, sunny, clear, and crisp. It was good day to be outside after the early morning chill had been burned away.

A reviewing stand with red and white and blue bunting had been erected in front of the old church. There was a speaker's podium where John Taggert stood observing the festivities.

Food vendors moved through the crowds. Now and again fire crackers would explode, followed by children's screams and squeals. There was certainly electricity in the air as the breeze carried on it the trail of bagpipes in the distance. The sounds grew louder and more raucous as the contingent from the 79th New York Cameron Highlanders came into view, resplendent in their full Highland dress including kilts. They skirled "Blue Bonnets Over the Border" as the crowd cheered lustily.

John Taggert stood with his hands on the podium, his politician's smile firmly in place, watching the proceedings. With all the commotion going on no one noticed immediately when he slumped forward. It was only after the weight of his body had toppled the podium that people screamed and yelled for help or even noticed that anything unusual had happened on the stand.

By the time Jim Seisse and Elijah Edwards reached the body, Taggart's breathing was already ragged. He was dead before a doctor could reach the scene. Jim and Elijah looked at each other incredulous at what had just taken place in full view of everyone.

"Elijah", said Seisse, "I can't figure this. I had men stationed all over watching rooftops and windows. No one in the parade was armed. I had them all checked too. How could this have been done?"

Elijah's brow wrinkled as he spoke, "I don't know, Jim. It seems like you had all contingencies covered. You'll have to go through the formalities of an investigation of course. I will help where I can, but my heart won't be in it. I think Taggart deserved what he got."

Seisse nodded. He understood, but he still had to follow procedure. He stood aside as Doc Isdel labored up the steps of the reviewing stand to examine John Taggart. The two men knew it was futile. They had both seen too many dead men in their lifetimes.

Weeks passed and the furor over the murder of John Taggart died down. The press found new things to write about, and even Jim Seisse was relieved of pressure from the paper. The death was attributed to person or persons unknown.

One morning when Constance and Elijah were having their breakfast at the Circle M Constance expressed worry over Elijah's behavior and spoke forthrightly while buttering her toast, "What is bother you? You haven't even read the latest Strand magazine. That's not like you."

Elijah sipped his coffee and responded, "You are right. It's this Taggart case.

Deep down I know that Ian MacGregor did the deed. I just don't know how. He has to be the answer. I must say I'm not sorry Taggart's gone, though his passing caused Jim Seisse some grief."

"Why don't you just ride over to Ranger's Rest and ask him?"

"Ian was already questioned by the police as to where he was and what he saw that day," Elijah replied.

"Did anyone ask him if he did it," repeated Constance.

"No, I don't believe anyone asked him right out."

"You know, Elijah, he wouldn't lie to you. You've just got to decide what to do with what he tells you."

"You are probably right", Elijah said. "I believe I will follow your advice. I think old Jack Hays needs to stretch his legs a bit anyway. I expect I'll be back by dinnertime. Thanks."

Elijah Edwards kissed his wife and squeezed her hand and walked off to go and saddle his horse. She smiled as she watched him go.

Ian MacGregor waved when he saw Elijah approaching. The old ranger sat whittling on the porch as Elijah dismount and tended to his horse, turning the animal into the corral.

"Ian, you are looking good," said Elijah as he strode forward to shake hands.

The two men made small talk for a few minutes then Elijah got to the purpose of his visit.

"Constance told me just to ask you straight out. I guess that is the best way after all. I don't believe I have any other choice. Did you kill John Taggart?"

The old ranger stopped whittling and through his knife into the wooden porch floor where it stuck. Then he smiled, "I was wondering how long it would take you to figure it. I surely killed Taggart and it felt good finally to do it."

Elijah sighed, "I don't suppose you'd like to tell me how?"

"You mean your detective skills haven't come up with the answer?"

Elijah shook his head.

"We had no weapons, remember? The police checked. What would I have used as a weapon?"

"All you had was your instrument – your bagpipes.

I remember commenting that they looked different from the ones I had seen you play before. You said they were special."

"And, so the were," said MacGregor, smiling.

The old man went inside and returned moments later with the pipes and handed them to Elijah.

"Relax, he said," let me tell you some things.

I hope they won't make you think less of me.

"First, I had changed my mind about killing John Taggart until those fellows attacked Terrell and me. I didn't tell you, but that boy talked before he died. John Taggart or his man hired them. That made me mad, Terrell too."

He paused to gather his thoughts then continued. "During the war there were all sorts of plans that never were carried out. I was involved in one of them. The South was desperate for help from the British.

The question was how to get them to commit to aiding the Confederacy.

"This plan had me infiltrating the 79th New York Cameron Highlander, my brother's outfit. We resembled each other considerably, and I could play the pipes.

"The Highlanders were sometimes called upon to entertain visiting dignitaries, especially British dignitaries who enjoyed Scottish bagpipes. There was talk of a possible trip to England to appear before the Queen herself.

"I had bagpipes specially modified by an uncle of mine who was a gunsmith and had experimented early with metallic cartridges. The outside tenor drone was steel lined with a spring loaded pin activated by a lever."

The old ranger leaned forward to demonstrate on the pipes for Elijah. Edwards was suitably impressed by the ease of mechanical operation.

"If a high ranking British official was killed or wounded by a member of a union military group, it might help turn Great Britain against the North.

"I realize now it was pretty far fetched and had little or no chance of succeeding, but I was young then, adventuresome and idealistic, dedicated to a cause and didn't care about consequences. I had been educated with the classics and pictured myself as a knight of the round table on a mission. It never happened though, and then I was wounded. I did keep the bagpipes though."

Elijah had a somewhat puzzled look on his face. "Even Sherlock Holmes couldn't have figured this out" he finally said.

Ian continued, "I made sure I marched on the outside in the parade. When we reached the reviewing stand, I was directly beneath Taggart. I fired the bullet. It worked better than I expected. The pipes, fireworks, and crowd voices drowned out the shot."

Elijah shook his head. "I would never have believed it," he said.

"Yes, I was lucky I guess," responded MacGregor.

"Now what?"

Elijah pondered the situation. It bothered him. "Jim Seisse has had a hell of a time with this case. He's my friend."

He paused for a moment more then continued, "But, you're my friend too. I'm not an officer of the law anymore, so I just have to use my own judgment here. I can't say I agree with what you did, but I understand the why of it. It's the kind of thing I probably would've done myself. It's best if this remains with you and me."

Elijah stood then and did Ian MacGregor. They shook hands, Elijah said, "Don't go killing anyone else."

"I have only killed people who needed killing," responded Ian, "Just like you, I can live with it."

"I guess I can too, said Elijah as he stepped down from the porch to go and get Jack Hays.

That night over dinner Constance asked Elijah if he had found out what he wanted. He said he had. She never asked him more, knowing that he would be obligated to tell her. There were things she felt she didn't need to know.

"Now, with your mind less troubled maybe you can read that new Strand magazine that came recently," said Constance smiling.

She had a dazzling smile and Elijah took her hand and smiled also. "Yes, he said, "my chair and lamp await and, my dear, I believe the game may be afoot."

Sunset Lady

AUTHOR'S NOTE

Even though the years are piling up on me, I still try to ride horseback whenever I can here at the ranch. It's a good way to see the country and it helps me think. Since I've started writing these little "campfire tales", horsebacking provides a little break from my desk, but it also helps me remember a little more clearly.

I've been raising horses here for close to forty years. I started with some blooded stock from my friends, the Tenners, and some Indian ponies given to me by the Comanche.

I've got a great horse trainer, Luke Taylor. His father, L.B. Taylor, was probably the best horse handler I ever saw. He wasn't the best rider, but he seemed to understand the animals and could sort of communicate with them. He passed away just two years ago, natural causes, no accident with a horse, even though he was still active and working on the Tenner ranch.

In the story that follows LB is one of the characters. Luke has heard it so often that now, when he reads it, he can tell <u>me</u> if I've stretched the blanket any.

Grant Kirby
Santa Fe, 1919

CHAPTER 1

We saw them put the rope around the young Negro's neck. There were four of them on horseback, a little wobbly, probably from a jug that they were passing around.

Even from a distance we could hear the boy shouting that the horse wasn't stolen. It was his. He wanted them to look at a letter in his jacket pocket.

Clay Ellis and I had left Houston a few days earlier and were bound for the Tenner ranch near San Antonio. Clay was a former Texas Ranger and law officer, known far and wide as a top notch shootist. He and John Tenner were old friends. He left his position as a peace officer in Houston to accompany me on my journey. I had just completed a quest to avenge the death of my good friend, Reese Tenner, John's eldest son. (That tale was recently published under the rather lurid title <u>TEXAS</u> <u>BLOOD</u>).

We approached the group, our horses moving slowly, but attentively, with ears pricked forward as they saw and probably scented their own kind.

Clay turned to me and said, "Grant, I know this ain't our business, but these fellows seem bent on lynching that boy without giving him any chance to prove himself innocent. He's only asking them to look in his coat".

I had to agree. "Someone about to be hung ought to at least be given that courtesy. Do we take a hand in this?"

"Well, I'm not a lawman now, but I've carried a badge a long time and this don't seem quite lawful to me," he replied. He grinned and opened his coat, revealing a brace of Navy Colts. I followed suit to make sure I too had easy access to my weapons.

The four men near the hanging tree caught sight of us and paused momentarily. Understandably, they were probably a little wary of us too. As we drew closer, the Negro called, "Please, help me! They say I stole this horse, but she's mine and I've got papers to prove it! Just look in my pocket!"

As we stopped, Clay addressed the man adjusting the rope. He was small and lean with a pock marked face and a broken nose. He was quite a bit older than the other three and appeared to be the leader.

"Howdy," Ellis nodded. "You think you got yourself a horse thief here?"

The boy opened his mouth to speak, and the lean man slapped him hard, almost unseating him.

"Yes sir," the lean man whined in a high pitched nasal tone, "we got us a goddamn nigger horse thief here, and my boys and I are aiming to send him straight to hell where he belongs."

The three boys smiled at that, looking from one to the other. The fellow in the middle was tall, the other two shorter, but they were all slim in stature and there was a facial resemblance too. Clay continued, "Are you sure this darkie stole that horse? Did you check for that paper he was screaming about?"

The lean man responded, "Look at that horse he's on. You ever see a nigger on a horse that fine that wasn't stolen? Few white folks ride such good animals."

The mare was a beauty. She was a bright sorrel with a blaze face and four white socks. She had a well muscled hip and a broad chest. She looked like she could run.

"You got a point there mister," Clay agreed. The lean man seemed to relax a little then. His three boys took their cue from him and followed suit. I, however, still kept my eyes on them. Clay spoke again, and this time there was a little sharp edge to his calm voice. "But, it'll only take a second to check his story, and I think we'll all feel better then."

Clay nudged his horse forward while I stayed put, keeping in position for action against the three sons if necessary. The lean man moved his hand away from the rope and closer to the handgun shoved in his belt. "This is really none of your business Mr. Whoever you are. He ain't just a horse thief. He's got a hankerin for my daughter, and me and her brothers won't stand for that from any decent man let alone from a black buck like him."

"That's not true!" screamed the Negro. "I only talked to her, passed the time of day, nothing more."

"So, this isn't really about horse stealing is it mister?" asked Clay.

He then turned to the three sons.

"Did your sister tell you he done something he shouldn't have?"

They thought a moment then the taller boy in the middle spoke. "No. She only said he was right friendly and a pretty talker. We don't want no pretty talking nigger around Ellie."

Clay turned back to the lean man.

"Well then, we can't be hanging people for being friendly or talking pretty can we? I think you better cut him loose".

"Look, you son of a bitch, who are you to be telling me what to do?"

I was just about ready to pull my pistol and dive off my horse when Clay answered.

"My name is Clay Ellis and I killed my first man because he insulted my mother."

When the lean man heard Clay's name, he sort of froze, and his three Sons just turned and stared at one another until the middle boy spoke. "Are you Clay Ellis of the rangers?"

Clay nodded. "Yes, I rode with Captain Tenner some years ago chasing Indians and bandits and such."

The oldest son continued, "You shot three men to death in San Antonio just after the war!"

"Killed two outright, the third died about a week later. They were horse thieves like this boy is supposed to be," Clay replied.

This was the first time I had ever seen what effect a reputation could have on some people. The lean man moved away from the young Negro. He was noticeably frightened and made sure his gun hand stayed far away from his waist. The lean man's sons stayed very still also.

Clay moved forward until his horse was next to the sorrel mare. He reached inside the young Negro's pocket and extracted an oil skin which he unrolled. He sat for a couple minutes reading.

"This here says your name is Lawrence Bradford Taylor and that Colonel Beau Taylor was your pappy."

This was the first time that I noticed that the boy's skin was not really black but more like coffee laced with cream. His features too were a little different. His nose was sharp rather than flat and his lips were thin not thick. His hair was kinky like a Negro's but the color was a lighter brown, not dark or black.

"Yes sir," replied L.B. Taylor, "He lost the plantation after the war, took sick, and passed away. All he could leave me was some clothes, a little money, this fine mare, and my freedom. I headed west because the South holds nothing for a half-breed like me."

Clay took the rope off the boy's neck and with his belt knife cut the ropes that had bound the young man's hands behind him.

"Well, we're headed down San Antonio way if you're interested. It's safer traveling together. You're welcome to come. I'm sure Grant won't mind."

He looked my way and I nodded in agreement.

We rode out leaving the lean man and his sons, never having learned their names. They made no move at all to stop us. I guess going against Clay Ellis was not in their plan that day.

L.B. Taylor expressed his thanks over and over as we rode. He was a smart fellow. He came about as close to death as anyone can and lived to tell about it.

CHAPTER 2

On our journey southwest L.B. Taylor proved talkative, more than willing to share his life with us. His father, Colonel Beau Taylor, was much more progressive about slaves than most of his southern counterparts. Acknowledging the fatherhood of his mulatto son was a first big step. L.B. thought it may have been because Beau's wife, Mary, had died in childbirth, and the premature infant son she bore had passed away weeks later.

Beau had quite a reputation and was certainly eligible, but he never showed interest in any other southern ladies. Rather, for reasons known only to himself, he took up with a young slave girl, Jane. They stayed together until after the war.

She died soon after he did. L.B. thought she just didn't want to go on without him.

Even though this was not uncommon behavior at that time, that kind of activity was usually kept quiet. Beau was completely open about the relationship, especially after L.B. arrived. This didn't endear him to Kentucky society.

Beau Taylor's passion was horses. His family raised some of the best horseflesh in the South. But, the war seriously depleted their stock and, by the time of his death, there wasn't much left. The mare L.B. rode was one of the last foals.

L.B. spoke like an educated man. His father had broken more rules by teaching his mixed son to read and write and introduced him to the marvels of the plantation library.

L.B. looked like a gentleman too. He wore an elegant dove grey traveling suit with matching hat. He did tell us though that it was the only complete suit of clothes he owned. Swapping stories made the miles slip by easier. I related briefly my participation in the Civil War and how I met Reese Tenner on a riverboat. I told about accompanying him to the Tenner ranch, about Reese's subsequent death at the hand of Comanche's supplied with guns from Comancheros, and about my desire for vengeance which lead me to Houston and ended with the death of two men on my hands.

Clay, of course, had had the most colorful life. His days as a Texas Ranger seemed filled with action and adventure: Comanche raids and ranger retaliation; running fights with roving bands of bandits; and gunfights in the streets.

We had a great time and almost forgot that we had entered that vast land that the Comanche regarded as their own. Clay Ellis reined his horse in and dismounted. We did the same.

"Hold my horse a minute," he said, handing the reins to me. He proceeded to examine the ground carefully.

"Unshod ponies come through here not long ago. Tracks are pretty fresh. They seem to be heading due west."

"You mean there are red Indians about?" questioned L.B. Taylor nervously.

"Well, we hope not," answered Clay, "but they been through recent. We best keep our eyes moving and our ears working too. We better just keep quiet and pay attention. I don't trust this trail, and I trust them that made it less. Enjoying each other's company and storytelling has made me a little careless."

We made a wide sweep to see if the Indian trail continued west. It did as far as we could tell. Then it veered north and we lost it. We proceeded on our southwesterly path, a little more alert now to possible danger.

We had just dismounted to walk our horses a bit. Had I been in the saddle, the bullet would've probably caught me in the middle of the back. As it was, it burned a furrow across the top of my bay gelding's head right between his ears, causing him to jump and squeal in pain.

We swung into the saddle, and I looked back to see a half dozen Indians headed our way. Their screams were enough to send shivers down my spine. I wondered how they affected L.B. who had never encountered a fierce western Indian before.

The young negro was riding hell bent for leather on his sorrel mare. Even in that rugged, broken, Texas hill country, she was fast. Clay Ellis and I had a hard time keeping sight of them. The Indians were gaining on us but not on L.B. who was fairly flying. The Indians, Comanche we found out for sure later, didn't waste any more bullets but kept up their hellish howling, no doubt intent on running us to ground. Over the pounding hoofbeats, I called to Clay. "Horses are tiring. We're going to have to pick a place to make a stand."

We saw L.B. reach the crest of the next hill.

"Yo, there," shouted Clay. "Dismount up there."

As we struggled the last few feet, cursing and spurring, we sprang from our horses and were shocked by four smiling faces. John Tenner and two of his hands, Tip Lomax and Cord McNab, were standing there with rifles in their hands. L.B. Taylor was holding the reins of all the horses.

The Indians kept coming having seen us reach the crest of the hill and then disappear.

John Tenner spoke with authority like the leader of men he had been and still was, "We'll take care of greetings later. Grab your rifles!"

I pulled my Henry from its scabbard, levered a shell into firing position, and moved forward. Clay Ellis did likewise. The five of us stood on the crest looking down at the approaching Comanche whose cries upon seeing us stopped abruptly. They tried to stop their horses and swing around to retreat. The footing and the speed at which they were traveling made it extremely difficult. The gunfire we directed at them made it a nightmare.

The squeals and cries and gunshots lasted only a few seconds. We left four dead horses and three dead Indians at the bottom. The other three beat a hasty retreat with one wounded man riding double. "Should we go after them Mr. Tenner?" asked Tip Lomax.

"We could catch'em easy."

"Not today, Tip" replied Tenner. "We've got old friends to greet and a guest to make welcome."

Then he smiled at Clay, L.B. and me. Even though I'm Indiana born and bred, it sure felt like I'd come home.

As we moved down the hill to check the casualties, Clay turned and called to L.B., "Ain't you glad you decided to come to Texas?"

He laughed then and so did the others. I don't think L.B. Taylor saw the humor in it.

CHAPTER 3

The homecoming was a marvelous time for us all. The whole family turned out to greet us. John Tenner's lovely wife, Martha, a small, pretty woman with gorgeous auburn hair, hugged the "stuffings" out of me. I shook hands with their sixteen year old son, Josh, who was almost as tall as his father and with Sam, the ten year old, who seemed to have grown a foot since last I saw him. The last hug was delivered with gusto by eight year old Jennifer, a beautiful little girl who was the apple of her father's eye.

But the Tenner ranch wasn't populated by just one family. John's good friend, Britt Jones, his wife Emma, and their two children, Ben and Belinda, lived there also. I went through similar greetings with them.

The Jones family really surprised L.B. Taylor because they were negroes. They were free and independent negroes living and working side by side the Tenners. L.B. felt comfortable with the Tenners right away. Having the Jones family on hand was almost too much for him to believe.

Late that evening as L.B. and I walked, he asked me about Britt Jones.

"Britt Jones came to Texas a slave, but his master, Jacob Jones, was a kind and fair man and treated him well", I replied.

"The Comanches raided the Jones place when Britt was away helping a neighbor. Jacob was wounded and his wife and daughter taken captive.

"Britt was friendly with the Tonkawa Indians, enemy of the Comanche. With their help he immediately got on the trail of the raiders, caught up to them, killed them, and rescued Jacob's wife and daughter before they were too badly abused. He became a hero and was rewarded with his freedom."

"But how did he get hooked up with the Tenners?" asked L.B.

"Britt learned a lot from the Indians about tracking and became an excellent scout. John Tenner, when he was a Texas ranger Captain, always tried to use the best men he could get. He employed Britt on many occasions against the Comanche. Jones also saved Tenner from harm three different times. One time it almost cost him his own life."

"That's amazing!" exclaimed L.B.

"I guess it is when you really think about it," I replied. "He's a good man; someone you can depend on."

"He asked me to stay with them in their house."

"That's mighty nice L.B. I'm sure you could stay in the big house too. I don't believe the Tenners would mind one way or the other."

"I'm going to accept their invitation if you don't think it would be improper. I just want to experience staying with a complete free black family. It's something I've never seen."

"I think that would be fine," I replied. "Now, I'm tired and am going to turn in. I'll see you in the morning."

He walked toward the Jones house and I went into the big house where John Tenner and Clay Ellis were still reliving old times. I bid them a good night.

It was time to sleep. It had been an eventful day: I had almost been killed, chased by Indians, rescued by friends, and had been a participant in a joyous homecoming.

These thoughts all whirled about in my head as I lay in the dark. Finally, relaxed and exhausted, I fell into a deep slumber.

CHAPTER 4

Breakfast the next morning was a feast as had been supper the night before. Martha Tenner and Emma Jones worked wonders with eggs, bacon, potatoes, fresh bread, butter and preserves, along with real coffee. It had been quite a few mornings since we had eaten that well.

Conversation ranged from our trip and escape from the Comanche to my experiences in Houston. With the children around I tried to gloss over it as best I could and was successful. It wasn't something I was willing to talk about anyway.

"How's the cow hunt coming?" I asked, changing the subject.

"We've done well," replied John Tenner. "We've been working together with a Mexican rancher southwest of us near the Rio Grande. Benito Chavez is his name. His family has been in Texas from before the war for independence. He fought against Santa Anna. He hasn't gathered as many cattle as us, but we aim to take some of his along. In return he's going to supply some hands for the drive. His vaqueros are some of the best."

"What about the bandits you were telling me about last night?" interjected Clay Ellis.

I hadn't heard anything about bandits, but there was so much going on the previous evening it didn't surprise me. Perhaps they had discussed it after I went to bed.

Tenner responded, "We got some real bad ones running north of the border all right. A feller they call the Coahuila Kid, I don't know his real name, has got himself about thirty riders. He's been causing lots of trouble down south. He hasn't been up here that we know of."

L.B. Taylor rolled his eyes. "So, you've got bandits to the south and Indians to the north. I don't want to ask what's west of here."

There was a general chuckle that rolled through the room. Britt Jones responded, "Son, it's a lot better than it used to be."

L.B. almost gagged on his coffee at that, and real laughter filled the room this time.

John Tenner continued, "This is a big, hard country. People coming out here don't realize it till they see it. It may take a lot of years yet, but one day it'll be a fine place. I guess we all enjoy bein' amongst the first before it can get spoiled."

"L.B.," interjected Clay Ellis, "let me change the subject a bit. I been meanin' to talk to you about your mare, but yesterday, in all the excitement, I didn't get a chance to. She can certainly run. Is she a racer?"

"She comes from a long line of runners. Her sire, Taylor's Sunset, was a champion in Kentucky before the war. She's never really been raced, but I know she's got it in her."

"What's her name?" asked Martha Tenner.

"Taylor's Sunset Lady."

"A pretty name for a pretty animal," commented Emma Jones. "Benito Chavez has got a black stud he fancies quite a runner," said John Tenner. "They'll be making a trip up to San Antonio in a short while so we can finalize plans for the drive. Maybe we can convince him to bring along El Negro. We could liven things up with a match race."

"Now that's to my liking!" exclaimed Clay Ellis, "Something I can bet on."

John offered a suggestion.

"Boys, as soon as we finish up here, let's take a ride out to the nearest cow camp. I want Grant to see part of what he's got his money invested in."

I had given the Tenners some money I had earned gambling to help them with the proposed cattle drive. You see, Texas was cash poor but cattle rich after the war. The profit to be made selling Texas cattle in the north was tremendous. The Tenners had given me cattle for dollars, and I stood to make a tidy sum if the drive proved successful. "Sounds good to me," I said.

We finished our meal and saddled up to go and look at what would become the savior of the Texas economy; mean, half wild Texas longhorns.

CHAPTER 5

The days passed quickly as Clay, L.B., and I pitched in with the work on the ranch. As I've said before, a cowboy's work has got to be one of the hardest, most dangerous jobs around, Working with crazy cattle, there was never a dull moment. Roping steers that ran, dodged, and ducked over that rough terrain provided exciting moments. Just riding some of those cowponies could also be an adventure. They were sometimes a little wild too. Every once in a while a horse would take to bucking or pitching with a cowboy clinging to its back. The others at the scene would hoot and howl while the rider would spur the animal on each jump.

L.B., however, spent most of his time working with Sunset Lady. He and Tip Lomax worked on a makeshift racing track around the ranch. They cut out some brush and mesquite so that it was relatively clear. They ran a couple of ranch horses against her, but, after two or three hundred yards, she left them in the dust.

A couple of riders had been sent to the Chavez ranch informing them of our plan and inviting them to take part. They sent work back that they were wholeheartedly in agreement and would look forward to the occasion as a festive one - almost like a fiesta. In fact Benito Chavez indicated that he was bringing in his family.

San Antonio was bustling when we arrived. The town was quite full. We could tell there were a lot of visitors, unfamiliar faces. A lot of outlying ranches seemed to have planned their supply trips to coincide with the race.

Justin Worth, the proprietor of the Casa Blanca hotel and good friend of the Tenners, had been passing the word about Sunset Lady and handling bets on the race. He greeted us when we arrived, his totally bald head glistening in the sun.

"Good to see you all," he called as he came out to greet us. He offered Martha his arm and walked with her into the hotel lobby, followed by our whole entourage; the Tenners, the Jones family, Clay, L.B., myself, and Tip Lomax. The cowboys had drawn cards to see who would come as the ranch couldn't be left completely untended.

"The Chavez family has already arrived. They got here early yesterday," said the tall, heavy hotelman. "After you get settled, I'll let them know you're here."

A little later that afternoon the families all gathered in the spacious Casa Blanca dining room.

Benito Chavez, though short and slim, was a very handsome man. His matching black tailored and embroidered pants and jacket made him appear taller. The outfit highlighted his thick steel grey hair and pencil thin mustache.

His wife, Estralita, didn't have a grey hair on her head that I could see, so she seemed younger. She was also short, but quite stocky. Her dazzling smile made everyone feel comfortable. The third member of the family was their daughter, Elena, at sixteen already a gorgeous, young woman with raven black hair, exquisite features, and a pleasant demeanor.

After rather extensive introductions and small talk, the conversation turned to the race. Chavez spoke excellent English with that hint of an accent that almost makes the words sound better than if spoken by a native American.

"John, this is an exciting event. People have traveled miles to see the match. I hope we won't disappoint them."

"I don't think so, Benito," responded Tenner. "We have a fine mare and she's ready to run. I've had one of your vaqueros, Jesus Cisneros, and one of my men, Tip Lomax, mapping out a route. We want to start and end right here in front of the hotel. How does that sound to you?"

"Very good John. We should begin at ten tomorrow. That will give the opponents a chance to go over the course. Also, we will finish before the heat of the day."

"That'll be just fine. Why don't we meet back here for supper. Justin says he's bringing in mariachis for entertainment. Might even be some dancing."

With that statement the female faces in the group began to beam. I must say I looked forward to it myself. Dancing with Elena would be a most pleasant experience, and I had noticed some other lovely looking ladies on the streets of San Antonio also. Good food, good music, and good people awaited me that evening.

CHAPTER 6

The evening's festivities were marvelous. Cool breezes and invigorating music added to the enjoyment of the night. I loved watching John and Martha Tenner dance. For all his size John was pretty light on his feet. He and his wife moved smoothly across the dining room floor that had been cleared of tables and most of the chairs.

I danced with some town girls whose names escape me now. I guess I only had eyes for Elena. She was a cultured young lady, light as a breeze to guide over the dance floor. She even made a fellow like me look good, and that's quite a task. I really didn't get to dance with her much though. She was very popular. There were a lot of young fellows waiting their turns I was just one of a number.

When not on the dance floor, I simply observed the people. It was quite a mixture; Anglo, Mexicans, and a few negroes. I noticed right away that many people were tolerant of Britt Jones and his family but not overly friendly. I guess they respected him for what he had done with and for John Tenner. Those facts were well known. I figured that, to some folks, being polite was all that was necessary. L.B. saw it too.

"The folks around here are like most southerners I've ever met, not too friendly to people of color," stated L.B.

"It looks that way," I replied. "You got little groups here and there talking together. Not much mixing."

"I think I'll just stick to dancing with Emma, Belinda, and Mrs. Tenner," L.B. continued. "I don't want to cause a problem by asking anyone else."

I nodded in assent. L.B. was too new here and different. No sense in pushing things until people got to know him.

"That Belinda seems to keep up with you right well," I said, trying to change the subject. L.B. scoffed at that.

"She's eight or nine years old. What are you talking about?"

"How old are you?" I asked.

"I'm fifteen. Be sixteen in another month."

"Right now it seems silly, but wait till Belinda's sixteen. You may think differently. She's going to be a pretty young lady."

L.B. Taylor had to admit it was a possibility, no matter how far fetched.

As I surveyed the room, I spied a young Mexican who seemed to stand out from the rest. He was rather short and slim but stood arrow straight which made him appear taller.

He was dressed a little more elegantly than some of the others. He wore a ruffled white shirt and a black velvet vest. His black pants were trimmed with tiny silver conchos which were tucked into highly polished black boots. He held a pair of silver trimmed spurs in his hand which he gave to a friend when he wanted to dance. His companions, three of them, were less formally attired than him. They had on plain clothes but looked clean. The best word I could think of to describe them was coarse. The man in black and silver was refined. They were coarse.

The fancy gentleman circulated through the crowd dancing with one of the young girls now and then. He seemed to keep an eye on the Chavez family. They took no special notice of him except Benito who once I saw stare directly at the fancy fellow. Chavez's eyes turned cold, and he abruptly shifted his gaze away. I thought it was a bit odd. However, I wasn't watching over a lovely young daughter who was sought after by every eligible man present.

The evening ended with toasts and good wishes for success and safety in the race tomorrow.

I walked with L.B. to check on Sunset Lady. We then went back to our rooms at the Casa Blanca and to bed.

Chapter 7

The race the next morning provided the excitement that everyone was expecting. People gathered all along the raceway to watch the event. The best seats available, however, were probably on the rooftops of buildings. The folks up high could see the horses all the way.

Jesus Cisneros rode El Negro and L.B. Taylor was aboard Sunset Lady. The stallion was nervous and fidgety, as stallions often are, especially around mares. He pranced and pawed and was sweating quite noticeably. On the other hand, Sunset Lady appeared calm and paid little attention to El Negro except to lay her ears back when he came a little too close to her.

Justin Worth, the official starter, strode forward and addressed the riders. "Are you both ready?"

L.B. and Jesus nodded. Sunset Lady stood still waiting for the cue from her rider. El Negro kept moving about, causing Jesus to spin him around to get the horse in position to start.

The hotel proprietor held his gun aloft and cocked back the hammer. "Ready," he yelled. Then a second later he pulled the trigger. The shot exploded, the crowd roared, and the horses burst forward.

The race ran pretty much as L.B. had predicted it would. The black stallion took an early lead. He was several lengths ahead after about four hundred yards. Then Sunset Lady began to close the distance. She caught him at about five hundred yards and just kept going. By the time they spun into the last turn, the sorrel mare was leading by three lengths and pulling away.

Cheers and whistles greeted the contestants as they crossed the finish line. Benito Chavez offered congratulations, and L.B. Taylor beamed with pride. Above the noise I heard him tell L.B. he wanted to talk to him after the horses had been cooled and put away.

In the Casa Blanca we had refreshments and enjoyed relaxing conversation while Justin Worth went about the task of settling up on race bets.

L.B. returned to more congratulations, back slaps, and hand shakes. I do believe all the people from the Tenner ranch took special pleasure in the young man's victory.

"Senor Taylor," called Benito Chavez, a toast to you and your beautiful mare."

The crowd cheered and raised their glasses.

L.B. Taylor responded, "I would like to offer a toast also, to a very worthy opponent. I'm glad that the race wasn't shorter."

Again glasses were raised and the jubilant crowd vocalized their feelings once more.

When all were seated at the table, Benito Chavez rose to speak.

"Senor Taylor, in front of all our friends here I have a proposition for you."

We quieted down to hear what would be offered.

Chavez continued, "You have a magnificent mare, your Sunset Lady. She is as beautiful as her namesake and she runs like the wind. Even though El Negro lost, our stallion too is a great animal. I would love to buy your horse, but I won't insult you by asking. I know you wouldn't sell. Neither would I in your position. Rather, I suggest that we blend our bloodlines. The offspring could only be magnificent. As winner of the race, you would be entitled to the first foal. If the mating proves successful, as I think it will, we can make further arrangements later."

To tell the truth I was a little uneasy. All this talk of breeding with ladies present didn't seem proper. They, however, didn't appear embarrassed but instead intrigued by the possibilities such a match might produce.

Britt Jones leaned over to L.B. and said, "Son, this is quite an opportunity. People are always looking for good horses and they'll pay to get 'em."

John Tenner heard the exchange and nodded in agreement. "If she has a good healthy foal, it's likely she could produce for the next eight or ten years. You could stand to earn a mighty nice sum of money from this."

L.B. grinned, "I made a nice sum of money already today."

"Did you bet on yourself?" I asked.

"Yep," he answered and smiled again.

"Well, Senor," interjected Benito Chavez, "what do you think? Do you accept my proposition?"

L.B. paused a moment, took a deep breath, and then said, "Yes, I believe I do. I think I can make something of myself in this country, and this might be the start of it."

Martha Tenner added, "Young man, you'll just have to become part of the Tenner ranch. We can't let a horseman like you get away from us."

"Thank you all," replied L.B. Taylor.

Strange how things sometimes work out in life. L.B. Taylor had known security on a big plantation then lost it all. He had almost been hanged by prejudiced people even though he was innocent of wrongdoing. Now, a very different assortment of people were all instrumental in helping him strive for success and a new kind of security.

Chapter 8

We spent the rest of the race day in San Antonio celebrating and also picked up some supplies. We headed for home the next morning. There was a bit of a change, however. Benito Chavez invited L.B. to visit the Chavez Rancho as the two were about to become partners of sorts. At the request of Elena, he also extended an invitation to Clay Ellis and myself. She was perceptive enough to realize that L.B. was unfamiliar and would probably end up feeling uncomfortable without someone around whom he knew a little better.

We said our goodbyes about mid morning.

"We'll be back in a few days." Clay called.

"No hurry, cattle don't give a damn," John Tenner responded. Then he waved as the wagon disappeared over the hill.

We traveled on a couple of more hours pleasantly conversing. We paused when the sun was high to stretch our legs and refresh ourselves with cool water.

The clatter of hooves and the jingle of spurs announced the bandits' approach as they simultaneously appeared on all sides. There must've been twenty five or thirty of them, all armed to the teeth and very menacing.

We were certainly frightened. Clay and I were ready to make a fight of it even though we knew it would be futile.

Both of us were lightly armed - no rifles, just a couple of Colts. Benito Chavez stopped us before we could act.

"They will not harm us," he said.

"How can you be sure?" asked Clay.

"Just trust me. Do you think I would not fight to protect my wife

221

and daughter? Believe me. You will come to no harm as long as you cooperate."

"I didn't like it one bit. I felt helpless. I knew we didn't stand a chance, but I figured I'd rather go down fighting. However, Chavez was so confident it convinced me.

The handsome, young man from the dance the other evening approached us. He still looked the dandy. Not only was he now wearing those silver mounted spurs, but his saddle was also trimmed in silver.

What followed was a rapid conversation in Spanish between Benito Chavez and the young man. I couldn't understand what was said, but there was anger behind it. Words were fierce and gestures violent. The women huddled in the wagon, looking at Chavez in amazement and then casting the same gaze of astonishment at the handsome, young Mexican.

When it was over, Chavez, an anguished look on his face, turned to us.

"Give them your weapons," he ordered.

Clay looked like he had just been slapped in the face.

"No one takes my guns," he said, "unless I'm dead. "

"I promise you Senor, you will be if you don't do as I say."

We were surrounded by hard looking men who wouldn't hesitate to kill us once given the opportunity. I remember thinking about L.B. Only a few short hours ago his life had been looking so good. Now he was in a tenuous situation again.

We did what we were told. Then Chavez instructed Jesus Cisneros and L.B. to dismount. The look on Taylor's face was indescribable. They were taking his mare and Chavez's stallion, and there was nothing we could do about it.

Jesus was a young man without the maturity the situation called for. He simply moved when he shouldn't have. Several shots rang out and he hit the ground dead. It was cold blooded murder.

L.B. had been nearby. Bullets caught him and knocked him to the ground too. He had been hit in the arm and the leg. Clay and I examined the wounds and tried to bind them quickly before too much blood was lost. L.B. moaned in pain as the women screamed.

With a wave of his sombrero and a dazzling smile, the handsome, young man led his bandidos away. They had packed our guns on Sunset Lady and El Negro.

We were without weapons, but we did have the wagon and two saddle horses.

The women were tight lipped and very grim. They didn't say anything or look at Chavez. They just stared out into the hills.

Clay marked the direction the bandits were going. "We've got to get back to the ranch. If we cut due east and ride hard, we might make it before dark. We've got to get L.B. back quick as we can."

"What then?" I asked.

"They made three mistakes today." said Clay.

"Three? What do you mean three?" I asked.

"One, they shot L.B., two, they robbed us, three, they left us alive," replied Clay. "I don't know who that fancy bastard is, but I guarantee you he'll know me sooner than later. I didn't get my reputation by steppin' aside or given' in."

"But, he's got twenty or thirty guns. We can't go up against that. We're talking about a pretty well armed bunch," I concluded. "Is your reputation worth dying for?"

"Grant, I don't have much else. But, it ain't just that. You forgot we both got friends near here. If those bandits are this bold, they're only going to get worse. No one will be safe. Look at L.B. and Jesus.

"John Tenner and I have seen this before. They got to be stopped now. there's lives at stake. They don't know it yet, but they just grabbed a tiger by the tail."

There was positively a gleam in his eyes. I know L.B. saw it too. Clay Ellis looked a little crazy.

We had almost forgotten about Benito Chavez.

"I think Senor Ellis is right. I've fooled myself for years into believing it could be avoided, but now I know it can't. I'm sorry for this. I'm ashamed for myself and the way I've treated my family. That bastard you referred to is really a bastard, my bastard. Down here he's known as the Coahuila Kid."

Now the reactions of Elena and Estralita were clear to me. They hadn't known. Benito Chavez had somehow kept a secret from them for a great many years. In one fell swoop the young man known as the Coahuila Kid had administered a crushing blow to the Chavez family and had made some bitter, unforgiving enemies.

I don't know how Benito Chavez was able to retain even some semblance of dignity, but he did. He spoke quietly in Spanish to his family for a few moments. Clay and I moved away. Even though we really didn't understand what was being said, it didn't seem right to listen.

"We'll accompany you to the Tenner Ranch. Then I will go with you to do what I should've done earlier," he said.

A few moments later Chavez called to us. I could see tears in the eyes of his wife and daughter.

We put Jesus' body in the wagon and loaded L.B. next to him. Thankfully, the young man had passed out. The Chavez women watched over him as we swung east. Only the sound of horses' hooves and creaking wagons could be heard.

Chapter 9

We were able to reach the Tenner Ranch by night fall. Needless to say, they were surprised to see us and shocked at what had taken place.

Martha immediately took charge of L.B. One bullet had gone through his arm. The other bullet in his leg needed to be dug out. Luckily, it was near the surface. Though bloody and painful, I'm sure, neither wound was critical. After quick makeshift surgery, L.B. was cleaned up, bandaged and carried into a bedroom to rest and recuperate.

Martha knew immediately that her husband would organize a group to go after the Coahuila Kid. That was his way. Men turned to him in times of trouble, and he provided the leadership.

It's a little hard for today's generation to realize how thin the law was stretched back then. There were too few men and too many miles to cover. Out of necessity people had to handle their own problems. They couldn't wait for help. To survive they had to act quickly and on their own.

John sent Sam to fetch everyone for a meeting in the main house. Martha put the coffee on to boil and little Jennifer put the cups on the table.

When they had all arrived, John told them what had happened to us. They listened somberly.

"Clay's right," Tenner said, "him and I have seen this kind of thing. The Kid's getting bolder. Now that he's moving this far north of the border he becomes our problem too. It was horses this time. You all could've been killed easy. L.B. is lucky and so are the rest of you. But they're still murderers.

"As many men and horses as they have, they won't be hard to follow.

I'm sure they figure they're safe because of their numbers. Well, they've stolen their last horse and shot their last citizens up this way."

It was decided that our expedition against the bandits would include; John Tenner, Clay Ellis, Benito Chavez, Britt Jones, Tip Lomax, Cord McNab, and myself.

We spent the rest of the evening planning what would be needed. We checked weapons and ammunition, made a list of food stuffs and amounts, and decided which horses would be used. Tenner asked Britt to bring along his bow and a quiver of arrows. He also asked Britt to pack some coal oil, extra gun powder, and blankets.

As everyone dispersed and headed for their beds the former ranger Captain announced, "We'll leave right after breakfast in the morning. Enjoy this night. It'll be your last sleep in a bed for a while."

The Chavez family was made comfortable by Martha. She was very good at that. She was able to make people feel right at home. She did not yet know about Benito Chavez and the Coahuila Kid, but I was sure it would only be a short time before she would find out the whole story. After all, L.B. Taylor had been there so he could explain the situation when he was well.

It took quite a while for me to fall asleep that night. I knew we were heading into a very dangerous situation. I couldn't see how so few were going to prevail against so many. But, I had confidence in John Tenner and Clay Ellis. They knew what they were doing. I had seen both in action. If the others felt like I did, I thought, we just might have a chance.

CHAPTER 10

Goodbyes are always hard, but they are especially hard when those leaving are headed into battle or danger of some sort. That certainly included our group. There were hugs and kisses and "be careful" was whispered more than once. We then mounted and rode off to pick up the trail of the Coahuila Kid and his men. We took off our hats as we passed by the hastily dug grave of Jesus Cisneros.

Our horses were fresh that morning so we covered ground rather quickly and arrived at the spot where the bandits had left us. The trail was easy to see because of so many horses. Britt Jones didn't even have to dismount to read sign. "Looks like due south from here," he said.

We put our horses in motion again and followed the wide bandit trail hour after hour. There wasn't much discussion until evening camp. John Tenner began conversation with a question.

"Benito, you seem to know more about the Coahuila Kid than anyone else here. Can you tell us anything about him that might help?"

I was sure this was an opening John gave Senor Chavez so the man could say as much or as little as he chose to.

"John, I am not proud of this," Chavez replied, "but I feel I must tell you about the Coahuila Kid and me.

"Some years ago on a trip to Mexico to buy cattle and horses I met a girl in a cantina. She was young and quite beautiful and attracted to me. I was a younger man then too and the owner of a large rancho north of the border. The tequila flowed, the music played, and as time passed her attraction for me became mutual. I admired her. I desired her. We became lovers.

"Even though I had passionate feelings for Rosa, I still had a wife at home whom I loved. To complicate matters even more, Rosa became pregnant with our son.

"I made excuses to increase my trips so that I could spend more time with my mistress and our new son, Antonio. I supported them, making sure they lived comfortably.

"As Antonio grew older, he became resentful of my now more infrequent visits. Rosa, too, tired of the arrangement and became involved with a man of low reputation, Gilberto Alcala.

"After my daughter was born, I knew I would have to choose. I couldn't deceive my wife any longer about my trips. I made one final journey to tell Rosa and Antonio that I wouldn't be coming back."

Chavez paused to sip some coffee. The flickering flames of the fire revealed tears welling in his eyes. Then he continued.

"Rosa took the news well. What we had felt for one another had long since passed. Antonio, on the other hand, was angry, understandably so. He swore to get even with me and ruin my life as he thought I had ruined his. I couldn't even answer him because he was right.

"I gave Rosa a generous sum of money and left, feeling empty inside and hating myself for what I had done. Antonio's curses were the last words I heard as I rode off.

"My son followed in the footsteps of Gilberto Alcala. He learned to love easy money and how to live outside the law. Because of his personality, men gravitated to him. He built a reputation as a daring thief and an expert gunman. He built a large hacienda on the Rio Grande, and has grown in strength and boldness, raiding both side of the border.

"When he heard about the race, he saw it as an opportunity to embarrass me in front of my family and to impress his men by being so daring as to steal horses so close to San Antonio. He accomplished both goals."

"But, we hear he's been more than a thief," interrupted Clay Ellis. "his bandits have left dead bodies wherever they've gone."

"That's true," replied Sanchez. "Whether he personally is a killer, I don't know. I find it hard to believe that such a sweet child as Antonio had been could grow up to do such things.

But, I know people like Jesus have died, and he must bear responsibility even if he didn't pull the trigger."

"I'm glad you understand that, Benito," commented John Tenner. "You see, we've got to drive those bandits away or kill 'em. They'll have to leave this country or be buried in it.

"I know," answered Chavez, "he has to be stopped. I can't help but hope that he hasn't turned all bad. He did spare our lives."

It was my turn to talk.

"That might've made him look more powerful to his men," I said, "like a king showing mercy to his subjects. Maybe he also figured we'd be less likely to pursue them if no one else was hurt."

"You're probably right," said Clay. "I do hope he'll be surprised."

"He better be surprised, the way he's got us outnumbered," interjected Britt Jones.

"I figure we've got to whittle down those odds some," said John Tenner. He called to Tip Lomax and Cord McNab who had been taking care of the horses. When everyone was gathered about the fire, Tenner spoke again.

"The odds against us here are pretty high. We're going to reduce 'em. First off, they don't expect no crazy gringos to chase 'em all the way down to the border after a couple of horses. Second, they feel safe with so many guns. Third, ain't none of 'em fought in this country as long as Clay, Benito, Britt and me. We're going to whittle 'em down, little by little."

I think we all began to feel a little better about our chances. John Tenner was so sure of himself that it began to rub off on the rest of us.

"We won't be able to make any specific plans just yet," Tenner continued. "We got to see the layout. There's no rush. We'll just move slow and easy and smart."

I know I fell asleep that night with a sense of cautious anticipation instead of fear. I really began to believe that shortly the Coahuila Kid and his men would no longer be crossing the border to raid Texas ranches.

CHAPTER 11

The Coahuila Kid and his men lived in a very nice hacienda just south of the Rio Grande. The adobe house was surrounded by a low wall with a large gate in the front that faced north and a smaller gate in the rear. In the back the wall attached to a long, low shed which served as a barn. Behind that structure were two corrals.

John Tenner had brought his field glass so we were able to stop some distance north of the river and still be able to spy on the compound. There was little chance of us being seen in that fairy flat, brushy country, especially if we weren't expected.

"They've got tents set up inside the walls," said the ex—ranger captain. "Some men must sleep there and others in the house. They got guards on the four walls, but they ain't very interested in their jobs. The one on the north seems to be watching. The man on the east wall appears to be napping. The other two are standing in the southeast corner passing the time of day. They must feel real secure here."

"Let me take a look, John," said Clay Ellis.

Tenner passed over the glass. The rest of us hunkered down on the ground while our horses browsed through the brush for something edible.

Benito Chavez rubbed his aching rump. It had been quite a while since he had ridden this hard. He had gotten used to soft beds and easy living.

Clay handed the glass back.

"What do we do first?" he asked.

"We'll rest up till nightfall," responded Tenner. "Then we'll split up. I'll take Grant and Benito. We'll travel east and find a ford. The rest of you will go west and do the same. Make a big loop. Get the lay of the land. We got to travel slow and quiet. All we're doing is looking. We'll meet back here before dawn. Now let's try to get a little shut eye. We'll take turns keeping watch."

I took the first watch. After about an hour I woke Tip. I don't think any of us were very successful sleeping. But, at least we rested.

We dined on jerky and water. As the sun was setting, we split up and rode off.

John, Benito and I only had to travel about a mile or so to find an appropriate ford. The water came only hock high on the horses and the footing was sandy, but didn't bog down the animals. We were able to cross quickly.

As we moved southward, we picked up a gully or arroyo that wound roughly in a half circle from the south to the east and then petered out.

It's end point was about four hundred yards directly to the rear of the hacienda.

"This is good," whispered Tenner. "This arroyo provides good cover. I bet they couldn't see anyone even in daylight hiding down here."

We also spotted a well which was outside the wall next to the horse corrals. It looked like a more recent structure, but it was hard to tell at night.

We sat for a while and observed. We could see lights on in some of the hacienda's windows. When the breeze was right, the strains of soft guitar music reached our ears.

Tenner instructed us to cut some mesquite. We retraced our steps and obliterated our tracks as best as we could. It took quite a while, but we still made it back to our rendezvous point before dawn.

Clay, Britt, Tip and Cord were waiting for us. "Anything?" John Tenner asked.

"Nothing helpful," Britt replied. "There's a hogback that runs about five hundred yards long. It's about two miles south of the hacienda."

"How far did you have to travel to cross the river?"

"Not far at all," answered Clay. "The river looks like it's shallow for a few miles here."

We told them about the arroyo and the well.

"Boys," John Tenner smiled, "we're going to start evening the odds tonight. Grant, you and Cole and Cord start cutting and piling mesquite. I want two large stacks about fifty yards apart.

"Britt, break out your bow and arrows, that coal oil, some of that gun powder and an extra blanket."

Obviously, we were all curious as to what this all meant. John continued.

"Britt and I are going to go back through that arroyo. I think we can belly up to the base of that well and plant a little package of gunpowder. We may not be able to blow it up, but we can damage it.

"The rest of you boys are going to set those two brush fires. Then cross the river south. Split up on either side of the trail to the fires. Let 'em cross the river and begin to head back. They'll be back lit for easy shooting. Stay low to the ground and try to move so they can't spot you by sound or barrel flash.

"There'll be five of you. One of you, Tip, can hold the horses in the arroyo. The rest of you will have to make it back there on foot. After, we'll ride south and east till we reach that big hogback.

"The key here," John continued, "is to hit hard and fast and move quick. Make every shot count. While you're sending them to hell down by the river, I'll have Britt send a few fire arrows into their feed stacks in the corrals. If we damage that well, it should affect their water supply. This could be a good night's work."

It was a lot to digest at one time. Tip, Cord, and I began gathering the mesquite. Afterwards, we checked weapons and ammunition and tried to rest till nightfall.

CHAPTER 12

We watched the hacienda, off and on during the day. John Tenner saw about a half dozen riders saddle up and ride of f to the south. Otherwise there wasn't a lot of movement. Late in the afternoon the riders came back heading a few head of cattle which they placed in one of the horse corrals. Some of the men looked to be carrying foodstuffs. For the first time Tenner saw a few women moving around in the compound, greeting the men, taking the food.

A little later on we faintly heard the bawl of a cow. John looked to see that they had slaughtered one of the cattle.

By evening the faint scent of cooking beefsteak reached us on the strong south wind that had picked up.

We crossed the river with Cord McNab left behind to start the mesquite fires. Britt had splashed a little coal oil on the stacks to insure a fast start. We wanted Cord across the river and far away before the fires really became noticeable.

Benito Chavez and Clay Ellis stationed themselves on the west side of the trail to the river. Clay was a little closer to the bank.

On the east side of the trail I was closer to the bank. Cord was a little further south as was Benito on the other side. Clay and I were good shots. We figured being close we'd have more light and probably be more successful.

After the first couple of volleys we planned to fall back and move south. Then Benito and Cord would open fire. After a few shots they would move westward and eastward respectively then northward toward the river. Clay and I would begin shooting again drawing the riders to us. We hoped to catch them in a four way crossfire.

We planned to shoot from a prone position as much as possible. That way we would be firing up at the horseman and would reduce the chance of hitting one another accidentally.

John and Britt made their way down the arroyo. There were good luck wishes all around. We would be out of touch for quite a while.

Cord ignited the fires and then hightailed it across the river past my position. He would leave his horse with Tip and make his way back on foot.

It didn't take long for the two giant stacks of mesquite to become huge flaming orange balls.

It took a while, but eventually we heard the thunder of horses' hooves headed our way.

From my experiences in the Civil War, I learned that waiting is especially hard because you're ready, primed for action. Thankfully, we didn't have too long to wait.

The bandits slowed as they passed by us and drew nearer to the river. There was excited chatter among the riders but nothing I could understand.

As they splashed across the river, I counted a dozen, certainly enough to go around. For a few moments they were highlighted very clearly against the roaring flames that were consuming the mesquite, but we held our fire. We wanted to catch them in the water if we could.

The riders circled the stacks then gathered together at the ford to head back to the hacienda. There was some discussion then they began to cross, weapons in hand.

Just as the first riders reached the southern bank I opened fire, followed by Clay. The lighting wasn't bad, and I levered shells into my Henry as fast as I could. I fired four times, and I know I hit two men, maybe a third, and probably a horse also. Then I fell back.

I didn't really have time to pay much of attention, but there was a lot of shooting. Most of the riders were armed with handguns, but I heard rifle fire so I knew we were doing fine.

I saw a flash from Cord's gun as I crashed through the brush. I was scraped and cut but nothing serious.

I looked back to see the riders, more dimly now, racing back toward the hacienda. The crossfire plan seemed to be working as men and horses appeared confused and fell in all directions. Three riderless horses sped past me as I cautiously stood. I heard a faint explosion and saw flames in the distance that indicated to me that John and Britt had been able to accomplish their part of the plan.

Benito and Clay emerged from the west side of the trail. We surveyed the carnage. It looked like all the bandits were down along with a half dozen horses.

"Where's Cord?" called Clay.

"I'll check up toward the river," I said. "Why don't you see if any are left alive. They could be useful to us."

I stumbled toward the Rio Grande, falling face down in the brush. Cursing, I rose to find the body of Cord McNab. I never really knew him and now would never have a chance to. The shame was we couldn't even bury him. We had to move fast. I grabbed his rifle and ran back.

When I returned, Benito and Clay had a wounded bandit up on his feet. His mouth was stuffed with a bandana, and they had strapped his left arm to his body using shell belts. His right arm hung limp, bleeding profusely.

"Where's Cord?" Clay asked again.

"Dead," I answered.

Benito crossed himself and said, "Not another one."

Clay viciously slapped the prisoner across the face so hard it spun the bandit around. "Goddamn it!" he cried.

"Let's go," I said. "Others will be coming."

We moved off into the darkness toward the arroyo, our horses, and hopefully, our friends.

As we walked, I thought about the good man we had lost and how we had reduced the bandit numbers. In the army our skirmish would've been considered extremely successful. I guess that's one reason why I never gave a thought to staying in the army after the war. I couldn't handle that military mentality. To me any life lost was too many. But, I never let it affect my fighting. In fact it made me madder than hell. We had lost two good men to those bandits, and a third was wounded. I guess I had tasted blood and wanted more.

CHAPTER 13

Britt, John and Tip were waiting for us in the arroyo.

There were smiles and handshakes as we emerged from the dark. Then Tip asked the inevitable question. "Where is Cord?"

"He didn't make it," I answered. We left him down by the river. I brought you his rifle. Since you were friends, I figured he'd want you to have it."

Tip took the gun and cradled it in his arm, looking like the life had gone out of him.

"He was my best friend. We rode many a trail together. I'm gonna miss him something terrible."

"We all will, son," added John Tenner. "He was a good young fellow. We'll make those bastards remember him and all of us."

"We already did, John," said Clay. "We evened the odds nice. Eleven dead by my count. And we brought you this one as a present."

All eyes went to the prisoner. Trussed with shell belts, a neckerchief stuffed in his mouth, and with that limp, bloody right arm, he was quite a mess. The bandit was probably in his twenties, of medium height, with a horribly scarred face. He had probably been in a few knife fights.

"We've got to ride now," said John Tenner. "Put him on Cord's horse. We'll question him later."

We mounted our horses and rode due south of the arroyo. Then, we turned west and headed for the big hogback. That put us on a little higher ground, and gave us a good view of the hacienda.

We dismounted and began to chew on jerky while John used Benito Chavez to question the prisoner.

"Benito, ask him how many more are down there. We need to know what we've got to deal with yet."

Chavez spoke rapidly in Spanish. Then he pulled the bandana from the bandit's mouth. The bad man spat on the ground and proceeded to launch into an angry tirade.

"Ain't he something," laughed Clay. "He's figurin' to put on a strong face in front of us."

"He calls us some bad names, John," said Benito. "He refuses to help us. Says we can kill him before he talks."

"He's not only mean, but he's a stupid son of a bitch to boot. Don't he realize the fix he's in?" questioned Clay.

John waved to Britt Jones calling him over.

"We're going to smarten him up right away. Britt, bring your knife over here. You're like an Indian with that tool, and I'm going to let you use it. Let's start cutting him till he talks. Clay and I will hold him down."

John and Clay grabbed the bandit by the shoulders. He couldn't struggle much because of his wounded arm and constraints.

"Stuff that bandana back in his mouth." Tenner motioned to Benito who followed instructions.

Britt drew his knife, and the man viewed it with true terror in his eyes. The black frontiersman then sliced the tops off the bandit's two ears, like cutting bacon for the skillet.

The bandit screamed in pain though the sound was muffled somewhat by the neckerchief in his mouth. When the scream reduced to moans, Clay told Chavez to question him again.

"Benito, now ask him what we want to know. Tell him if he don't talk we'll cut off his nose next and then move down to his privates."

This time the prisoner spoke freely. The tough facade was gone. I guess he'd been cut by a knife too many times before and wasn't about to endure what John Tenner and Clay Ellis had in mind, especially when he saw how Britt Jones handled a blade.

According to the bandit, ten men had gone on a raid north. That left the Kid and nine men. There were five women too. They cooked and washed and performed as prostitutes.

"They're down to ten," I said. "We are six. We're still on the short side but better. Whatever we do, we can't wait long. If those others return, we're badly outnumbered again."

"Yes, I know," said John. "And we can't surprise 'em no more. They don't have to come out. They're protected. They can just set there and wait."

"We're limited on food and ammunition," offered Britt.

"They don't know that," responded Tip. "They also don't know how many of us there are.

It was good to see his mind get off of Cord's death and back to our most serious situation.

"Senors, if we can't get inside, we won't finish the job and I'm not going back without the Coahuila Kid, dead or alive. I think we may be able to surprise them once more." Benito Chavez looked directly at me, and got the uneasy feeling that I was part of the surprise.

CHAPTER 14

The plan Benito had did include me along with everyone else, but I would be one of the main players helping to provide a diversion.

I was about the same size and build as the bandit prisoner. In the dark wearing his wide brimmed sombrero and silver concho trimmed vest, I could probably get by fooling the guard on the front wall. It was necessary, however, for me to learn a couple of Spanish phrases.

I was to ride up with Benito Chavez appearing to be my prisoner, fire my pistol, and announce this good news and then ask if the Coahuila Kid would like to come and greet us. Meanwhile, Britt, with his bow and quiver of arrows, along with John, Clay and Tip were to have positioned themselves near the south wall. As soon as Britt heard my shot, he was to take out the guard on the south wall, quietly, with a well placed arrow. My four friends would then advance cautiously into the compound.

Benito was to be center stage next. He would scream about not entering the place where his bastard son lived, and that he would rather die in the dust. He hoped that this would bring the Kid outside the walls.

Hopefully, by this time, Britt, John, Clay, and Tip would've been able to infiltrate through the corrals and barn.

If the plan even succeeded this far, we'd be lucky. But, each man would be on his own from this point.

That's how it was planned. Here's how it worked.

Benito and I waited until we were sure the others had time to get into position at the rear of the hacienda before we approached. It had only been a couple of hours since we had attacked the bandits at the river. I imagined that the rest of them had to be a little anxious about their compadres. I

239

wondered how smart it was to try to sneak up from the rear again. I was sure they'd be very aware of that southern approach. Benito tried to calm my fears.

"Certainly it's dangerous," he said. "They will be watching more closely because of the explosion at the well. But they still feel safe within their walls. They didn't show a lot of intelligence by riding straight into our trap. I don't think they've gotten smarter in the last hour. Remember, sometimes the most unexpected, unlikely things work. Often it comes down to luck."

He made me feel a little better, but I was still skeptical. It was a calculated risk, but one we had to take or turn tail and leave. The bandit we had left tied in the brush had told us about riders due back from the south. We couldn't handle more opposition.

We had rigged a breakaway rope on Benito's hands so they looked bound, but he could pull free easily. His holster was empty. He had placed his revolver in his waistband in the back under his jacket.

I didn't have to fire my pistol because the guard on the wall fired his rifle, alerting those inside the compound. I screamed out what I had been taught; that I had a prisoner, Benito Chavez. Then Benito began his tirade about not going inside alive.

It was only a matter of minutes but seemed an eternity as we sat our horses waiting. The gates of the compound finally swung open and three men strode out. Two of them held torches in their hands. In the middle of the trio walked a smiling Coahuila Kid.

I slouched a little in the saddle and pulled the brim of the bandit's sombrero lower over my face. I rested my right hand on my Colt. I had another pistol on the left side and a third handgun shoved into my rear waistband under the vest. Whatever happened now would probably be close work. My Henry was in its saddle scabbard.

As the Kid approached, Benito spoke in English, probably so I could know what was transpiring.

"Now you finally have what you've always wanted - me in your power."

"Why do you speak as an Anglo?" asked the Kid as he moved closer.

"I don't want these other bastards to know what I say."

"They are not the bastards. I am," replied Benito Chavez's illegitimate son, his smile slowly fading. "You are right. I have been waiting for his moment for a long time."

"You use the circumstances of your birth as an excuse for this kind of life." shouted Benito angrily.

I nervously watched the other men. The light from the torches made me more visible. As long as most of the attention was on Benito and the Coahuila Kid, I was safe. If they looked closely at me, I would have to act fast. I'm not too proud to say that my heart pounded so hard I thought it would burst through my shirt.

"You are a butcher," continued Benito. "You rob and kill. You don't do this to get even with me. You do this for yourself."

There was livid anger in the Kid's eyes now and the dazzling smile had been replaced by a grimace.

"I do what I do, old man, for my own reasons. And what I choose to do now is to finally rid myself of you. At first I thought that ruining your happy life would be enough but it wasn't. I'm glad you're here. You make it easy for me."

The Kid then lunged for Chavez, pulling his father off his horse. Benito's animal shied sharply right knocking into my horse as I reached for my Colt.

I figured it was the time to act. I swung down to the right side of my horse, Comanche style, and fired under his neck catching the nearest torch bearer high in the chest.

My horse squealed as bullets slapped into him. Both the other torch bearer and the guard on the wall had fired. My weight on my animal's right side helped pull him down on me. I got my left leg free, but my right was stuck. The horse was tossing his head about and thrashing so much that I had to shoot him in the head myself. I couldn't afford to be knocked unconscious by the dying animal.

Laying on the ground pinned under my horse, I had some very inadequate cover. Also, my position was very awkward for shooting accurately.

A quick glance to my left and I saw the other torch holder drawing a bead on me. His gun exploded. A split second later mine did too. The slug hit me in the left shoulder and knocked me flat as if I had been clubbed by a sledge hammer. My bullet found the bandit also. He was slammed backward and his torch fell igniting the surrounding brush to match the flames from the other fallen torch.

Through the flickering light I could see Benito wrestling with his son.

I think the Kid was surprised to find that his father's hands were not really bound.

My shoulder began to hurt seriously. I couldn't move my left arm, and I could feel my shirt becoming soaked in my own blood. Since I only loaded five shots in my Colt, I had two left. I had lost one of my guns in the fall, and I couldn't reach the other one in my position and condition.

I could see a half dozen bandits advancing through the gates. I could taste my own fear, and I fought to stay conscious, hoping to take one or more of them out before I was shot dead. I couldn't see if Benito had subdued the Kid or not. And, truly, my mind was on my own predicament.

I tried to steady myself and aim. I had a fat Mexican in my sights and drew back the hammer. However, before I could pull the trigger, the bandit fell forward and into the dust and brush. An arrow protruded from between his shoulder blades. His compadres stared incredulously. A sigh of relief escaped my mouth. Somehow, Clay, Britt, John, and Tip had been successful coming in from the rear. All the commotion we had caused had pulled the bandits' attention to the front of the compound. This allowed Benito's plan to work.

I couldn't see any of my friends, but, judging from the rifle fire being poured into the bandits, they must've gotten up on the walls. The bandidos tried to scramble for some sort of cover, but there wasn't any. Withering fire including two bullets from me cut them down to the last man.

I fell back onto the ground. My leg under the horse was beginning to go numb. My shoulder ached and throbbed, and I felt weak and nauseous.

I looked to my left to see what had become of Benito. It wasn't good. The Coahuila Kid had his father in a headlock with a pistol pointed at the old man's temple.

"Senors," he shouted, "you will let me pass or I will kill him."

I saw Britt, John, Clay and Tip walk through the gates and around the bodies of the bandits. Behind them women scurried about in the compound.

"Do not let him leave, John!" screamed Benito. "I came here willing to die to rid this country of him. I failed to do it myself. You must help me. Shoot him!"

The Coahuila Kid looked quite smug as he cocked the hammer on his pistol.

"Last chance senors. Let me pass or he dies. You are not the kind of men who want this on your conscience."

"You realize you're a dead man no matter what you do Kid," shouted John Tenner. I had never seen him acting calmer.

"I've lived in this country most of my life. My conscience has learned to be very selective."

"I have more men Gringo," responded the Kid. "I can start over. They are like children. They only need someone to lead them. My life goes on and so does his." He gestured with his gun barrel at Benito's head.

"No," said John Tenner coldly as he raised his rifle and then hesitated. The dazzling smile lit up the Coahuila Kid's face again.

"John," shouted Benito Chavez, "please, compadre, don't worry about me. End it. At least then I can leave this life…"

His words were cut short in the roar of gunfire. The Coahuila Kid simply looked forward and pulled the trigger. The side of Benito's head was literally blown off. At the same time the Kid screamed as John Tenner's bullet struck the base of this throat. He collapsed with his dead father's body still in his arms. That's when I fainted.

CHAPTER 15

When I came to, Britt Jones was bandaging my shoulders.

"Welcome back," he said.

"How long was I out?" I asked.

"Not long. You lost some blood, and we had to get that bullet out. You was lucky you fainted."

"How about you and the others?"

"I tripped and fell. Banged up my knee and busted my head. Tip got his left earlobe shot off. That was a mighty close call. John and Clay, those two old warhorses, didn't get a scratch. Ain't that amazin'?"

I smiled. It sure was. With all those bullets flying to not get hurt was almost a miracle.

I could see John, Clay, and Tip busy digging makeshift graves.

"Are they burying all these bodies?" I asked.

"No," chuckled Britt, "that would take days. John wants to bury Benito, Cord, and the Kid. I don't know why he don't just leave the Kid lay. That young fellow brought nothing but trouble and death."

"Maybe because he was Benito's son and could've grown to be a different man if Benito had accepted him."

"Maybe."

"Britt, how could John shoot, knowing the Kid would kill Benito?"

"I think Benito knew he wouldn't be coming back from this. He done something and tried to hide it, keep it separate from the rest of his life. You can't do that without paying a price. Life has a way of evening things out. It was time for him to accept responsibility. He knew he hurt his family and through the Kid lots of other folks suffered and died. I don't think he wanted to live with that anymore."

I digested Britt's thoughts for a moment.

"It was the only way to end it wasn't it?" I asked.

"I didn't see no other. Neither did John. There's bad things in this life that got to be done. Most people are lucky they don't have to do many of 'em. John can live with it. I imagine he gets through thinking what it would be like if he didn't do 'em. There'll always be men like John, and the rest of us should probably be grateful."

"What about the bandits?"

"We'll leave 'em where they lay."

"The one we caught?"

"We cut him loose. He's wandering around being thankful for his life, I reckon."

"The women?"

"We can't take 'em with us. They got food and water and a roof over their heads. They're better off now than before we came. They got less men to deal with."

I watched as the bodies were placed in the graves. It was too bad we couldn't take Benito and Cord back, but it was too long of a trip. Besides, it's not where you're buried that counts. People who care will keep you in their minds always.

Tip, Clay, and John collected all the ammunition they could use and any of the good guns. They tossed all these into a wagon they had found in the back of the barn. Afterwards they approached me.

"How you feeling, Grant?" asked John Tenner. There was true concern on his face.

"Like hell. How about you?" I replied.

He looked a little puzzled for a moment. Then he smiled and answered, "I'll be fine." Tip stared down at me. I could see the blood congealed where his earlobe had once been.

"How's your ear?" I asked.

"I'm sure it ain't pretty, but I can hear. It don't hurt much. Are you ready to go?"

"Sure he is," interjected Clay. "He don't want to be here when them others return."

"But, this wagon will slow us down," I stated.

"You can't ride," responded John. "So this is the way it has to be. We've been able to replace ammunition we used, and we got food and fresh horses. Tip turned their other stock loose. If they want a fight of it, we'll oblige.

In open country you got nowhere to hide. You need grit for that kind of fighting. I don't think them bandits have it. But, I guess we'll find out. Time to move."

With that they lifted me into the wagon. El Negro, Sunset Lady, and three other horses were tied to the back. Britt and Tip mounted up. Britt took the lead. John and Clay rode in the wagon and Tip, with the keenest eyesight of the four, rode drag. He spent half the time swiveled around, scanning the horizon for signs of anyone trailing us.

I fell into an uneasy sleep. I was grateful because the bouncing and jarring of the wagon did my shoulder no good.

CHAPTER 16

It was late the next morning when Tip yelled, "I see dust!"

We all turned and looked where Tip pointed. It was a noticeable cloud and not that far of f.

"They should catch us within the hour, Captain," said Britt.

"Are all you handguns loaded?" asked Tenner.

The men out of habit proceeded to check their loads. Tenner turned to me.

"Grant, you better get out of the wagon and stand behind it. T h i n k you can handle a pistol?"

"Yes sir," I said, as I painfully climbed out of the wagon bed.

John and Clay mounted their horses.

"If it comes to it, we'll charge into 'em," stated John. Tie your reins in a knot so you don't lose 'em. Try to guide your pony with your knees. Fire your pistols with both hands. When they're empty, throw 'em down and grab another. Don't bother aiming. Just point. You'll hit just as well that way."

I was reminded of Reese Tenner giving me similar advice when I first came to Texas and faced screaming Comanches. It was something I knew I'd never forget.

Clay looked at John and said, "Old Times." John nodded.

The bandidos slid their lathered horses to a stop, completely surprised to see us waiting. John Tenner gave them no time to think. He, Clay, Britt and Tip moved forward at a walk. It was all I could do to keep from mounting a horse and trying to follow. But, I knew it was impossible. I was still too weak. I would have to do my best on foot behind the wagon.

There were ten of them, probably the ten that had gone south on the raid. I couldn't tell if the fellow we captured was with them or not, but I doubted it. I imagined he had had enough of us.

My friends advanced until the two groups were about one hundred fifty yards apart. Then John drew rein and called in Spanish asking if any of them spoke English. A thin, bearded man mounted on a spirited grey horse answered yes.

My four compadres moved their horses forward another fifty yards and stopped. This time Clay spoke.

"Start the ball if you've a mind to, but remember, we left around twenty of your gang dead south of the river, your leader among 'em. You can turn around and ride away or join them. Your choice."

"Who are you, Gringo," shouted the thin bandit.

"I don't see that it matters much, but I do suppose a man has a right to know who his killers are," Clay answered. My name is Clay Ellis."

He then motioned one by one to the rest of us.

"This is Captain John Tenner, Britt Jones, Tip Lomax, and back yonder by the wagon is Grant Kirby. Don't bother introducing yourselves or we'll be here all morning. Besides, I don't give a damn anyway. Now, we're hungry and tired and in no mood for more talking. Pull your weapons or git."

With that Clay, John, Britt and Tip each drew a brace of pistols and moved forward at a deliberate walk.

The bandits milled around undecided, jabbering excitedly among themselves. No doubt they were thinking of the twenty or so dead men back at the hacienda. No doubt at least two of the names they heard were known to them. No doubt, faced by men who weren't running but advancing, the rest of the Coahuila Kid's gang were puzzled and maybe beginning to become a little frightened. No doubt when John Tenner yelled, "At my signal!" it was psychologically more than they could handle because they turned their horses and spurred away.

I had never seen anything like it. Those were hardened men who had robbed and killed and they turned away. Later, I asked why. John, Clay and Britt all had some explanation.

"They was mad about what we done," said John, "but not stupid. They saw that we weren't no dirt farmers. I think hearing our names carried some weight. Clay and I rangered in this country for some time. Britt scouted for us. They probably figured if you and Tip was with us, you must be good hands".

Then Clay added his opinion.

"You see — doing something is one thing. Knowing that you can do it is another. And, when others also believe you can do something, well, you've got a full hand."

Then Tip asked, "What are you getting at?"

Now it was Britt's turn.

"Them boys saw the bodies we left behind. They saw we wasn't backing down. Didn't show fear. Instead we pushed them ,, like we wanted to fight , like they didn't have a chance against us. We just twisted their minds some."

"I was glad we didn't have to fight," said Tip Lomax. "I had my fill of fighting and killing on this trip."

"Son," said John Tenner, "I couldn't agree with you more. Let's go home."

Tip helped me into the wagon, and we continued our journey north to the Tenner ranch, a place that had become like a home to me.

As usual the homecoming was marvelous. It encompassed cheers and tears. The Tenners, Britt Jones' family, and a healthy L.B. Taylor greeted us joyously. Elena and Estralita Chavez had gone to their home ranch. After some needed rest John said he would ride there personally to break the news.

It may not surprise you to know that eventually John Tenner's son, Josh, married Benito Chavez's daughter, Elena. This union bonded together two families and two ranches. L.B. Taylor who originally thought Belinda Jones was just a child did change his mind after a while. He married her. Their son, Luke, is my horse trainer as I've mentioned before.

Sunset Lady turned out to be a great mother and El Negro a fine stallion. They produced some wonderful sons and daughters which certainly helped improve the horse herds on the Tenner and Chavez ranches. L.B. Taylor was in charge of the breeding program and spent his time happily training horses.

So, you see, even as I get older and more and more of my contemporaries pass away, I never forget them. All I have to do is look out at the grazing horses in my pastures and some of those old friends come alive for me again.